P9-CFS-483

Praise for

Say the Word

An ALA Best Book for Young Adults

★ "Powerful and compelling. . . . This sensitive and heart-wrenching story . . . unfolds into a gripping read." —*Booklist*, starred review

"Garsee has created an intense, frank novel with fragile, resilient, believable characters. . . . A mature and gripping coming-of-age story." —*SLJ*

"Compelling, emotional, and down-to-earth, *Say the Word* is a wonderfully written novel. . . . Garsee is an author to watch." —The Compulsive Reader

"[This] novel hits the ground running and doesn't let up. . . . Garsee presents a compelling portrait of a young woman growing up and coping with an overwhelming array of problems." —*PW*

"Garsee . . . gives readers plenty of food for thought about families, loyalty, and identity, so Shawna's experience will elicit much discussion." —*BCCB*

ALSO BY JEANNINE GARSEE

Before, After, and Somebody in Between

Say the Word

JEANNINE GARSEE

BLOOMSBURY

NEW YORK BERLIN LONDON SYDNEY

First published in the United States of America in March 2009
by Bloomsbury Books for Young Readers
Paperback edition published in February 2011
www.bloomsburyteens.com

For information about permission to reproduce selections from this book, write to
Permissions, Bloomsbury BFYR, 175 Fifth Avenue, New York, New York 10010

The Library of Congress has cataloged the hardcover edition as follows:
Garsee, Jeannine.
Say the word / Jeannine Garsee. — 1st U.S. ed.
p.   cm.
Summary: After the death of her estranged mother, who left Ohio years ago to live
with her lesbian partner in New York City, seventeen-year-old Shawna Gallagher's life
is transformed by revelations about her family, her best friend, and herself.
ISBN-13: 978-1-59990-333-0 • ISBN-10: 1-59990-333-4 (hardcover)
[1. Family problems—Fiction. 2. Lesbians—Fiction. 3. Homosexuality—Fiction. 4. Grief—Fiction.
5. High schools—Fiction. 6. Schools—Fiction. 7. Only child—Fiction. 8. Ohio—Fiction.] I. Title.
PZ7.G1875Say 2009   [Fic]—dc22   2008016476

ISBN 978-1-59990-613-3 (paperback)

Book design by Daniel Roode
Typeset by Westchester Book Composition
Printed in the U.S.A. by Quad/Graphics, Fairfield, Pennsylvania
1 3 5 7 9 10 8 6 4 2

All papers used by Bloomsbury Publishing, Inc., are natural, recyclable products
made from wood grown in well-managed forests. The manufacturing processes
conform to the environmental regulations of the country of origin.

This book is dedicated to my sister, Karen Margosian, and to the memory of our mother, Myrlin Moeller Fischer.

1

When the phone slashes a machete through my brain at six fifteen a.m. it can mean only one of two things: Dad somehow found out I was sucking face with Devon Connolly last night. Or somebody's dead.

I lean over LeeLee's semi-lifeless body to snatch up the receiver. On second thought it might be my grandmother, Nonny: *Shawnie, your grandfather's fallen and he can't get up!* Yes, people say that. Nonny's said it so often, EMS threatened to bill her if she hounds them again. "Hello?"

"Shawna?" A voice I almost but don't quite recognize. "I need to speak to your father."

LeeLee flips over with an irritated grunt. I stretch the phone cord, trying not to garrote my best friend. "Who is this?"

"It's Fran."

Fran? Francine Goodman. Dubbed the Frankfurter by LeeLee and a few nastier names by my dad. I make it a point not to call her anything at all.

"Is your father there?"

"N-no," I stammer, awake now, but confused. "He's in California." At a medical conference at Cedars-Sinai, I could add. But it's none of her business. Fran stole my mother away from me when I was seven years old. Why is she calling my house at the crack of dawn?

"When will he be back?"

"Why don't you just tell me what's going on?"

No answer. I can picture her clearly although I haven't seen her, or Mom, in three years. Short bristly haircut. A round face, deceivingly motherly. Brown eyes circled with spidery laugh lines, though Fran rarely laughs. Mom's the "laugher" of the two; she takes nothing seriously. Only her photography, and Fran, and Fran's precious little boys with the funny Jewish names. No wonder the last time I visited them in New York I almost dropped dead from appendicitis. Mom blew it off. At least Fran figured it out.

Fran draws a quavering breath. "Honey, I'm sorry, but—well, your mom had a stroke last night. The doctors don't think she'll make it. You really should come." She chokes, and adds, "I'm so sorry, Shawna," before hanging up on me.

I sit there, phone in hand, breathing in one breath after another. LeeLee, sensing something awful, drags the pillow off her face to peer at me through mascara-smudged eyes. "Huh? What?"

"My mom had a stroke."

"Shut up!"

"That was the Frankfurter. She had a stroke. She's not gonna make it."

LeeLee scrambles up. "No way. Are you sure?"

"Yes, I'm sure!"

LeeLee bites her lip, maybe waiting for me to go berserk, or faint, or something equally dramatic. Breathe in, breathe out . . . breathe in, breathe out . . . My chest hurts, but the rest of me feels numb.

"Are you gonna cry?" LeeLee touches my hand as I shake my head hard. "Want me to call your dad?"

"He's probably not up. It's only three in LA."

"God, Shawna, who cares what time it is? Call him! Now!" But my limbs refuse to work, so LeeLee grabs the phone out of my hand. "What's his number?"

"I don't know." It's programmed into my cell phone, but I can't remember where I left it.

LeeLee punches zero and magically connects to Cedars-Sinai Medical Center in Los Angeles. Then she punches more numbers, yells, "This is a dire emergency!" and then slams the receiver down in triumph. She takes my hand again, her fingers hot against my icy skin. "They'll give him the message. You sure you're okay?"

"I'm fine. I promise."

And I burst into tears.

2

My life wasn't always this complicated. And Mom wasn't always a lesbian.

Once when I was eleven and still hoping she'd come back, I said, "Maybe it's not true. You don't *look* like Fran"—who, at the time, looked pretty butch to me. "So maybe you're not really, you know. One of *them*."

Mom snapped back, "I'm a lesbian, Shawna. *Les-bi-an*. Why are you so afraid to say that word?"

But what lesbian looks like a ravishing, Scandinavian faerie? Pale blond hair, Nordic eyes, a reed-thin frame—all of which I inherited, minus the ravishingness. People don't expect Drop-Dead Gorgeous when they hear the word "lesbian." They think crew cuts, Harleys, and a wallet in the back pocket.

I haven't seen Mom since I was fourteen. I've spoken to her on the phone, but mostly in grunts and monosyllables.

Now the worst thing I ever said to her springs to my mind: "Don't come. I hate you. Just leave me alone."

3

LeeLee toasts me an English muffin and coaxes what might pass for a chai latte out of my espresso machine. I sneak the muffin under the table to my mini dachshund, Charles, who licks my fingers clean with joyful slurps.

The phone shrills. LeeLee whips up the receiver. "Hi, Dr. Gallagher. Yeah, hang on."

"What's going on?" Dad, of course, half-asleep and quite perturbed.

Unlike Fran, I can't ease my way into it. "Mom had a stroke," I blurt out. "She's not gonna make it, and Fran wants me to come to New York, and—"

As Dad shouts something unintelligible in my ear, I drop the phone and bolt from the kitchen with Charles scuttling beside me on stubby, excited legs. I hear LeeLee mumbling to Dad as I curl up on the window seat in the dining room and stare out at the leaves on the trees, glinted with red and gold.

A minute later, she joins me. "You owe me a thanks. I convinced him you're not about to have a complete mental breakdown." She eyes me nervously. "You're not, right?"

I shake my head, my forehead pressed against the windowpane. "So what'd he say?"

"Well, after he got done bitching about how he's not pulling you out of school to go visit that beepity-beep mother of yours, and

I politely reminded him that, um, this might be your last visit . . ." LeeLee hiccups apologetically. "He gave me his credit card number and wants you to book your own flight."

That figures. "He's not coming with me?"

LeeLee knows a stupid question when she hears one. She answers it anyway. "No, he says he's got an awards dinner tonight."

I guess an awards dinner is more important than the fact that the mother of your only child may croak any second. Not that I blame him, I guess. Mom left *him*, and for a woman, no less. How humiliating is that? Of course he's bitter.

But I dread flying to New York alone. I dread seeing my mom, gazing into the gaping jaws of death. And I dread facing the Frankfurter, dread fighting to maintain my usual polite persona when, yes, I'm bitter, too. Because Fran's the reason Mom also dumped me.

LeeLee hands me the paper with Dad's credit card number. I crumple it up and toss it aside. "I know the number." Dad makes me use it a gazillion times a year to order stuff for the house, gifts for his employees, and flowers, or whatever, to impress his floozy of the week. He tends to forget I'm his daughter, not a live-in secretary.

"I wonder what happened." LeeLee touches her nose jewel thoughtfully. "Did she just, ya know, fall out? Did Fran find her?"

I hug myself. "Can we possibly talk about something else?"

"Okay," she says quickly. She drops down beside me and draws up her feet. "Um, so, wanna talk about last night? You and Devon Connolly? Wow, if I hadn't seen it with my own eyes . . ."

I can't believe I forgot about Devon Connolly. And it seems wrong to be talking about him at a time like this. "We were just goofing around."

"Yeah, right. I never knew you *liked* the dude."

Neither did I, till last night. I've known Devon my whole life—he's the twin brother of my ex–best friend, Susan—and I never thought of him that way. Last night sort of happened out of the blue.

"I can't believe Susan even invited us to that party," LeeLee goes on. She sticks a finger down her throat for emphasis.

"She didn't invite you. You crashed, remember?"

"Well, it was the least I could do for my BFF." She winds an arm around my neck. "Why don't you come over for breakfast? I'll make you a Puerto Rican omelet."

I lean my cheek briefly against her glossy hair. "Thanks, but I've got stuff to take care of. You know, call the airline . . ." Maybe clue in a few people. Like Nonny and Poppy, Uncle Dieter and Aunt Colleen . . . Oh, hell, I can just *hear* Aunt Colleen.

"Well, if you change your mind, *chica* . . ."

I'm tempted to go. I love the Velezes. They're so very different from my own uptight, neurotic, totally-*not*-down-to-earth family. Dinnertime at my house, for example, consists of me at one end of the table, Dad on the other, neither of us speaking as our house-keeper, Klara, dishes up broccoli florets and vichyssoise. Dinnertime at the Velezes means industrial-sized pans of beans, meat, rice, and tortillas planted on the table, a general free-for-all, every kid for himself. A sloppy, noisy house booming with Spanish music, where I can kick back, practice my *español*, and pretend LeeLee's brothers and sisters belong to me.

I know Dad would prefer me to find a more "suitable" best friend. Somebody *not* Puerto Rican. Somebody whose parents speak English.

Somebody who can afford to pay Wade Prep's heavy-duty tuition without depending on scholarships and grants. But who in their right mind would give up a best friend like LeeLee?

With a hug and a cheerful "*Adiós,*" LeeLee takes off.

I scoop up Charles and hug him, already wishing I'd gone with her.

4

Sometimes I swear I have three personalities.

Perfect Shawna is the one I present to the world. Perfect Shawna would slit her throat before she'd ever be unkind. She makes perfect grades. She makes her daddy proud. Perfect Shawna is polite to a fault, admired by everyone.

Pathetic Shawna hovers at the edge. She grovels for attention. She's the one who let Devon Connolly grope her boobs in the Connollys' basement last night. She can never make an independent decision of her own. She's also the biggest suck-up on earth.

Thankfully she's usually rescued by Perfect Shawna. Well, except for last night . . .

Evil Shawna lurks, always planning, always thinking. Always blurting out crap that neither of the others have the guts to say out loud.

Secretly, I kind of like Evil Shawna. But I'm scared of her, too. She could easily get out of hand and mess up my life.

Of course it's Perfect Shawna who makes the necessary calls.

Phone call #1: The airline ticket counter.

I find that I can't catch a flight to New York till seven a.m. tomorrow. When the unsympathetic booking agent drones, "Ma'am, you're lucky to get *that* one," Perfect Shawna jots down the info, and thanks her, no less.

Phone call #2: Nonny.

"Oh, dear God, oh, dear God" is all she says for five minutes. Then: "You're not thinking of flyin' all the way to New York by yourself?"

"I have to. Dad's in California."

"Oh, no! Oh, Shawna, dearie, why don't ye wait till he comes back? Then you—"

"She could be dead by then!" Instantly, I'm ashamed as Evil Shawna creeps in. Nonny and Uncle Dieter are the only ones who don't try to remind me every second how worthless Mom is. More quietly, I add, "Fran says she won't make it, so, well, I guess I should go."

"How will ye get to the airport?" Nonny pronounces it "*ayr-r-r-port*" in her husky Scots brogue. "Ye know I can't leave your granddad for more than a wee second." Of course not. Last time she left him for more than a wee second, Poppy rolled his wheelchair down the basement steps and blew out a hip.

"Nonny. I have a car, remember?"

I endure all the reasons why I should *not* drive myself to the airport. Then, after severe instructions to keep my valuables in my bra and not to drink anything on the plane that doesn't come in a sealed container, Nonny bids me a mournful good-bye. I hang up a teeny bit harder than necessary. Hello? I'm seventeen, not seven.

Phone call #3: Aunt Colleen.

Aside from Susan Connolly and her entourage of winged monkeys, Aunt Colleen's my least favorite person in the world. Her response explains why: "Well, I'm only surprised it's not cancer. That woman smoked like a chimney."

I clench the receiver. "That woman"—my mom—has a name. And I don't mean *dyke* or any of the other nasty names Aunt Colleen likes to throw around.

"Well, I'm leaving in the morning," I say curtly. "I thought I'd let you know."

I picture her battling the Botox to draw her face into a scowl. "How long will you be gone? What about school? You can't miss school! What about—" And on and on. Poor Uncle Dieter, who has to live with this witch.

Phone call #4: To my own cell phone, which I haven't seen since that party last night.

I call my number three or four times, but I can't hear it ringing, not in the house, not in my car. I must have left it at the Connollys'. Well, I am not climbing onto a jet with no link back to earth. I'll want to say good-bye to Nonny, at least, if a mad shoe bomber shows up.

Phone call #5: Fran, of course. After I work up the nerve. A male voice answers. "May I speak to Fran?"

"Who's this?"

"Penny's daughter. Shawna?"

"Are you coming?" he asks abruptly.

Annoyed, I ask, "Who is *this*?"

"Arye."

Oh, ri-ight, Arye, Fran's older son. My last impression of him: a chunky, bucktoothed, zit-riddled, short-tempered smart-ass. We met only once, on my last visit to New York. We did not hit it off.

"Well?" Arye prompts. "Mom's not here, she's with Penny. Are you coming or not?"

"Of course I'm coming." I rattle off my flight details, and everything grows quiet. I think he's waiting for me to ask about Mom. "Um, how's she doing?"

"She's on life support. You better fly fast." *Click.*

5

I dawdle on the sidewalk in front of my ex–best friend's house. Up until ninth grade we'd been tight our whole lives. Same baby playgroups, dance classes, Brownie troops, etc. Not only that, but we were kind of famous at one time. Susan's mom, a writer, and my mom, a photographer, did a picture book series called *Susie and Shawna*. For our first seven years, till Mom took off with Fran, we starred in over a dozen books, like *Susie and Shawna Go Trick-or-Treating*, *Susie and Shawna Have Fun at the Circus*, blah, blah. The books made scads of money. Everyone knew Susie and Shawna.

Susan dropped the "Susie" at the end of eighth grade. She also dropped me for a new best friend, the intolerably evil Paige Berry. That summer Susan had a sleepover and invited a couple of girls I barely knew: Brittany Giannelli, who could benefit from some serious nourishment through a stomach tube, and Alyssa Hunt, currently the top slut of Wade Prep's upper school.

And Paige, of course.

I admit Susan and I had already been drifting apart. In sixth grade I decided to become a doctor like Dad, while Susan decided she'd grow up to be the next Meryl Streep. Every year we had less and less in common. But we remained best friends, and closer than most sisters.

After swimming in Susan's pool we took turns in her shower. Susan came out of the bathroom wrapped in a towel, which slipped, like, one teeny inch. When she yanked it back up with an exaggerated shriek, I'd joked, "Chill out, Susie. It's not like you've anything to show off."

"It's *Susan*," she shot back. Then, slyly, "Yeah, you'd know—I've seen you checking me out." To the others she added, "Shawna's mom's a lesbian. Maybe it runs in the family."

Up until that moment nobody knew much about my mom. Clearly it's not something I brag about. I'd sworn Susan to silence. Evidently, she forgot.

Brittany and Alyssa stared. Paige exploded into giggles. "She is not! Is she?"

Delighted with the response, Susan explained, "She lives with somebody in New York, like, this total butch."

I sat there, speechless and humiliated, while they battered me with:

"Gross, really?"

"God, what does your dad say?"

"Did you ever see them, ya know, kiss and stuff?"

"Ew-w! I'd *die* if my mom ever did something like that."

Then, from Paige, "Are you really gay? Omigod! We took *gym* together last year."

Belatedly, I gathered up my stuff and stomped out. I wanted to die. I fully expected to die. Who could feel this embarrassed and *not* drop over dead?

Susan rushed after me. "Shawna, wait, don't leave. I'm sorry! I don't know why I said that. I have *su-u-uch* a big mouth."

And for that one instant I believed she was sorry. In that instant I almost forgave her.

Then: "God, whatever you do, don't tell my mom about this. She'll *kill* me. I'll be grounded for life."

Yes, Susan was sorry. Sorry her mom might find out what a bitch she was. But not sorry she blabbed about my mom. Not sorry she pretty much accused me of being a lesbian myself.

I left anyway. I've barely spoken to her since, and no, I never told Mrs. Connolly. What for? The damage was done. The news spread. When school started that fall I became known as "Shawna, that brainy chick. Her mom's gay or something." But at least nobody tried to pin the same thing on me. Aside from the occasional snide remark from Paige, that is.

I missed Susan. My only saving grace was that I still had two good but not "best" friends left: Melanie Katz and Danielle Walsh, both fellow science geeks and future physicians who *loathed* Susan and congratulated me on seeing the light.

Then LeeLee and I got thrown together, on a field trip to the science museum. Although she wasn't impressed, as I was, by the "living mouse stem cells!" or the interactive global warming database, we bonded over the exhibit of five-thousand-year-old skulls. She didn't have many friends; Wade Prep can be very, well, shall we say "snooty"? People sneered at her shabby secondhand uniforms and made fun of her double ponytails, a blatant fashion no-no. They resented the way she never groveled to the "in crowd" and how she peppered her comebacks with indecipherable Spanish insults. LeeLee's so un-herdlike. I love that about her.

As far as last night's party goes—yes, I was shocked when Susan invited me. I'd even wondered if this was her way of reaching out, of trying to make up. But Susan, who alternated between mingling with her deadly trio—Paige, Brittany, and Alyssa—and making out with Jake Fletcher, was too busy to say more than hi to me. Oh, and to snarl at LeeLee for barging in, uninvited.

I had one glass of beer. Devon likely drank twenty. LeeLee grazed at the munchie table, deliberately double-dipping. One minute Devon and I were flirting, acting silly, simply goofing around. The next thing I knew, we were entwined in a corner, actively sucking face to a thundering Mary J. Blige.

A simple drunken romp? Or a hint of things to come?

I press the doorbell, hoping to find out now and wondering if I remembered to brush my hair this morning.

The Connollys' notoriously rude housekeeper frowns through the porthole before she swings open the door. "Yes?"

"Um, I think I left my cell phone here last night. Do you mind if—?"

She bangs the door shut, and I stare at the ornate knocker in disbelief. A moment later the door reopens, and she holds my precious phone out between her thumb and index finger. "It's been ringing all morning, I'll have you know."

"Thanks," I say to the knocker as the door, once again, swings shut in my face.

Oh, well.

6

I oversleep in the morning, jump up to pee, let Charles outside to do the same, then rush around with last-minute packing. Nonny promised to come over to feed and potty Charles if she can get a neighbor or someone to stay with Poppy. Otherwise it'll be up to Klara, but she's only here during the day. I spread newspaper on the basement floor in case, and set bowls of food and water around in strategic places. I wish I could take him, but there's just no way.

At the airport, I park in the garage, then endure all but a body cavity search at the security gate, and finally board. I brought my sketchpad and a few colored pencils, but I'm aching for a nap. After mentally marking all the emergency exits, I shut my eyes till the plane is in the air, then stare bleakly through the glass into a black oval of nothingness.

I forgot my rosary. Well, too late now.

7

My mom left me without saying good-bye.

The final *Susie and Shawna* book had been released that week, so Mom and Mrs. Connolly threw a party at the Ritz-Carlton in downtown Cleveland. They signed books, drank champagne, and schmoozed with the big shots, including a Hollywood producer who promised to turn *Susie and Shawna* into an animated series. That was the first time I heard the expression about blowing smoke up some-one's ass.

Susan and I signed books, too. Fans fawned over us, stroked our matching blond ponytails, remarked over and over how darn *cu-u-ute* we were. Mom drank too much and worked up a sweat dancing. Dad didn't bother to show up at all. Later, too loaded to drive, Mom asked a friend to drive us home—and that's when I met Fran for the first time.

I liked her. I liked the way she called me "sweetie" and tweaked my ponytail. I liked the way she'd spout out a four-letter word, then clap a hand over her face and whimper, "Sorry!" as if she wanted me to like her, as if my opinion counted. I especially liked the way she swung Mom's hand as the three of us headed toward the car. Susan and I did that, too. Fran, I'd decided, must be Mom's BFF.

Back home, at three in the morning, I threw up a river of shrimp. If it weren't for this I might have missed the whole fight. I heard Fran's name shouted over and over. Finally, when it grew quiet, I ventured out to the kitchen, where Dad sat alone, with Mom nowhere in sight.

"She went out," Dad said in a funny choked-up voice. "Go back to bed."

I did, but I couldn't sleep. I heard Mom come back in, then closets and drawers slam open and shut. More shouting, more swearing, and then, oddly, screaming. Once again I crawled out of bed, tiptoed to their room, and saw something that, to this day, I try not to think about.

Mom left a second time during the night. In the morning, I peeked into her workroom and totally freaked out when I saw every table and shelf bare, every cupboard empty. I ran crying to Julie, my nanny, who tried to explain that Mom would be "visiting a friend for a while."

"She took all her stuff! Where'd she go? Where'd she go?"

Julie couldn't, or wouldn't, tell me, and I cried all day. When Dad came home later, agitated and disheveled, I found out the truth—Mom wasn't "visiting" anyone and it wouldn't be "for a while." She'd left us forever to be with Fran. Somebody she loved, Dad said, a whole lot more than she loved us.

Six months later, with no advance warning, Julie was gone, too.

8

Swinging my carry-on, I stagger down the ramp into the crowded terminal, where I wander aimlessly, panic creeping in. Where's Fran? Did Arye give her my message? Why do I feel I might spend the rest of my life here, tripping over bags and toddlers and stray bottles of Aquafina?

"Attention, please. Will Shawna Gallagher please report to the American Airlines ticket counter?"

After wrangling my bag from the loaded carousel, I follow the dubious signage to the ticket counter. Miraculously I recognize Arye, although the buckteeth are gone, as well as the zits. Stocky, shorter than me—well, a lot of people are—he now wears his dark curly hair tied back in a ponytail. He might strike me as cute if he didn't look so pissed off.

"I'm here," I announce unnecessarily. "How's my mom?"

Arye doesn't answer. Nor does he offer to take my suitcase. He sprints ahead, forcing me to trudge miles behind, huffing and puffing and growing more annoyed by the second. I didn't like this dude the last time around. Now I remember why: he hadn't liked me, either.

I catch up to him outside, the weight of my overstuffed bag wrenching my arm from my socket. I drop the load with a thud. "What's your problem?"

"I want to get back. Schmule's by himself. I didn't think it'd *take* this long."

"You didn't have to pick me up," I object. "I could've taken a cab."

"Mom thought it'd be too overwhelming for you," Arye answers through distinctly curled lips.

Luckily, a dozen eager cabs await us. Our turbaned driver spits on the ground, then snatches up my bag and throws it into the trunk. Inside, I'm knocked into Arye by a wild left turn. He shoves me off impatiently. Off we zoom, *way* over the speed limit, zigzagging pedestrians, clipping curbs, cutting off other vehicles at will. All I can think is, "Why did I get off that damn plane?" I could be somewhere a whole lot safer than New York City by now. Like Delaware. Or the bottom of the Atlantic. I rub my neck and shoot fireballs at Arye, who makes it a point to pretend he's on this death journey alone.

Forty minutes later, jammed in traffic, Arye glances murderously at his watch. "C'mon, let's walk. It's only ten more blocks."

"Thank you," Perfect Shawna calls to the maniac driver who just tried to kill her.

It's a *long* ten blocks. Dead on my feet after a trek through unimaginably people-packed streets, I wait impatiently while Arye unlocks not one, not two or three, but four fricking dead bolts to the front door of Mom and Fran's brownstone.

Schmule pops up anxiously from beneath an afghan on the sofa. "Is she dead?"

"No," Arye says shortly. "But you better get dressed if you want to go see her."

Schmule stares at me. "Did you bring your dog this time?"

"Why would I bring my dog?"

" 'Cause you freaked out last time. You thought nobody would feed him. You said you'd probably find his dead body under the kitchen table or something."

I don't remember saying that, but it's likely I did. "They don't let dogs on airplanes. Unless you crate them or something." Charles would never forgive me.

"Yeah, they do. Like, if you're blind."

"Well, I'm not."

He grins, revealing a mouthful of metal. "You could pretend."

Arye kicks the sofa. "C'mon, get some socks on. I told you to be *ready*."

Schmule stretches, then rolls off the sofa. His sandy hair hangs in overgrown curls and he has a smattering of freckles across the bridge of his nose. Long bony feet stick out comically from the bottom of his grubby jeans. While he gets his act together, Arye paces around, cracking his knuckles in an obnoxious way. Suddenly I wonder if he knows something I don't.

Is my mom already dead? And he's afraid to tell us?

9

I last saw Arye and Schmule three summers ago when Mom opened Sonia's, her Greenwich Village art gallery. Only strangers call my mom by her real name, Sonia. Otherwise, she's Penny. I have no idea why.

So wrapped up was she in preparing for the festivities, she paid no attention when I told her I was sick. I'd puked four times, my stomach was on fire, and I felt hot and cranky and just wanted to go to bed.

"I can't *stay* with you tonight, Shawna. A thousand people are expecting me." Mom flitted about in her usual self-absorbed daze, adjusting her pale blond hair, peering at her makeup, tugging fretfully at her slinky black dress.

Fran touched my sweaty forehead. "Pen, she does feel warm."

"Give her some Tylenol. She'll be fine." So I swallowed the Tylenol, which promptly came up again. Mom took this ver-ry personally. "Oh, Shawna. Of all nights for you to get sick!"

A fourteen-year-old version of Perfect Shawna assured her, "I'm okay now. I guess I can go," because who doesn't feel better immediately after they puke? This gallery, I knew, was a big deal to Mom; along with her latest work, plus photographs by a few "promising new artists," she was also displaying a ton of outtakes—photos that never made it into the *Susie and Shawna* series.

She wanted me to be there. She was counting on me, right?

Head stuck in a grocery bag, I made it to the opening in Mom's rented limo. Arye rode with us, and Schmule, too, who looked like a ventriloquist's dummy in shorts and a bow tie. Flashing cameras, thunderous applause, and then—*POW!* Someone tapped my face as I lay sprawled flat on my back

"Oh, my God, Shawna," Mom cried, "I *told* you not to wear those shoes." As if my new platform sandals were the reason I collapsed in the middle of a Manhattan media blitz.

Fran shouldered Mom out of the way. "Pen, she's burning up."

"Maybe the Tylenol hasn't kicked in yet." Gee, Mom, because I threw it all up? "Here, Frannie, help me get her out of the way—"

With a lead-melting glare at my mom, Fran hauled me to my feet, motioned to Arye and Schmule, and hustled us back to the limo. "St. Vincent's!" she barked at the driver, who mashed his foot down and zoomed off, getaway style, down Bleecker Street.

Arye whined the whole way. "Not fair, Mom! Why can't I stay with Penny? I'm missing the whole thing!"

"Shawna's sick, dammit. And I need you to keep an eye on Schmule."

Schmule squinted at me. "Um, you're not gonna die, are you?"

Lucky for him I was too sick to swing a fist. Fran said, "Of course not!" I think the fear in her voice might have scared me if I hadn't already believed I was dead.

Sixty minutes later, a surgeon sliced out my ruptured appendix. I later found out the docs gave Fran a hard time because she wasn't my legal guardian and couldn't sign any forms. What saved me was the fact that I had no blood pressure to speak of. This took precedence over their idiotic rules.

Dad showed up the next day, cussed out Mom and Fran and

every doctor and nurse in sight, then lugged me onto the first flight out of New York. I spent a week at the Cleveland Clinic on antibiotics till the doctors decided I'd survive.

The hospital phone rang as I was packing to go home. Dad was waiting downstairs with the car, so I was in a hurry, and tired, and insufficiently medicated. Seventeen staples in your stomach tend to make you pretty crabby.

It was Mom, calling from New York. "Sweetie! How are you? Guess what? We're flying in for a while, all of us, and we'll be staying with Fran's aunt in Cleveland Heights. So I was hoping we could spend some more time together. Of course," she added with a brittle laugh, "your father's giving me a hard time, as usual. But it's up to you. Are you up for some company?"

My ears rang. I tasted something funny in my mouth, either from the antibiotics, or possibly from her.

"Sweetie? What do you think?"

She didn't get that I almost died from peritonitis. All she'd cared about was her stupid gallery. And two "sweeties" out of her mouth in a single conversation? How lame, how fake. Even when she lived with us, she never called me "sweetie."

"No," I said. "I don't want you to come."

I sensed stricken disbelief. "What? Sweetie, don't be silly, I—"

"I said *don't—come*! I hate you. Just leave me alone."

After that, I never saw her again. Fran, not Mom, invited me back once or twice, but I always said no. Mom had a new family now, one that didn't include me. And Dad never missed a chance to tell me how much better off I was.

Maybe I was. But now it's hard to remember.

10

The three of us halt outside of Mom's hospital room. "You go in first," Arye directs me. "We'll wait in the lounge."

Schmule startles me with a lethal glare. "Hey, *I* wanna see Penny!"

"Shawna goes first."

"That's not fair!"

Oh, yes it is. Abandoning them, I take a deep breath and push open the door. First I see Fran, seated at Mom's bedside, reading out loud from a book: "'. . . once, indeed, seemed Beings Divine; / And they, perchance, heard vows of mine, / And saw my offerings on their shrine.'"

I know this poem—Brontë? Browning?—because it's one of Mom's favorites. I *hate* the sound of those words coming from the Frankfurter's mouth. I take a step in, then freeze in horror as the bed comes into view.

The bed, and the thing that used to be Mom.

A machine with glowing red numbers thumps and hisses, sending air through the tube that snakes out of Mom's mouth. Other tubes rise in a tangle, connected to bags on poles. On a box on the wall, more blinking numbers flash across a screen—99/39, 96/40,102/49. On and on, over and over. A silent litany to let people know that yes, Mom's alive.

One half-open eye, a slit of blue, watches nothing. When Fran jumps up, I jump, too. "Shawna! Thank God you're here." She steps closer, and I'm terrified she'll hug me. Something in my face must warn her off.

"Why is her eye open like that?" I ask uneasily.

"I'm not sure."

Well, I wish someone would close it. I inch closer. The room reeks of disinfectant and the underlying odor of dirty diapers. I inhale through my mouth, but sorry, it's too late. "Um, I think I'm gonna be sick."

Fran turns me smartly toward the adjoining bathroom. I snap the latch and hang my head over the toilet, but nothing happens. This is not good. How can I be so grossed out? I'm going to med school, dammit! I planned it my whole life. Not only because Dad expects it, which of course he does, but because I'm in love with the idea of curing diseases, saving lives. I want to join the Peace Corps so I can teach hygiene in Africa or India, inoculate kids, deliver babies—and now I'm ready to toss my cookies at the sight of a respirator?

I recover, mop my face, and slither out of the bathroom. The room still stinks. A nurse hovers over Mom with yet another tube in hand.

Fran picks at my sleeve. "Let's step out. The nurse has to suction her and, uh, clean her up."

My throat convulses at the same time my cell phone goes off. "No cell phones allowed in patient rooms," the nurse barks, like there's not a thousand signs around to remind me.

Sheepishly I follow Fran to the lounge, where Arye and Schmule are waiting. I glance at my phone: Dad, of course. I call him back and he answers abruptly, "Did you make it there all right?"

"I'm at the hospital now."

"How is she?"

Half-dead? "Not good. She's on machines and stuff, and—"

"Okay, I'm on my way. I'll see you tonight."

"You're coming here? Why?"

"We'll talk later." Dad clicks off.

Acutely aware of Fran's and Arye's stares, I confess, "My dad's on his way."

Fran looks displeased, but refrains from comment. Schmule bounces out of a chair. "Hey, it's *my* turn to see Penny."

"The nurse is busy with her now, sweetie," Fran says.

"Doing what?"

"Just stuff. We can go back in a few minutes. C'mon, let's get something to eat."

That, right now, is about the *last* thing I want to do.

11

There ought to be a law against hospital food. I'm a healthy eater who avoids grease and preservatives and, except for my chai lattes, as much sugar as possible.

This doesn't fly in a hospital cafeteria. I buy a semi-safe Diet Coke, while the Goodmans load up on fat and carbs.

"How was your flight?" Fran asks as we circle a vacant table.

"Twenty minutes late," Arye complains, chomping down on a buttered croissant.

"Good thing we didn't crash," I shoot back. "You'd still be waiting."

Schmule pipes up with, "Did you know that only thirty-two percent of all fatal airplane crashes are caused by pilot error? And I think sixteen percent are related to bad weather."

"Fatal?" I repeat. "Aren't all airplane crashes fatal?"

"Depends." Schmule pokes a straw into a carton of chocolate milk. "Anyway, the odds of dying in an airplane are only like, um, one in five thousand."

Can't he wait till I'm back in Ohio before spouting this crap? "Where do you get this stuff?"

"Discovery Channel."

Fran sips coffee and nibbles a muffin, her mind in another galaxy. She reminds me of an old hippie in her wrinkled, Indian print tunic and bleached-out jeans. I see she let her crew cut grow out, and it hangs to her shoulders in gray, greasy waves.

I almost ask for the details about what happened to Mom. Did she simply keel over, or had she been sick for a while? I'd like to know how she ended up a blob in that bed, unable to breathe without that *thump, hiss, thump, hiss.*

I decide against asking, because (A) I don't think Schmule needs to hear it, and (B) it might give me nightmares for the rest of my life.

"*Code Blue, Nine West! Code Blue, Nine West!*"

Fran leaps up so fast, her chair topples backward. "Oh, my God. Oh, my God."

"It might not be her," Arye says, face drained of color. Poor Schmule trembles visibly.

"It's her," Fran croaks. "Wait here. I'll go see."

Icicles drip down my spine. "I'll go with you."

"No, you won't. You stay here with the boys."

What makes her think she can order me around? I ignore her command and follow anyway. She doesn't speak in the elevator. She shifts impatiently, watching the buttons as each floor flips by with maddening slowness.

The hall outside Mom's room looks like a scene from a reality medical show. Bustling bodies, barked commands, and screeching equipment.

"Clear!" someone shouts.

A nurse grabs my elbow and ushers me out of the way. That's fine with me. I can't watch anymore! I find the lounge again, and languish there alone, shuddering uncontrollably, trying not to think about that awful scene down the hall.

12

I jump when Fran bursts into the lounge. "Shawna, why don't you go back downstairs and make sure the boys are okay?" Why is she always trying to get rid of me?

I notice the doctor behind her and bury my butt firmly into the chair. "Are you my mom's doctor?" Fran, annoyed, repeats her request, and *poof*! Evil Shawna reappears. "Look, you are not throwing me out. She's my mother, so leave—me—alone!"

Fran's lips part in shock. Then, resigned, she nods at the man.

"I'm Doctor Felker," he says after a little *ahem*. "First of all, I need to know if Ms. Sorenson has a living will."

I shrug, not sure what that is. Fran keeps quiet.

"Well, what about a durable power of attorney? That's the legal document that names somebody to make any medical decisions in case the patient can't make them on her own."

Fran admits, "I, um, don't have anything like that."

The doctor looks at me. Why would *I* have it? If Mom and the Frankfurter are supposed to be, you know, *married*, or whatever you want to call it, why didn't they take care of this before somebody got deathly sick?

"Does it matter?" Fran asks weakly.

"Well, the thing is, this doesn't look good. We got her back, but it's only a matter of time before it happens again. It could be days. It could be minutes." Dr. Felker's voice sounds gentle, yet strangely impersonal. I can't imagine giving anyone this news, but I bet he does it every day. Another part of this profession I won't find very pleasant. "The EEG we did yesterday showed minimal brain activity. This episode didn't help."

The room spins crazily. "Are you saying she's brain-dead?"

"Well, the damage is permanent. If she survives, she'll never wake up. I'm very sorry."

This isn't happening. His words can't be real.

"What are you saying?" Fran demands. "Are you asking us if you can pull the plug? You're giving up on her?"

Dr. Felker shakes a weary head. "I'll be happy to have her neurologist speak to you personally—"

"I don't want to speak to her damned neurologist. People come out of comas all the time! I just can't . . . I just can't—"

She stops to suck in a mouthful of oxygen. I stare at my hands, thinking, *Mom's gonna die, Mom's gonna die* as if it's the first time this idea occurred to me.

"—let her die," Fran finishes. Pale and sweaty, she drops into a chair and hides her face.

The doctor waits a sympathetic moment. "There's not much else I can say, except I'm sorry."

I believe him. I glance helplessly at Fran with her head drooping in her lap, torn between feeling, yes, really *sorry* for her, and yet more resentful than ever. *One* of us has to stay in control. Why does it have to be me?

I turn back to Dr. Felker. "My dad's a doctor. He'll be here tonight, so maybe you should talk to him about this—"

Fran's head snaps up, a cobra on high alert. "Shawna's father has nothing to do with this. He has no say in this at all."

"Neither do you," I say hotly. "You're not even a *relative*."

The doctor studies Fran with new interest. "You're not her sister?"

"Her sister?" I lose it for a second, spluttering giggles into my fingers. Sorry! I know this is serious. Obviously I'm cracking under the stress. But Mom has no living relatives. She has nobody but me.

Agitated, Fran crosses her heavy legs, then uncrosses them again. One stained leather clog clunks to the floor. She lets it sit there, twitching her toes in her sock. "Penny and I are very close," she says without looking at me. "She's divorced. We've been together for ten years. I'm the only *real* family she has."

Well, if Fran hadn't come along and turned her into a lesbian, Mom *would* have a family. Namely Dad and me. We wouldn't be having this conversation.

The doctor's pager goes off. He frowns, but I know it's a fake frown, that he's secretly ecstatic to be dragged away. "Sorry, I have to run. I'll keep you posted if there are any changes in" —he aims this at me, not at Fran— "your mother's condition. Ask one of the nurses to page me when your father shows up."

I sense a wisp of steam trailing out of Fran's ears. She jams a foot into her discarded shoe, pushes herself up, and stalks off without another word. Her clogs flap with each enraged step.

Not that Fran and I were ever "friends" . . . but something tells me I just made a serious enemy.

13

Visiting hours, which come at two-hour intervals, are over. I lurk illegally, peeking at Mom from the door. A nurse flits around, adjusting drips, scribbling on a clipboard. Mom looks no better, no worse. Maybe a shade closer to dead.

Thump . . . hiss. Thump . . . hiss.

The nurse notices me. "If you like, you can come back at two."

Rules are rules, and I'm not one to break them. But why can't they make an exception? The next time I see Mom, she might be dead all the way.

I do an about-face and ride the elevator to the first floor. I wish I'd brought my sketchpad so I could curl up and doodle; I left it at Mom and Fran's, and I'm in major withdrawal.

I browse through paperbacks in the gift shop till Arye shows up and catches me with a bodice-ripper romance. "Mom says we should take a break and go home."

"I don't want a break." Actually, I do. But it seems more appropriate to hang around and suffer.

"Oh, come on. You can shower and stuff, and eat some *real* food. We'll come back later."

"What about Schmule?"

"Mom wants him to stay."

"Why?"

"I don't know," he growls. "Man! Do you have to question everything?"

Well, yeah! Fran's throwing me out, but Schmule gets to stay?

On the other hand, he has a point. If I don't shower pretty soon, I'll end up as raggedy-looking as Fran.

Back at the brownstone, I shower, then pull on jeans, a T-shirt, and a cardigan knitted by Nonny in her few free moments between grinding up Poppy's pills and hauling him onto the toilet. Hair damp, I wind my way back downstairs and find Arye in an apron, frying pierogies.

"What?" he asks when sees me stop short.

"Cute apron."

He grins, tugs the hem, and dips his knee in a curtsy. I burst out laughing, and the sound of it stuns me back into silence. My mom is dying. I have no right to laugh. But crabby old Arye in an apron? Too funny!

I swing open a cupboard. Arye's grin vanishes. "What're you doing?"

"Getting some plates?"

"I'll do it. You'll mix them up."

"Mix what up?"

"The dishes. This is a kosher kitchen. You can't just mix stuff up."

"Since when do you guys keep kosher?"

Arye smacks my hand from the cupboard door. "Since Penny decided to convert."

"My mom converted? When?"

He seems pleased at my reaction. "Well, she didn't actually *convert*. But she started taking classes, and now my mom's all into it again. So, yeah, we're kosher. Don't *treyf* it up." Whatever that means.

"Why would my mom convert to Judaism? She never even went to church."

Arye pokes at the steaming pierogies. "Duh. Maybe that's why."

Steaming myself, I plunk down into a chair, too blown away to think straight. Mom wanted to convert to Judaism? Okay, I've heard of Jews accepting Christ and converting to Christianity. Maybe I'm naive, or just dumb—but how can a Christian become Jewish? How can you stop believing something you believed your whole life?

This is unbelievably weird.

No. It's Mom.

I pick at the pierogies Arye passes to me, squishing potato filling through the prongs of my fork. Yes, I know what it means to keep a kosher kitchen. Different dishes for meat and dairy, all of them kept in separate cupboards and drawers. I wonder what happens if a milk glass bumps into a meat platter. Does the kitchen explode? Are you then forced to go to the Jewish equivalent of confession?

Appetite shot to hell, I finish one mangled pierogi to be polite and wash it down with some cold milk. Whoa, wait'll Dad hears this one. He'll shit the proverbial brick.

14

Arye dozes on the sofa after the pierogies. I roam the house, looking at the pictures all over the walls and on every available surface. One catches my eye: a heart-shaped portrait in a silver frame of Fran, in a marginally feminized tux, and Mom in a white dress, a single red rose resting in the crook of her arm. Cheek to cheek, hands clasped, glowing with smiles. Their "wedding" picture?

I don't know why I'm so shocked that my mom planned to become Jewish. Isn't this the same woman who was married for ten years, had me for seven more, and then decided she was a lesbian? Nothing she does should surprise me anymore.

Tired of Arye's snores, I punch the sofa. "Are we going back to the hospital in this century or the next?"

Arye mumbles, "What time is it?" and then scrambles up, wide-awake. "Crap. Visiting hours are over at eight. Why didn't you wake me up?"

"Um, because I'm not your mother?"

"*Tha-ank* you."

"Knock it off!" Seriously, how much of this must I take? "You think this is fun for me? Am I having the time of my life? No, I don't think so. So stop acting like an ass."

Arye opens his mouth, then apparently thinks twice about antagonizing Evil Shawna. "Fine. Let's go."

Shawna, one. Arye, zero.

15

Back at the hospital, Arye and I are barely off the elevator when I hear a familiar boom: "Do you have any idea who I am? Get me your supervisor!"

Oh, no, Dad's playing his favorite *do-you-have-any-idea-who-I-am* card again. Of course the nurse doesn't realize, or care, that he's John W. Gallagher, MD, PhD. Nationally renowned expert on primary infertility. Nationally renowned expert on preconception gender determination. Emperor of Petri Dishes. Supreme Ruler of the Bulb Syringe, or whatever they use nowadays.

"Sir, our visiting hours—," the flustered nurse begins.

"Didn't you hear me just ask for your supervisor? I didn't fly all the way from California to be jacked around."

Arye lags back. "Uh, your dad?"

"Bull's-eye, Einstein."

"What's *he* doing here?" he asks accusingly, as if I invited him.

Part of me wants to run up and distract Dad so he won't explode in a way that'll turn the whole staff against me. The same thing he likes to do at school meetings, for example. But then a lady in a lab coat skittles up—the poor supervisor, no doubt—and edges Dad away from the quaking nurse. "I'm sorry, Dr. Gallagher, but my staff was instructed—"

Dad lowers his voice one decibel. "I know what they've been instructed to do. It also states clearly in your hospital policy that only immediate family members can visit in your ICU. Ms. Good-man's been in and out of here for two days. She is *not* a relative. How do you explain that?"

As the supervisor stammers, Dr. Felker shows up. Wilted, exhausted, he extends a hand. "Dr. Gallagher? I'm George Felker, the resident on call."

Dad turns an evil eye on this intruder. "Resident?" Contempt drips like fresh tar. "Where's her attending physician?"

"Home with his family, I imagine. What you see is what you get." Got to hand it to the guy, he's not easily intimidated. The nursing supervisor, I notice, has already snuck off.

I jump when Fran asks behind us, "What's going on?" Arye jerks a thumb toward Dad. Fran's eyes almost pop out of their sockets. "Oh, shit." She straightens her shoulders and marches over. "Hi, John. Fancy meeting you here."

Dad nods curtly. Then he spots Arye and me. "Shawna?"

Oh-h, God. I drag myself over. "Hi, Dad."

My dad, tall, massive-shouldered, generates an imposing figure in his gray Armani suit and red power tie, a charcoal coat draped over one arm. Stern, chiseled features. An aura of indisputable authority. When Dr. Felker suggests he accompany him to the lounge, Dad consults his Rolex as if he has a pending appointment. "Fine. Let's go." He adds firmly, to Fran and Arye, "You two can wait here."

Fran bristles. "Oh, no you don't. Anything that needs to be dis-cussed, we can do it all together."

Dad informs Dr. Felker, "Ms. Goodman isn't a relative. She's my wife's roommate, nothing more—"

"*Ex*-wife!" Fran interjects.

"—and I happen to hold a durable power of attorney."

Silence. Fran deflates.

"So," Dad continues in that same smooth, icy tone he uses when I career into the house four seconds past curfew, "as you can see, Ms. Goodman has nothing to do with any decisions that need to be made."

"Stop talking about me in the third person," Fran barks. "I'm standing right here."

Dr. Felker raises a hand. "Please. For now, let's just get out of the hall."

Dad prods me ahead of him as the doc leads the way. Fran and Arye follow anyway. Schmule, thankfully, is sound asleep on the sofa. I move his feet and ease myself down. Fran and Arye sit, too, but Dad remains standing so he can tower over us and intimidate everyone in the room.

Now that he has a captive audience, Dr. Felker launches into an account of Mom's condition. He uses the word "grave" three times and "critical" twice. Mom's kidneys are shutting down. Her blood pressure is holding at 60/20. Heart rate in the thirties. An MRI revealed more bleeding in her brain. A repeat EEG showed "no significant brain activity."

In plain English, she's gorked.

"What I'm advising is that we discontinue the life support. Leaving her on," he adds carefully, "will only postpone the inevitable."

Robot-like, Fran stares at her hands. "No."

Dad whips an envelope out of his suit coat and hands it to Dr. Felker. "My wife made this out after the birth of our daughter. It states her wishes quite clearly. No extreme measures."

Dr. Felker scans the document as Fran studies her mangled finger-nails. I guess Mom's "wishes" must be pretty cut-and-dried, because all he says, after passing the paper back to Dad, is, "I'm very sorry."

Fran raises her eyes, glassy with rage. "People wake up from comas all the time. Hopeless cases. People who have been in comas for years! Don't tell me there's no hope. There's always hope."

"People in persistent vegetative states, maybe," the doctor admits. "It's rare, but it happens. But they're never the same, never normal. Regardless, this is different. Sonia's not in a vegetative state. She's brain-dead."

Somewhere along the line "Ms. Sorenson" turned into "Sonia" and, well, it hits me like a stray grenade. I realize I'm crying without making a sound, only tears dripping rapidly down my cheeks.

"I don't believe it," Fran insists. "Penny would *not* have wanted this. She would've wanted a chance, goddamn it. You're not even giving her a *chance*."

I try to stifle it, but the sob escapes me. Dad strides across the room and tows me to my feet. "My daughter's upset," he announces, as if nobody can tell. "Just give me the papers and I'll sign them now. Then Shawna can go in and say good-bye to her mother."

"Can't we at least wait for the rabbi?" Fran cries out.

"What rabbi?"

No one answers. It's up to me to break the news. "Mom's sort of . . . Jewish," I whimper between hiccups.

"She's what?" Without waiting for a reply, he snaps, "That is the most ridiculous thing I ever heard. I'm not waiting for any rabbi." He puts one arm around me and propels me toward the door, tossing over his shoulder, "Let's get this over with."

Schmule twitches in his sleep as Fran's howl cuts the air. Arye springs across the room, hugs her, and she sobs into his shirt. Seeing that, hearing her cry, makes *me* start crying harder, because *what if she's right?* What if there *is* a chance Mom might wake up?

I pull back. "Dad, wait!"

Dad stops. His big shoulders droop. Then, slowly, he pulls me close. I rope my arms around his waist as he smothers me to his chest.

"Shawna," he says softly into my hair, "the doctor's right. It's better this way. It's better for *her.* You have to trust me, okay?"

I nod into his suit coat, praying he's as right about this as he is about everything else. He squeezes me tightly for one long, warm moment. Then, linked together, we sidestep out of the room, leaving behind Fran's broken wails.

16

Dry-eyed, rigid, I stare at the person who used to be my mom. No ventilator. No tube in her throat. No more IV bags dangling overhead. Yet she breathes on. A ragged intake of air. A gurgling expulsion. A full minute of silence before her chest heaves again.

Earlier, after a brief, heated argument, Dad agreed to "allow" Fran, Arye, and Schmule to join the deathwatch. Schmule stares blankly at the bed, also measuring each breath. I think about the fact that Schmule's known Mom his whole life, that she'd been his mom longer than she'd ever been mine.

Dad didn't stay; he said to "page" him if anything happened. After he left, the rabbi showed up—not a bearded old guy in a prayer shawl and yarmulke, but Fran's aunt Rina who flew in from Cleveland Heights. When she prayed in Hebrew, she didn't call my mom Penny, or even Sonia. She called her Shoshanna, Mom's soon-to-be Hebrew name. At first I thought she'd said "Shawna," which totally rattled me.

One foot, purple and mottled, sticks out from under the sheet. Mom hates having her feet covered up in bed. So do I. I always hang mine off the edge. If I had the energy, I'd get up and uncover the other one.

I lean my head back for a second, and that's when it happens: Mom's pale blue eyes flicker wide open. I blink, and watch her pull herself up by the metal side rail.

She fluffs the sheet and says unconcernedly, "That father of yours *still* gets on my nerves!"

17

Mom nods at Fran, listless and unseeing. "Poor thing," she says sadly. "And she's worried about me?"

No, no, no. *This is so not happening.*

"Are you listening, Shawna?"

"Yes," I whisper.

Nobody else hears me. Not Arye, who sits right beside me. Not the rabbi, quietly reading out loud. Not Schmule, resting his head on Fran's shoulder.

"He barges in, takes over, then he's too chicken to watch me die." A thoughtful pause. "Fran always said he was a royal prick. He thinks he knows everything. Everyone else is an idiot. How do you stand it, Shawna? Don't you wish you could tell him off?"

"He's my dad," I say faintly.

"Ri-ight." Her fingers follow the monitor wires attached to her chest. A Star of David on a silver chain rests against her throat, the same place she once wore a cross. "Are you shocked?"

"Not really. You always did do . . . weird things." With fingers as blotchy as her slender feet, Mom touches the six-pointed star. She smiles, and I blurt out, "Mom, are you happy?"

"Very happy."

In one swift movement she yanks the monitor wires off and tosses them into the air. An alarm shrills as she throws back her head and sings out, " 'But careless gifts are seldom prized' "—the buzzing grows louder, and her fingers dance, Fosse-style, high over her head—"'And *mine* were worthily despised'"—and louder and louder—

 —and I jerk my head up as the nurse slaps the monitor off for good.

18

Part of me wants to go back to the hotel with Dad, sleep in a strange, impersonal bed, and dream of nothing. The rest of me longs to return to Mom and Fran's cozy, cluttered rooms—the same rooms my mother touched only two days ago. Maybe if I can touch her things, if I can smell her scent, it'll give me a better chance to say good-bye to her.

What saves me is that it's after midnight. All my stuff is back at Mom and Fran's, including the tampons I'll probably need any minute now. I don't say this outright, but Dad gets the hint.

He taps his toe and fiddles with a cuff link. "Fine. But I'll *send* a cab for you first thing in the morning. Don't try to get one by yourself. This city is full of maniacs." He pecks my forehead and I catch a whiff of his cologne. "Call me tonight." This is a royal command, not a concerned request.

Fran asks Rabbi Rina, "You'll take care of everything? You'll stay with her?" Rina, an older version of Fran right down to the limp gray hair and crinkly brown eyes, promises her she will, and the four of us cram into a cab in the crisp autumn night. Fran doesn't speak to me the entire ride back. Does she blame me for this? I didn't pull the plug! I had no say in it at all.

I seethe silently, my breath fogging the cab window. Back at the brownstone, I pull on my long purple nightshirt, brush my teeth, and crawl under the afghan on the saggy flowered sofa. After a quick call to reassure Dad I wasn't abducted by a desperate pimp, I tap in LeeLee's number and wake her up. "It's me. It's over. My mom died."

"Oh-my-GOD! Are you okay?"

"I guess so. I'm at Fran's right now."

"Does your dad know she died?"

"Yeah, he's already here."

"At the Frankfurter's?"

"No! At a hotel."

"So when will you be back?"

"After the funeral, I guess. Look, I gotta go," I add as I hear a toilet flush. "I just wanted to let you know."

"Thanks. And I'm so sorry, *chica*. I know you guys were kind of on the outs, but—"

"I know. But she's still my mom. Well, I mean . . ."

"Yeah," LeeLee agrees softly. "Okay, love ya! Call me tomorrow?"

"I'll try. Love ya back."

Homesick, I punch Fran's extra pillow into a suitable lump, the lines of Mom's poem racing through my mind. I know it had been a dream, a hallucination, and yet it had seemed so real! Her flickering fingers, her glowing face. All of her alive and real enough for me to reach out and touch.

I drag the pillow over my head, tired of thinking, tired of feeling. And already tired of missing my mom.

19

Starved by morning, I devour a bagel and cream cheese, then feel highly guilty for enjoying it so much. Mom's been dead for twelve hours. How dare I think about food?

Fran, who has barely said a word to me, flies across the kitchen when the telephone rings. I drift out to the living room, where I find Schmule glued to an anime cartoon involving flying dragons and large-breasted women. "Where's your brother?"

Schmule's head bobs under the afghan. "I dunno."

"WHAT?" Fran screams from the kitchen. "Whose idea was this?"

Schmule throws off the afghan, eyes bright pools of alarm. *Now what?*

"No fucking way! I will not—allow—it!" Fran listens intently, her spine growing more rigid by the second. "No, you do not have my permission to release the b-body . . . *What?* Bullshit! I'm calling my lawyer right now." The receiver slams and then she punches more numbers. "Seymour? Fran. You will not believe what that man's pulling now!"

Something tells me that "that man" is my father.

Schmule scrambles up and heads for the door. "I'm gonna find my brother."

I catch his arm. "Wait! You need a coat."

"I got a hoodie on," he protests.

"You need shoes, too, unless you want to catch pneumonia and di—" I bite my lip.

Unfazed, he informs me, "Pneumonia's a virus, duh. You don't get it from being cold. And only, like, one in forty-four hundred people even die from it, anyway."

Can you believe this kid?

Arye's crouched outside on the stoop, sipping coffee. "Mom's on the phone," Schmule announces, flipping a leg over the rail, "yelling at somebody named Seymour." He slides all the way down, landing in his bare feet on the sidewalk.

Arye lifts his eyebrows. "That's Mom's lawyer. What's she yelling about?"

I shrug. Schmule busies himself at the curb, poking damp brown leaves with a stick. When I sit down next to Arye, he scooches another step up. At five foot ten, I'm two or three inches taller. Guys have a complex about that. I'm sure Arye's no exception.

The prolonged silence gnaws at my nerves. "So, do you like living in New York?"

"So, do you always have this compulsion to involve others in mindless chitchat?"

"Why don't you like me?" I demand, surprising myself.

"Who says I don't like you?" I scoff openly, and Arye adds, "You don't know me and I don't know you. Right? So let's leave it at that."

I can't. "Why are you treating me like the enemy? It's my mom who died. And it's *your* mom who asked me to come in the first place."

"Yeah, well . . ." Dismissing this, Arye yells over to Schmule, "Put your hood up, goofball!"

"Hoods are for nerds!" Schmule retorts without looking back.

"Hoods are for people," I say, "who don't want to get sick. Cold lowers your resistance and makes you susceptible to bacteria."

"Blah, blah, blah." Schmule drops the stick in the gutter. "What are you, a freakin' doctor?"

Before I can inform him of my life's plan, not that he cares, Fran appears at the door. She says icily, "Shawna, get your things together. Your cab will be here in ten minutes."

"You talked to my dad?"

She slams the door without answering. Arye hops down to the sidewalk to drag Schmule out of the gutter, and pushes us both inside. "Mom. What's wrong?"

"I'll tell you what's wrong," Fran explodes. "And Shawna, I'm sorry, I know this has *nothing* to do with you—but I've never met a bigger son of a bitch in my life!"

Schmule tucks his hands into his armpits. "Who?"

"My dad," I say. Gee, Fran. Tell me something I don't know.

"Dr. Gallagher," Fran rages to the boys, as if I'm not here in the same room, "wants to have Penny's funeral in Cleveland."

Arye shoots me that familiar look of blame. "Can he do that?"

"He's already done it. As soon as they finish the autopsy he's shipping her right out."

I clear my throat. "They're doing an autopsy?"

"Yes. Your father *insisted*," she adds sarcastically.

Not that I'm on their side, okay? But Dad's barely spoken to Mom in years. How can he insist on anything? More important, *why?*

"I spoke to my attorney. He's hoping to get an injunction. But your father, apparently, already made the arrangements."

Spinning on one heel, too furious to go on, Fran starts banging crap around the kitchen, filling a kettle for hot water, ripping mugs from the cupboards. Don't mix 'em up, Fran, I silently warn. Unless God doesn't care if you screw up under duress.

She stops to grip the edge of the counter. "Your mother has a will," she says hoarsely. "It's never been updated. Your father's the executor. And he's listed *everywhere* as her next of kin." Her whole body sags. I pray she doesn't end up on the floor. "Oh, God, I begged her, begged her, *begged* her to change that will! I can't believe it. I just—can't—believe—this!"

I can. It's so typical of Mom. Once, in first grade, after I was out with the chicken pox, Mom sent me back to school without a doctor's note. My teacher freaked out over one leftover spot, so they forced me to sit in the office till Julie came back to pick me up. Later, of course, I had to hear about it from Mom: *What do you need a doctor's note for? Are they idiots? Can't they tell by looking at you you're not contagious? God, I hate bureaucracy!*

Yes, Mom hated bureaucracy. No doctor's excuse? No biggie. But leaving Dad's name on her will because she couldn't get around to it? Not making sure Fran could be in charge if anything happened to her?

No wonder Mom didn't take me to the hospital that night. Forget the gallery. She just dreaded the paperwork.

Arye asks uncomfortably, "What—what kind of funeral will it be?"

Fran rests an elbow on the counter and mumbles into her hand, "I think you know."

Silence. I get it: no Jewish funeral for Penny/Shoshanna, who, unsurprisingly, never got around to converting.

Nobody speaks as I gather up my things and move toward the door. Unnecessarily, I offer, "I'll wait outside."

I turn the knob with a shaky hand and let myself out, thankful that these people, all of them, are so out of my life.

 20

LeeLee, true friend that she is, cuts school on Monday. She watches dubiously as I lace my vintage Frye boots up to my knees. "You're not seriously wearing those."

"Why not? You gave them to me." One of her better thrift shop finds.

"Because you're Shawna Gallagher? Because your old man will kill you if you show up looking like some punk-rock bag lady in thirty-year-old boots?"

I smile. My face hurts from the effort.

Dad's not happy about me taking my own car to the funeral; he thought I'd "prefer" to ride in some ghastly limousine. How they plan to stuff Poppy into a limo, I have no idea. And I honestly can't deal with Aunt Colleen right now.

In the car I ask LeeLee, "What are you hiding in there?" She's been very secretive about the contents of her bulging hobo bag.

"You'll see."

I drive a white, five-year-old, moderately geeky Camry. I say only "moderately" geeky because it's a convertible, and loaded. We reach the church and crawl into a space at the end of the lot. LeeLee, at last, reveals her surprise: two unlabeled bottles of red wine. "Are you nuts? You want me to breathe booze on Father Bernacki?" To say nothing of my relatives.

"Have a swig. You deserve it. Anyway, it's sangria. Homemade! Hardly any booze at all."

I look out one side of the car, then the other, and glance out the back to be safe. No cops in sight. Hopefully the police force has more pressing things to do than patrol church parking lots in search of underage drinkers. I take a couple of sweet, fruity swallows and then hand the bottle back. "Thanks."

After a few healthy swigs of her own, LeeLee twists the cork back in place. She shoves both bottles under the seat, ignoring my protests about the open booze bottle laws. "We'll drink it later. You're not gonna be driving around with it, okay? Trust me."

"Okay. But if it leaks, you're dead."

Inside the church, Aunt Colleen hugs me viciously. I nearly slice open a lip when my face hits her lacquered red hair. "Oh, Shawna. What a perfect nightmare!" she declares with a glance of revulsion at my battered boots, making me wonder if she means Mom, or what I'm wearing on my feet.

I unwind myself from her tentacles with a polite murmur, then scan the crowd for familiar faces. Mr. and Mrs. Connolly are here, but no Susan. And, sadly, no Devon, either. Other than Danielle and Melanie, who hug me before slinking self-consciously to a back pew, it seems only LeeLee bothered to take the day off from school.

Five minutes later we sit in a rigid row: LeeLee, me, Dad, Aunt Colleen, Uncle Dieter, and Nonny. Poppy, hunkered in his wheel-chair, gets planted in the aisle. I sense a flash of Dad's ire, and instantly see why: Fran, Arye, and Schmule just wandered in.

"Well, well. Watch the roof cave in." Aunt Colleen fires orbital daggers over her shoulder.

Uncle Dieter hushes her, and Nonny says at the same time, "They're not hurtin' anyone, Colleen."

"All of you hush." Dad gives me a significant poke, although I'm the only one who kept my mouth shut. Then, rethinking this, he rests an arm around my shoulders.

"It's not too *laaate* to run back to the *caaar*," LeeLee sings in my ear.

I wish.

Sit, stand, kneel, pray . . . I could do this in my sleep. I have to force myself not to doodle on my program as I listen to Father Bernacki. You can tell he never met Mom in his life; his droning, generic words could apply to anyone. As he wraps it up in obvious relief, I notice a growing commotion—and then Schmule's voice rises from the back of the sanctuary. "No, I *want* to! Why can't I?"

Father Bernacki squints out over rapidly swiveling heads. "Ma'am?"

Fran, flushed, half rises from the pew. She swipes for Schmule, missing him by an inch. Schmule rushes down the aisle, dodges Poppy's chair, and runs up the steps to Father Bernacki's podium. God must have hit the master pause button of the universe; aside from Dad's rapidly crunching jaw, nobody else moves. Even Poppy's rhythmically bobbing chin halts for the moment.

"I have something to say," Schmule announces, glancing anxiously at Father Bernacki. Father B. smiles, adjusts the microphone, and smoothly steps back. "My name is Schmule Goodman—" He jumps back in horror as his voice thunders through the speakers. Recomposed, he adds, "I want to say some stuff about my mom."

LeeLee whacks me with her knee. I know what she's thinking: why does Schmule want to talk about Fran at *my* mother's funeral?

"I loved my mom a lot," Schmule begins. "And so, when my other mom asked me *why* I loved her so much, I started to think about all the things that made me really love her. So I guess this is gonna be, like, a whatchamacallit, a eulogy?"

"Other" mom? This isn't about Fran at all. Oh, God! If there's anyone here who doesn't know about my mom, they're about to find out—and Dad's going to spaz!

Don't blame Schmule, Shawna. You're the only one who ever kept me a secret.

Not true, Mom. *You* moved two states away. If you were so proud of being gay, why didn't you hang around?

How twisted must you be to carry on a conversation with your dead lesbian mother in a Catholic church? I pick up the missal and thumb pointlessly through the pages.

"I loved my mom because she was the smartest person I know. When I asked her a question she always knew the answer. If she *didn't* know the answer, she'd make me look it up. And if I couldn't find it, she'd say, well, it must not be important."

That's Mom, all right.

"I loved my mom because she liked poetry. She used to read it to me all the time. I liked listening to her read. I really miss her voice."

Funny how *I'm* still hearing it . . .

"I also loved her 'cause she liked to take pictures. Sometimes she'd follow me around all day with her camera. Once when I was little, she took a picture of me crying. That really made me mad, so I told her to throw it out. I'm like, 'Quit taking pictures of me, it gets on my nerves.'" Schmule pauses. "But then she said that someday I'll grow up, and that if she didn't take my picture *now* she'd forget what I look like. She said she wanted to keep, like, pieces of me. I said she already had lots of pictures, so she should throw that one away. I didn't want people to see me crying like that."

He stops again. The church stays silent except for the relentless tapping of Aunt Colleen's pointy-toed pump on the padded kneeler.

"But Mom said she wanted *all* of my pieces. Not just the good ones. She said that when I grow up I won't be able to cry like that anymore, that men don't cry. And even if they do, they never let anybody see 'em. She wanted to keep that picture so that when she's an old, old lady she can look back and remember what I looked like that day."

LeeLee reaches for my hand. Dad removes his arm from my shoulder so he can play, irately, with the band of his watch. Aunt Colleen's shoe tap-tap-taps. I blink, and one tear splats on the missal.

"After that, I let her take pictures of me whenever she wanted. But then she died last week and nobody expected it . . . so now she'll never know what I'm going to look like when I'm grown. I'm sad because she'll never be that old, old lady and I won't be able to take care of her like she took care of me. I keep thinking of all this stuff I'd like to tell her, but now it's too late. That's kinda the worst thing of all, not telling her stuff."

His breath shudders into the microphone. The shoe tapping stops. I hear Poppy snore.

"So now when I grow up, I'll think about all the stuff she'll never know about me. That'll make me miss her even more, so then I probably *will* cry. Even if I'm, like, forty or something." Another ragged breath, and then he finishes so softly I have to strain to hear him: "I think she was wrong. I won't even care if anybody sees me."

21

After the service I endure condolence hugs from people I never met in my life. Melanie and Danielle take off as soon as they can, not that I blame them. If it were the other way around, I'd run back to school, too. There's not much you can say when your friend's mother drops over dead. At least they showed up, unlike Susan the Bitch Connolly.

All I can think about is the sangria waiting in the car. But just as I'm about to grab LeeLee, a cluster of women walk in—three neatly dressed in somber-colored pantsuits, but two others with very short haircuts and masculine clothes—followed by a group of, well, sort of swishy guys, one with a lavender scarf around his neck.

As I nudge LeeLee, I hear somebody ask behind us, "Do you believe that?" and another person add in a hushed tone, "What a bunch of freaks."

"Who are they?" LeeLee whispers.

"Friends of Fran, I guess." I see a few people gawking openly at a hefty woman with tattoos crawling up both arms. Others studiously turn away while most, I'm happy to say, pay no attention to her at all. "Omigod. What a dyke."

LeeLee narrows her eyes at me. "Nice. You sound just like your aunt."

Heat flames across my scalp. It does sound like something Aunt Colleen would say, and I have no idea what possessed me to say it. And friends of Fran, I realize, means friends of my mother as well.

I hear Mom again: *Yes, Shawna, gay friends of your gay mom. What did you think? That all my friends were straight?*

I shake my head. She sounds so close, so real. Can this be the first sign of a nervous breakdown?

Quickly I turn to seek out Dad's reaction to the newcomers—and bump into Arye.

"Hi," he grunts.

"Oh, you must be Arye!" LeeLee ogles his yarmulke. "Shawna told me *all* about you."

Arye's nostrils flare. "No kidding?"

I squeak, "Where's your mom?" Arye jerks his head, and I see Fran and Schmule making a beeline toward her friends. "How's she doing?"

"Why don't you go ask her?" Not quite sarcastic. But damn close.

LeeLee flies into his face. "Hell-oo? Are we not at a funeral? Isn't there, like, some kind of decorum here? Do you have to be such a, such a—?"

"Putz?" Arye suggests.

"Yeah. Putz." She spouts the *P* in a very unladylike fashion.

Perfect Shawna stares at Fran, knowing she should take the initiative to welcome her and thank her for coming. When Fran notices, though, she turns away.

Evil Shawna thinks, fine, be a bitch. I'll never lay eyes on you again.

Leaving Arye and LeeLee nose to nose, I slip out a side door. Uncle Dieter, indulging in a cigarette, jumps guiltily. Here he's been telling us all he quit three months ago. "Oh, you are so-o busted!"

Red-faced, he taps an ash. "Don't ever pick one of these up.

You'll be a slave to it your whole life." I don't mention that I'm headed out for a drink myself.

"I don't get it," I burst out. "This funeral. Everything. Why did Dad do it? To get back at Fran?"

"Is that what you think?" I flick my hand, and Uncle Dieter adds thoughtfully, "Well, you might be right. To have a Catholic mass when he knows your mom was trying to convert to Judaism. Plus the embalming, the viewing. Jews do none of that, you know."

No, I didn't know. My only Jewish friend is Melanie, who's about as kosher as a cheeseburger. "How do you know so much about Jewish customs?"

Uncle Dieter scratches his buzz-cut head. I love how his eyes twinkle when he smiles. "I'm an old, learned man, Shawnie. I like to think I know it all." He takes one last drag and grinds the butt under his heel. "Honestly? I don't think he did it just to piss off Fran. I think he did it for you. For closure, you know? And maybe some guilt thrown in, too." Before I can zero in on this, he adds, "Plus, he did love her at one time."

"You'd never know it the way he talks about her," I remind him.

"Well, he did. You know how they say 'opposites' attract? Your mom and dad, they're the classic example. The thing with your mom was, yeah, she was flaky. But she was a strong woman. Strong, and stubborn, and very talented. When her career took off, your dad had a problem with that. He wanted her home. He waited a long time for you, and didn't want you raised by a nanny. It didn't sit well with him, and . . . well, you know how he gets when things don't go his way."

Tell me about it.

Uncle Dieter steps away as I mull this over. Self-consciously, he shakes out his suit coat. "Here, take a whiff. Do I smell like tobacco?"

I sniff. "You reek. Aunt Colleen's gonna kill you."

"I'm used to it, kiddo."

He holds open the door. Reluctantly I go back inside because I can't think of a good excuse to run to my car. LeeLee's gabbing with someone I don't know, a girl in camo-patterned pants, skimpy tank top, and a long red sweater. Nice outfit for a funeral—not. Animated, LeeLee chatters so intently she doesn't even see me.

Fran and her gay pals stir in a tiny clique, avoiding the Black Death otherwise known as my father. I can hear snatches of conversation from other milling guests:

"Did you know Penny was gay?"

"Who was that boy?"

"Poor John. How humiliating for him."

"His daughter seems to be holding up pretty well . . ."

Suddenly, I can't stand it. I can't stand people talking about us. Worse, I can't stand the realization that I've let all Aunt Colleen's anti-gay blather over the years rub off on me so well. I mean, LeeLee and I share a table in art with Jonas Dunn. *He's* gay, he doesn't care who knows it, and I've never had such nasty thoughts about him. If he'd shown up today in a lavender scarf, I'd hug him to death.

So what's different about this?

I don't know. I only know I have to get out of here.

22

I pop the cork and raise the wine bottle to my lips, being especially careful not to spill a drop on my dress. I nearly choke to death when the passenger-side door swings open and Arye slides in without an invitation.

"What're you doing?" I howl.

"I needed a break, too."

"Can't you break somewhere else? I'm kind of busy right now."

He squints at the more-than-half-empty wine bottle. "That any good?"

"I'm saving the rest for LeeLee—my *friend?*—who should be here any second."

"Good luck. She's busy with Tovah."

"Who's Tovah? That chick in the camo pants?"

"Yeah. You know that guy with the purple scarf, and the guy who's with him? Tovah's their daughter."

"Gimme a break. They don't let gay guys adopt little girls."

Arye stares.

"What?" I ask loudly.

"I was gonna ask you if you grew up in a cave. Then I remembered you grew up in O-*hi*-o, so I guess it's not your fault you're so ignorant."

"Ha, ha." He snatches the bottle away, and I warn, "Better not. It's not kosher. I'd hate to see you go to hell."

"Jews don't believe in hell." Arye closes his wicked grin around the spout.

"Seriously? So, what's to stop you, then, from acting like an asshole?"

Arye splutters sangria on his pants. "You don't know much about Jews, do you?"

"Probably as much as you know about Catholics." But I'm smiling again for the second time today. Is it the wine? Or the fact that Arye's not treating me like a leper for a change? Or maybe he is and I'm too buzzed to tell the difference.

We polish off the wine, and I hide the bottle under the seat, where it clanks against number two. "So what'll your dad do," Arye asks, "if he catches you drinking out here?"

"I hope *not* to find out." But I glance around anyway. "I'd better get back. People will think I'm antisocial."

"So what? Jeez, it's your mom's funeral. Maybe you don't *feel* like mingling."

"It doesn't matter how I feel. I'm kind of the hostess here, and—"

Arye hoots. "Hostess? You think this is a party?"

"No! But she's my mom, right? I should be in there talking to people. Not sitting around out here getting drunk with *you*." I grab my keys, jump out, and wobble back to the church.

Arye doesn't follow. I hope he doesn't find that second bottle.

23

"Did you see Arye?" Fran asks me at the door. It's the first time she's spoken to me since the day I walked out of her house.

Tipsy, I fib, "I thought he was right behind me."

"Well, we have to leave. We're flying back home tonight."

The wine has mellowed me. Perfect Shawna returns. "Don't you want to stay for lunch?" Then I picture the food downstairs: cheese cubes, pepperoni, and iced shrimp cocktail, all stacked on the same table, undoubtedly touching in some way.

"Thank you, Shawna. But I don't think we'd be welcome." Fran nods to Arye, who saunters up behind me. "Are you ready?"

"*Been* ready," he says significantly.

Fran wraps a wooden arm briefly around my shoulder. "Take care now." Off she heads toward her rented car. No "keep in touch." No "call me sometime." With Mom gone, I guess she has no reason to pretend.

The boys lag behind. Arye offers me a piece of paper—his e-mail address with his name spelled backward: EyraG. Ooh, clever. "E-mail me one of these days, okay?"

Shocked, and yes, suspicious, I tuck it away. "Thanks."

Arye trudges after Fran. I reach out to smooth Schmule's long, light brown curls. "Hey, I liked what you said about my mom. I meant to tell you that."

Schmule digs a shy toe into the asphalt. "Well, um, she was my mom, too, ya know." And he dashes off after his brother.

# 24

All the way home LeeLee blabs nonstop about Tovah. "Shawna, she's a blast! You know how you meet someone for the first time and you just kinda click? We could've talked for hours. I can't believe how much we have in common!"

I keep stern eyes on the road as she raves on: Tovah's a freshman at NYU. Tovah's majoring in journalism, which is LeeLee's dream. Tovah's parents were killed in a Jerusalem bombing, and she was sent to the U.S. to be adopted by her uncle Will, and Uncle Will's partner, Leo.

Smart. Funny. Gorgeous. Unique. One more gushy adjective out of LeeLee and I swear I will scream. Astonished at this roaring surge of jealousy, I force myself to remember that this is LeeLee, not Susan—that she won't dump me for Tovah the way Susan dumped me for Paige Berry. Besides, Tovah lives in New York and only flew in for the funeral.

Hopefully she'll fly back out ASAP.

"Hello?" LeeLee knocks on the dash. "You still there?"

I snarl back, "It's not like you're giving me a chance to talk."

"Ouch. Sor-ry."

Why am I jealous that LeeLee made a friend?

Maybe because today, of all days, I wanted LeeLee to myself. I want her to hang around and make me laugh even though I should be crying my eyes out, missing my mom.

"You coming to school tomorrow?" LeeLee asks as I halt the car at her driveway.

"Might as well. I already missed two days."

Back home in my blessedly empty house, I lug my sweet, lonely Charles upstairs and curl up with him on my bed. I try to focus on Mom, to remember the "good times"—that's what Father Bernacki stressed in his sermon.

It's too damn bad I can't think of a single one.

Charles burrows his snout into my armpit. My thoughts drift back to LeeLee, and I wonder again why I feel so jealous, so abandoned. Is this what happens when you only have one best friend? You depend on them so much, you're afraid they'll disappear?

25

"Hey, Gallagher!" Devon Connolly tugs my hair as I drag myself toward first-period Anatomy and Physiology. "What're you doing back? Don't you get a vacation when someone dies?"

LeeLee smacks him. "Moron! Do you own a single manner?"

I'm barely insulted by his inane remark because, omigod, Devon touched my hair! Okay, he yanked it. But my scalp tingles deliciously.

Devon plunges ahead of us, and LeeLee grimaces at my dazed expression. "Just tell me, please, what do you see in that *pendejo*? He's related to Susan, remember? They shared a *womb*, for God's sake."

Good question. What *do* I see in him? Aside from the fact that he's undeniably gorgeous with that shaggy blond hair, brain-nuking smile, and hockey star thighs? Does he *remember* making out with me in the basement last week? He doesn't act like it.

LeeLee takes off to her own first-period class. I slide into the table I share with Mary Therese Montgomery, my queen-of-the-geeks lab partner, who's revving up her tape recorder. Mr. Twohig grunts his sympathy and tosses me some handouts, and here, in A&P, I'm finally back in my element. Neurons and synapses. Mitochondria and DNA. Memorize, memorize, and then out the door. Math and science are so safe, so predictable. No surprises.

Melanie and Danielle share the table next to mine. Pale, willowy

Melanie tucks her tidy auburn pageboy behind her ears and leans closer to whisper, "You doing okay?" Danielle, with her fabulous sun-streaked hair and a leftover summer tan, wiggles her fingers in a wave.

"I'm fine. Thanks." I'm kind of tired of saying this.

Mel and Danielle are tight the way LeeLee and I are tight. Even when the four of us hang out, we always pair off. Without LeeLee in this class—because she'd never be caught dead slicing open a rabbit—I tend to feel like the odd geek out.

Devon, on the other hand, *is* in this class. He pokes my back as I shuffle through my handouts. "Gallagher. Got an extra pencil?"

I always have extra pencils on hand. How could I not? I'm always drawing. I hand one back to him, though not one of the sacred mechanicals I use to take notes. He smiles. I smile back. How could he possibly forget he almost swallowed my tongue? How could he forget that his sweaty hands once groped the cups of my padded bra?

I watch in dismay as his green gaze roams and then rests on the exposed legs of Alyssa Hunt, top slut. Alyssa wets her lips with a feline flick of her own tongue. Devon's smile stretches, and suddenly I'm invisible.

I slouch, tapping my pencil. No, Devon will never ask me out, and here is why: picture me at fifteen dating Kevin Nguyen, a sweet, normal guy. We were lab partners in pre-chem. We study-dated a *lot*.

Then Dad got to meet him.

Dad: "I don't want you going out with that boy anymore. He's Asian."

Me: "No, he's not. He was born *here*."

Dad: "No interracial relationships, Shawna. End of discussion."

After that, I made up excuses whenever Kevin asked me out. Finally, he quit asking. We say hi in the halls now, but that's about it.

Okay, picture me again later that year: Andrew Klinger, the geeky-yet-sexy computer genius who couldn't wait to get his hands on my, um, modem.

Dad, prerecorded: "I don't want you going out with that boy anymore. His father works in a bar."

Me: "His father *owns* that bar." A chain of them, actually.

Dad: "Bar owners aren't the kind of people I want you associated with. Besides, they're Protestant."

Then, the best one of all: Danielle fixed me up with her brother, Philip. We hit it off right away and dated for two months. Dad, hard as he tried, couldn't come up with a single criticism except that Philip, a senior, was "a bit old" for me. A nice, Catholic, Irish American boy on his way to Harvard to follow in the footsteps of his lawyer parents. Perfect, right?

When Philip asked me to his senior prom, I spent four months' allowance on a dress, double pierced my ears, and risked skin cancer trying to build up a tan. A week before prom, Philip took me to the movies. Later, we parked. We didn't go all the way— hello, I was fifteen—but we did lose track of time. A full hour past curfew we gunned up the driveway. Luckily Dad possesses no firearms.

My father loomed menacingly as Philip began, "Dr. Gallagher, I'm so sorry, but—"

Dad: "Shut up."

Me and Philip: (stunned silence)

Dad, taking in my messy hair and disheveled clothes: "Did you have sexual intercourse? Did you use a condom?"

Me: "WHAT?"

Philip—once he recovered from the shock: "S-sir?"

Dad: "A condom. A condom. Surely you know what a condom is?"

Me: "Dad, Dad, Dad—"

Dad: "Did—you—or—didn't—you—use—a—condom—tonight?"

Philip: "Sir, we didn't do anything—"

Me, at the same time: "*No, Dad! We did not use a condom!*"

Poor Philip took off like a chipmunk. He didn't take me to the prom, or anywhere else again. He graduated and went off to Harvard, of course. I never told Danielle what happened. I doubt Philip did, either.

But that's not the "best" part:

A couple of days later I found a sample-sized box of Trojans on my bedspread. Ribbed, no less. Pre-lubricated. Assorted colors! And a typewritten note from Dad: *Shawna, this does not mean I approve of premarital sex. I sincerely hope you never need these. But IF YOU MUST ENGAGE IN SEXUAL INTERCOURSE, please promise me you will use a condom.*

I stashed the condoms in my closet and never looked at them again. Never dated again, either. By junior year I'd established myself as a die-hard science nerd, with minimal social skills and an ayatollah for a father. No male heterosexual with a brain would ask me out on a date, and I'll *never* bring another guy home to meet my dad.

I yelp as Devon flicks my shoulder. "Got a sharpener?" he whispers.

I fumble in my purse . . . where is it, where is it? Noting his sigh of impatience, I give up and relinquish one of the pristine #7 pencils I reserve for impromptu sketches. I'm sure I'll never get it back.

My reward, though, is his heart-melting smile. "Thanks, Gallagher. You rock."

26

Just like in the movies, there will be a reading of Mom's will. The same will she made out, like, twenty years ago.

Dad leans close to the beveled mirror in our front hall, smoothing the sleeves of his dark suit, adjusting his tie. Is he deliberately trying to look the part of a grieving widower?

"Will Fran be there?" I ask, curious.

"I hope not. I've had enough of that woman. As far as I know she's back in New York."

"Can I come?" If Fran won't be there, it might be interesting.

"Don't you have an English test today?"

One thing about Dad, he knows my schedule down to the minute. Wade Prep posts every detail on the school Web site: exams, assignments, due dates, etc. Big Brother in action, making sure your parents can track every grade.

Yes, it's an English test. No, I didn't study. I've been a bit busy, you know, with death and all.

"Yes." I sigh, and add, "Hey, you look handsome today," because he really does. No wonder Dad has so many girlfriends. Not shabby at all for an almost-sixty-year-old dude.

"I do?" Dad jerks his tie one last time, then shrugs, businesslike, into his coat. He pecks my forehead. "Thanks, honey. You have a good day."

I grab a bran muffin, head off to school, and drag my way

through A&P, trig, English, lunch, economics, study hall, Spanish, and then art. No after-school extracurricular activities this year. Thank God I already fulfilled my requirements for college. After three years of Spanish Club, Tech Club, Mathletes, and Greenpeace, I am so taking a break.

After school I peek in the mailbox. Since I'll technically have enough credits to graduate this winter, I already sent out a gazillion applications. Kenyon, though, is the only college I want. Dad took me to visit the campus over the summer and I fell in love with those old Gothic buildings in the middle of nowhere. I almost didn't apply anywhere else, but Kenyon's a bitch to get into. Besides, Dad made me.

Nothing for me in the mailbox. I shower Charles with attention and then check my e-mail, but it's only the usual butt-cluster of spam, jokes, and chain mails. Then I notice the wrinkled paper on my desk with Arye's e-mail address. Was he serious about keeping in touch?

Impulsively, I type a short note: *Just wanted to say hi. Hope you had a safe trip back and thanks for coming. Say hi to*—how do you spell Schmule?—*your brother for me.*

Perfect Shawna adds: *Say hi to your mom, too. Talk to you soon.*

Talk to you soon? Ha, not likely. I bet he forgot all about me the second he jumped onto that plane, happy to escape the evil clutches of the Gallagher clan.

I hit SEND anyway. Now he has my e-mail address, too.

27

Too old to go trick-or-treating, too lazy to hand out candy, LeeLee and I hit the mall on Halloween night. In a fitting room at Sears, the only store she can afford, I watch sympathetically as she tries to force a pair of jeans over her, um, voluptuous rear end.

"I'm so fa-at," she moans, adding a few self-directed insults in Spanish.

"You are not fat. You're Puerto Rican. You're supposed to be curvy."

LeeLee sniffs. "Ugh, so stereotypical. What, because I'm Puerto Rican, I'm supposed to shop in the fat lady department and be happy about it? These piece-of-shit jeans are supposed to *stretch*."

"So go up a size."

"This is a four-*teen*!"

She bitches some more, and ends up buying nothing. We head for the food court, and while waiting in line at Auntie Anne's—not that she needs a giant pretzel after her fitting room meltdown—her cell phone rings.

"Hi!" she squeals. She holds it away from her mouth. "Omigod. It's Tovah."

She gave Tovah her cell number?

"Yeah, I mean, no, we're at the mall. Shawna and me." LeeLee smiles so broadly I'm surprised her cheekbones don't splinter. "Yeah, I know! I'm so glad you called—" Jabbering, she drifts out of line, phone glued to her face like it was stitched there by a Beverly Hills surgeon.

Dismissed, I buy a whole wheat pretzel and stake claim to a bench. As I munch despondently, who comes along? Susan Connolly and her winged monkey, Paige Berry.

"Hey," Susan greets me. "What're you doing here?"

"We sure didn't expect to see *you* here, Shawna," Paige adds sweetly.

I swallow a bite of pretzel and dab my lips. "Why not?"

"Well." Susan tosses her mane and glances at Paige, who smiles evilly as she twirls a mahogany curl. "Because of your mom and all."

I—simply—cannot—*stand*—these—two. "I'm not allowed to go to a mall because my mother died?"

Paige's frosted lips twist with amusement. "God, Shawna. Why are you so touchy?"

I'm not touchy, Paige. I simply hate your guts. Every word you say in my presence only tempts me to jab a fingernail through your phony purple contacts.

"Do you want to hang with us for a while?" Susan asks, disregarding the fact that Paige's reception to this couldn't be any colder if she'd dumped a bucket of ice water over my head. "Saks is doing makeovers. C'mon. It'll be fun!"

Not too long ago I would've jumped at the chance to hang out with Susan, *sans* Paige, of course. Even now I can feel the old fantasies creeping in: *Susie and Shawna Cruise the Mall. Susie and Shawna Find a Great Deal on Estée Lauder Mascara. Susie and Shawna Make Peace, Blow Off College, Tour Europe for a Year, and* . . .

"Yo, Gallagher." Devon ruffles my bangs. "'Sup, blondie?"

Susan groans. "God, Devon. Do you have to follow me *every-where?*"

Devon jerks a thumb in the direction of his hockey pals. "I'm not following you, freak. I'm here with my homies."

"Devon, you're white," Paige says flatly as I sit there with my half-eaten pretzel and stare straight up into Devon's devastating green eyes. "You don't have homies."

Ignoring this, Devon smiles at me. "You look great tonight, ya know?"

"Thanks," I croak, happy I washed my hair and remembered lip gloss.

"Yeah," Paige coos. "You do look nice. I mean, for a while we were really worried about you. Those bags under your eyes? We thought you were *sick* or something."

Interrupting my thoughts of homicide, LeeLee marches over and fakes astonishment. "Wow, happy Halloween! I see you losers remembered your costumes."

Susan levels her with a chilly gaze. "Got enough pockets on those pants?" she inquires, nodding at LeeLee's cast-off cargos.

"Yeah," Paige echoes. "Better watch it, Velez. I hear they're cracking down on all the shoplifters around here."

LeeLee holds out a flat, talk-to-the-hand palm. "Bite me, bitches."

My pretzel tumbles to the floor as I jump to my feet. Devon picks it up and hands it back, as if I have any desire to eat it now, and runs his hand deliciously along my forearm. "Gotta run. See you Monday, right?"

"Sure," I say faintly, heart clanging.

Paige yanks Susan's purse strap. "Let's get some coffee. I'm, like, jonesing here."

Susan sends me a weirdly apologetic look. But before I can analyze it, LeeLee drags me away. "I hope they sprinkle it with arsenic. Two less rats in the world."

I stare longingly over my shoulder as Devon joins his band of hockey buddies. "Do you think he remembers that night? Seriously."

LeeLee blows raspberries. "Seriously? I *so* think you need to get over that dude. It's one thing to suck face when you're drunk at a party, but—"

"I was not drunk."

"—but you can do a lot better than *him*."

"Really? With whom? You see anyone lining up?"

She avoids that one with: "Why do you care so much about having a boyfriend?"

"Why do you *not* care? When was the last time *you* had a date?"

"Please. I'm on scholarship. What rich WASPy dude's gonna ask *me* out?" Whether this is true or not, she doesn't seem concerned. I really envy that. "You're so hot for him," she adds slyly, "why don't you ask him to the Snow Ball?"

I consider this halfheartedly. "What if he says no? What if he already has a date?"

"Ooh, I guess you'll just shrivel up and *di-ie*, then."

LeeLee dances off. I follow, disgruntled. At an alpaca kiosk, she raves over a beautiful red scarf while I try to decide if I should blow sixty bucks on a doggie sweater for Charles.

"I bet Tovah would *love* this." She fingers the soft fringe. "It looks like something she'd wear."

"What did she want?" I ask, since LeeLee brought her up. "And why'd you give her your number? You hardly know her."

"Well, I do now." Anticipating another Tovalogue, I don't press for details. "I really like her, you know?"

"Yeah, so you said."

LeeLee stops. "Why are you acting so weird? I mean, we met at your mom's funeral, so we decided to keep in touch, and—"

"What-ever." I roll my eyes.

"I'm so sorry that bothers you!" she finishes angrily.

Instantly ashamed, I grab her sleeve before she can walk away. "Wait! I'm sorry." LeeLee flexes her jaw as she looks up, looks down, looks everywhere but at me. "I'm, I don't know, I'm just not me, I guess." My voice breaks. I haven't cried since Schmule's eulogy.

LeeLee relents. "Oh, Shawna." She hugs me. I hug her back, tears spurting. "I'm sorry, too. I mean, you just lost your mom, I know you're depressed—"

"I'm not," I sob. "I'm just, just . . ." I don't know what I am! Or why it has to hit me in the middle of a crowded mall.

"It's okay, okay? God, Shawna. You *know* you're my best friend. You are, forever! I absolutely swear it."

I cry harder, and she's kind of bawling by then, too. Then I see Susan and Paige strolling back, lattes in hand. When Paige nudges Susan, they exchange identical smiles. Thankfully they pass by with no snippy remarks. I shut my eyes, hug LeeLee harder, and pretend not to notice them.

28

As I'm surfing the Net for some new art supplies—I wore my pastels down to nubs with a life-sized portrait of Charles—I hear the unmistakably cheery: "You've got mail!" I click on my mailbox to find an e-mail from Arye.

My jaw drops when I see: Tell your dad THANKS A LOT FOR NOTHING!

What? Quickly I add his name to my buddy list. Good, he's on. I click on the message box and type: What are you talking about?

I wait, taking mental bets whether or not he'll ignore me. A second later I get an IM back: Like you don't know.

Me: I DON'T know! What did he do?

Him: Go ahead. Play stupid. YOU know what's going on.

No, I don't. But I'm not in the mood to argue in cyberspace. I wait, fuming, till a second e-mail arrives and "EyraG" disappears from my buddy window.

I click on the message: Let me FILL YOU IN. Penny left a will—AS YOU WELL KNOW. It's old and she never changed it—AS I'M SURE YOU ALSO WELL KNOW! OK, that's her fault. But this really screwed us over.

Your dad gets EVERYTHING! He gets the GALLERY. He's making us SELL OUR HOUSE because Mom can't buy him out. He's even after Penny's STOCKS! It's going to probate, but it looks like he'll GET EVERYTHING! Like you didn't know? He never said ONE WORD?

Mom's freaking out! We can't afford to stay anywhere in NY, so guess where we're moving to? CLEVELAND! IN THE MIDDLE OF MY SENIOR YEAR! To live with Aunt Rina!

Shawna—do NOT bother to respond to this. I am seriously pissed off and I do NOT want to talk to you. This SUCKS! So do me a favor and ask your dad—WHY IS HE DOING THIS? WHY DOES HE WANT TO RUIN OUR LIVES?

Shocked, I can't budge. Dad said nothing about that reading of the will. I never asked because, well, who cares? But he wants half of Mom's house? He wants her art gallery, too? Hello, it's not like we have no money of our own.

Arye said not to answer, but I do: I swear I didn't know this. And stop blaming me. It's not my fault! YOU ask him why!

I hit SEND. Apparently Arye blocked my IMs because I get a second e-mail back: I'm not asking him anything. And I know it's not your fault. Right now I'm REALLY PISSED OFF. Just let me know if you find anything out.

"I'm not letting you know anything!" I shout at the screen.

It makes no sense. I can't even believe it's true.

29

Over the weekend Dad throws a dinner party for some colleagues.

Correction: Dad "throws" the party; Klara and I do all the work.

Normally I make a terrific hostess. I like to plan menus and select flowers for the centerpiece. I enjoy deciding which set of china will look best on our formal, twelve-foot-long table. This only shows you how desperately dull my life really is.

I couldn't care less about this latest party. Beef brisket or chicken cordon bleu? Klara shuffles about in a tizzy, belly straining against her apron as she nags for my opinion. I'm like, "Order whatever." Chances are I won't be eating much anyway. Isn't it tacky to throw a dinner party only a few weeks after a funeral? Tacky, and creepy.

Tonight I follow my usual routine: greet guests, serve drinks, and place hors d'oeuvres in convenient locations. Charles, poor baby, has been banished to my room. As small as he is, he flies below radar and has been known to trip unsuspecting guests. I intend to eat as quickly as possible, then make a gracious and inconspicuous escape. I like *planning* parties. I just hate to participate.

With Arye's e-mail gnawing my brain, I peek around the table at Dad's mind-numbing guests: four male doctors, each with a collagened, liposuctioned trophy wife who added her own dead animal skin to the furry jumble in the closet. Then there's Babs, a life-sized Bratz doll with huge platinum hair and weirdly oversized eyes. Aside from her massive boobage, she's frighteningly thin. She can't be a doctor. A lab experiment gone wild?

She keeps calling me Sharon. Like, "So, Sharon, your daddy tells me you're thinking about medical school!"

"Not thinking about it," my daddy corrects her. "She already made the decision." He arranges his napkin fastidiously across his lap, then rearranges it when it doesn't suit him the first time. "Yep, she's keeping with the old Gallagher tradition. Three generations of physicians. My own father, you know, delivered more than ten thousand babies before he retired . . ."

I sigh heavily, remembering what Poppy is like now: eighty-five years old, immobile, and demented. Every morning Nonny rolls him to his old office at the back of their house, where he sits with his sippy cup, a stethoscope around his neck. Does he ever wonder why no patients show up?

Babs asks, "Where are you going for premed?"

Dad, who so far has already answered every question directed at me, says, "Kenyon. My old alma mater. She's already been accepted, I'm happy to report."

I was?

"Already?" Babs pretends to look ver-ry impressed.

"Well, she has more than enough credits to graduate in January," Dad brags. "God knows why she wants to hang around for the whole second semester."

"No point in rushing it," Babs babbles, a wee bit tipsy. "Enjoy high school, Sharon! You'll have a tough enough road ahead."

Another guest asks if I'm majoring in biology or chemistry, but I'm still too shocked to utter a word. First of all, I didn't *know* I'd been accepted. Dad must have opened the letter and neglected to tell me. I slice my eyes at him, but he's too busy refilling Babs's wineglass to realize the significance. He does, however, notice enough of Babs's cleavage to splatter a few drops of wine on my snowy linen tablecloth.

Perfect Shawna, at last, answers politely, "Biology, sir."

But Evil Shawna hopes Dad'll trip and land face-first on Babs's astounding bosom. Maybe impale his skull on one of those jutting collarbones.

Mom says in my ear: *Call him on it, Shawna. He had no damn business opening your personal mail!*

Pathetic Shawna ignores her.

"Well, congratulations!" Babs raises her lipstick-smudged glass. "I hear Kenyon's one of the hardest colleges to get into. Your grades must be excellent."

"Not bad," Dad agrees, no longer fawning over her mammaries.

Chicken and spinach form a lump in my throat. I grab a hasty gulp of water. "What do you mean, not bad?" I ask, not very modestly. "Have you seen my GPA?"

"Well, if I remember correctly, didn't you finish off last year with a B in English? That was disappointing."

Well, thanks for memorizing every frickin' grade I ever made.

"It was a B plus for the semester. My final grade was an A," I clarify in case anyone cares.

Certainly not Dad. "How can you fail to make an A in your own native language? Haven't you been speaking it for seventeen years?"

Babs picks up on my mortified vibes and nudges Dad with her pointy Bratz elbow. "Oh, John, leave her alone. I'm sure Sharon's just as brilliant as you are. Good luck, sweetie," she adds with a sugary smile for me.

I'm twenty-five percent grateful, twenty-five percent humiliated, and fifty percent ready to barf on my Limoges dinner plate. And I hate that Babs had the audacity to call me "sweetie," of all things.

"Excuse me, but I have a test to study for. An English test," I add meaningfully. Transforming myself back into Gracious Hostess, I simper, "So nice to meet everyone. Thanks for coming." Amid a chorus of good nights, I fly upstairs.

I phone LeeLee, and scorch her ear for five minutes. ". . . and he just about embarrassed me to death!"

"Did you call him on it?" she asks, eerily echoing Mom's imaginary nagging. "Did you tell him he embarrassed you? To say nothing of committing a federal offense."

"You mean in front of everyone? Of course I didn't."

"Why not?"

I splutter, "How could I? It would've been, well, awkward. It would've made everyone uncomfortable."

"I know, right? Because *you're* the only one who's allowed to be uncomfortable. On top of it all, he insulted you!"

"You don't get it," I say tiredly.

"Oh, please. Why didn't you say, 'Gee, Dad, that was a shitty thing to say'? What's the worst he could do?"

". . . I don't know."

"That's because you never piss him off. Doesn't that get, like, boring?"

Now I'm sorry I called her. I wasn't expecting an attack.

"Are you mad because I said that?" she asks when I don't reply.

"No," I lie. But my chest hums painfully.

"Well, good. Because you really needed to hear it."

"Hear what? That I'm *bor*-ing?"

"Oh, is that all you heard?"

"That, and the fact you think my dad's a prick."

"Well. Isn't he? I mean, seriously, who cares if you got one damn B in your whole life? *Chica*, you aced the SATs! You got into Kenyon, your number one choice! Why aren't you freaking out from *happiness*?"

I let that sink in. LeeLee's right—I should be ecstatic! How many people get accepted to the one and only school of their dreams?

But I feel no joy, and why not? Because my inconsiderate father opened my mail?

"He'd never talk to me like that if I were a boy," I finally say.

LeeLee pauses. "Where did *that* come from?"

"It's true. He always wanted a boy, and he got stuck with me instead."

Nonny told me that when Mom's sonogram showed she was pregnant with a boy, Dad did everything but dance an Irish jig. But when I turned out to be a girl, he gutted the room he'd paid a fortune to decorate in a Cleveland Indians theme and told Mom do what-ever she pleased with it. Mom opted for unicorns and lots of pink.

"It's not like he says this to me," I clarify, so Dad won't come across as a total ogre. "But that's why he named me Shawna. For Sean, right?" The Gaelic version of John.

"Shawna, your dad's, well, your dad. He's mean to everyone." LeeLee giggles. "Hey, I know! You want to send him over the edge?

Change your major to art. Hasn't Pfeiffer been nagging you about that for, what, two years?"

True. Miss Pfeiffer, our art teacher, told me she has a friend in Boston, a teacher at MassArt, and if I'm ever interested in having him look at my work, yadda, yadda. This was after she confiscated the mock portfolio I threw together last year so she could use it for future classes. As a *good* example, I hope.

"You'll hate med school," LeeLee insists. "You can't even sit through a slasher movie."

"It's not the blood. I don't like to be terrorized, okay? And I will not hate med school." Why does she nag me about this? If I wanted to be an artist, I'd be an artist. I want to be a *doctor*.

"Shawna, don't you remember that psych class last year? All that 'self-actualization' stuff they stomped into our brains?"

"Right. And how many artists support themselves? Without going on welfare. Or selling caricatures on the street."

"Your mom did it."

"La, la, la," I sing out, because arguing with LeeLee's a lot like arguing with my dad. Totally exhausting. And totally futile.

30

Spurred on by LeeLee, yes, I eventually ask Dad, in a polite, round-about way, why he felt compelled to screw with my mail.

Dad brushes me off like a fleck of dandruff. "What difference does it make who opened the letter? The important thing is, you were accepted, Shawna."

"I know, and I'm happy, but . . ." I falter. "It was addressed to me. It might've been nice if I could've, you know, opened it myself?"

Dad pierces me with a look. "Since I'm the one who'll be paying that exorbitant tuition, I think I have the right to keep abreast of your college applications."

Yes, my college applications, and every other aspect of my life. Can we say "control freak" here?

"He said he opened it by accident," I report back to LeeLee. A teeny lie, but a simpler explanation.

"Ri-ight," LeeLee drawls, but doesn't pursue it.

She's spending the night. Dad's out boogying with the Bratz doll, so we have the house to ourselves.

"So, how's loverboy?" LeeLee asks.

I make a face. "Aside from bugging me for pencils, he barely speaks to me."

"Are you or are you not gonna ask him to the Snow Ball?"

"I haven't decided," I lie. The truth is, I'd never have the guts.

LeeLee sets her glass of Pepsi aside—I eye it nervously because

I'm not allowed to drink in my room—and drops backward onto the bed, arms and legs stretched to form an X. "God, I love your house. It's so big, and quiet, and . . ."

"Sterile?" I suggest, tickling Charles's stomach.

"Yeah, sterile. I love sterile. I love feeling pampered. Do you know how lucky you are not to have to share a bathroom? Can we please trade lives?"

"Trust me. You don't want to be an only child. At least your folks can focus on something other than you." Plus, as much as I love Charles, it must be thrilling to have someone to talk to besides a dog. She has no idea what it's like to have nobody but yourself. How lonely that can feel sometimes.

We fall asleep with the TV on. When I wake up at two a.m., LeeLee's not in bed, and she's not in the bathroom when I get up to pee. I pad downstairs, and hear her voice in the living room.

". . . yeah, I know it's a drag, but what am I supposed to do?" Then, "No, I'm sorry, I'm not ready for that yet."

Who is she talking to on the phone in the middle of the night?

"Who? Shawna?" LeeLee whispers. "No, she doesn't. God, Tovah. Do you think I'm crazy?"

Tovah. Big surprise.

"Yeah, I gotta go, too. I'll let you know. 'Bye!"

My first instinct is to race back upstairs. But (A) I wasn't listening in on purpose, (B) this is my house, and (C) LeeLee, my best friend, was discussing *me*. On the phone, in my living room, in the middle of the night.

She stifles a yelp when she walks into me in the dark. "Shit!"

I shush her by asking, "I don't what?"

"Huh?"

"You were talking about me. You said I don't—*what?*"

"Aw, jeez. It was personal, okay?"

"Personal about me? Something you had to tell Tovah at two in the morning?"

LeeLee pushes me to the sofa and collapses beside me. "This is *so* getting old. Are you jealous or something?"

"No," I say, louder than necessary. "But I think it's weird you have to sneak off to make a stupid phone call."

"Maybe I wanted some privacy. Maybe I didn't want you flipping *out* on me again."

I spring back up, twitching with resentment. "Whatever. Call her whenever. I really don't care."

"Wow," LeeLee drawls. "Thanks for your permission."

"But don't talk about *me*, okay? Just keep me out of your secret little conversations."

"Nobody told you to listen in."

Yeah, no kidding. Upstairs in my bathroom, I press my hot cheeks into my hands, wishing I'd kept my mouth shut and just gone back to bed.

Because LeeLee's right. I *am* jealous. And I don't know what that means.

31

To say Devon's eyes met mine would be so utterly Harlequin. But that's what happens on Monday morning.

"Hi," he says. "I was looking for you."

My heart flutters. "You were?"

"Um, yeah." Pencil time again. As I fumble with my purse, he casually adds, "So, do you have a date for the Snow Ball yet?"

My purse lands on my loafers. Crap flies everywhere. "A date for the Snow Ball?" I repeat like a demented parrot.

He squats beside me, scooping up keys, makeup, calculator, and lip balm. My face prickles as I swipe a tampon container out of reach. "Yeah. The Snow Ball."

This is unreal! Not only is Devon Connolly asking me out—*he's asking me to the Snow Ball!* Now! At this moment!

"Okay. That'll be fun," I say with incredible poise as I hide the plastic container under my regulation gray vest. "Thanks."

"Cool. I'll call you." Devon chucks my chin, and helps me to my feet. "Later, Gallagher."

If I'm not in heaven now, I'm definitely close.

32

"I don't think you should go," LeeLee says in my car after school.

We made up over the weekend, of course. We always do. But this is not what I expected to hear. "Why not? You're the one who told me to ask *him*."

LeeLee sighs. "Ever see *Carrie*? The pig blood?"

"You think Susan and Paige'll *pig blood* me?"

"No," she says slowly. "It's just a feeling I have."

"Well, I'm going, LeeLee. And I wish you were, too."

She yammers her thumb and fingers together in an imitation of my mouth. "Wish all you want, *chica*. I'm staying clear."

Annoyed that LeeLee destroyed my fabulous mood, I drop her off and drive home in a snit, only to discover an unread e-mail from Arye. More hate mail, no doubt.

Haven't heard from you, so I guess you didn't talk to your dad. Mom fired our worthless lawyer. Your dad already found a buyer for the house. We're moving in with Aunt Rina next month.

You guys WON. I hope you're happy.

I don't understand. What does he want from me? Sympathy?

I hit DELETE.

I wish he'd leave me alone.

33

Dad has another date, his second one this week. Go, Babsie! I study for midterms, watch some reality TV, and then take Charles for a walk in the chilly night air. Charles sniffs every dead leaf and pees neatly on every tree. By the time we get home I see a strange car in the driveway. Charles goes nuts when he smells the unfamiliar perfume, and races ahead of me as I push open the back door.

No, not the Bratz doll. I stare at the flippy dark hair and gray eyes, trying to place this person . . .

"Shawna! Long time no see, huh?" Julie, my old nanny, flings her arms around me. "Oh, my God, you're beautiful. And so tall! I can't believe it."

I stare at Dad over Julie's shoulder. This is Dad's date? What about Babsie?

Dad smiles back a smile I haven't seen in ages. "Surprise!"

Surprise, hell. What I'd like to do is scream at Julie: Where have you been? Why did you disappear? How could you do that after what *Mom* did to me?

I wriggle out of her embrace. "Wow. It's you," I say as politely as possible, remembering the morning I woke up, six months after Mom left, to discover Julie had bailed out, too.

"Yes, it's me, all right. I was in Europe last month, so I didn't hear about your mom. But then I ran into a mutual friend, and— well, when I heard, I called your dad." Julie moves forward as if to smother me again. I step back rapidly, pretending not to notice her puzzled expression. "I'm so sorry about your mom. What a horrible shock."

I take a closer look. She's plumper than I remember, but very cute except for a mole next to her mouth. I can't believe people walk around with those things. One quick zap with a laser is all it takes.

"Anyway, your dad and I kind of clicked. Isn't that wild?"

Wild, yes. Since when does my father date former employees? A former employee who's young enough to be my sister, no less. Why would he give her the time of day? She quit without notice, no good-bye, nothing. Dad threw a fit at the time.

Julie surveys me up and down. "Jack, truly, she looks just like Penny."

Oh, and where did this "Jack" come from? My mom called him Jack. Nobody else.

Perfect Shawna holds her breath against the waft of floral perfume. "So. What have you been up to, anyway?"

"Julie's an editor for *Cleveland Moves*," Dad says. He doesn't sneer when he says it, but I know he hates that magazine. He calls it a "liberal rag."

I wonder if Julie minds Dad's habit of answering other people's questions. But she continues to smile and her eyes continue to shine. Uh-oh, I know that look well. I've see it often enough on Dad's other bimbos-of-the-week. Usually about twenty-four hours before they disappear.

"I can't stay." Julie reaches for her coat. Dad practically throws his back out leaping to assist her. "I just wanted to make sure I got the chance to say hi. I'll see you soon, all right?"

"Sure," I say shortly. "Nice seeing you again."

If Julie notices the ice in the air, she hides it well. She blows both of us a kiss and disappears into the night. When the front door closes, I tilt my head to meet Dad's eye. Instantly he dissolves back into his frown of perpetual irritation. "What?"

"That was freaky. After all these years?"

"She heard about your mother. It was nice of her. Funny, I'd forgotten"—his frown melts uncannily into something like delight—"how much fun she could be."

Uh-oh, I've seen *that* look, too. Is he joking? Julie wasn't that much fun as a nanny.

"What do you think of her, Shawna?"

Well, this is a first. Dad never asks my opinion of his fawning floozies. "Why? Are you planning to propose? I did notice the way she was *gazing* at you . . ."

"Knock it off," he grumbles. "It was a dinner date, nothing else."

Now that I've ticked him off, I might as well go for the gold. "Dad. Did you really have Fran evicted from her house?"

Confused by the subject switch, he stalls by moving to the bar to mix himself a drink. "Evicted?"

"Well, not evicted. But you did make them move."

"No-o, I asked Ms. Goodman"—I love how he calls her that—"to purchase my share of the house—"

"Your share?"

"Yes, Shawna. Half of the brownstone was in your mother's name. She left everything to me, remember?"

Yes, in the will she never changed after she moved in with Fran.

"I did that woman a favor. She'd never afford those mortgage payments on her own. She doesn't even have a job, as far as I know. Your mother *supported* her." Dad rattles a shaker and splashes the contents into a glass. "And this, Shawna, is a perfect example of what happens to people who never learn to be self-sufficient."

"Well, it doesn't seem fair," I say, against my better judgment.

"How do you know about all this, anyway?"

I hesitate. No fast-enough lie pops into my brain. "Arye told me."

"Who the hell is Arye?" As if he doesn't know.

"Fran's son. You met him at the hospital? He came to Mom's funeral? He said he and Fran are moving back to Cleveland Heights."

He peers, steely-eyed. "Have you been talking to that boy?"

"Um, well, we e-mail occasionally . . ."

"I forbid it."

"Dad!"

"You heard me. I forbid you to have any more contact with, with, whatever his name is." I stay silent. "Would you like me to cancel our Internet service?" I shake my head. "Then stop e-mailing him. And I want you to block his address."

"What have you got against Arye? It's not his fault his mom . . . I mean, that Mom and his mom . . ." I trail off. There's no delicate way to put it.

Dad smacks down his glass and heads for the stairs. I hate when he does this. As if he thinks that by refusing to acknowledge me, *poof!* I disappear. I no longer exist.

"Dad!" I stomp my foot. "I want you to tell me why."

Because I'm normally not a foot-stomper, Dad halts in disbelief. "Why what?"

"Why are you selling the gallery? Why are you making them move? If Fran had time to find a job, maybe she could make those payments, and—"

"Because I can, Shawna. That's all there is to it."

34

Since Dad's not one to make idle threats, I think twice before e-mailing Arye back. Dad could cut me off from the universe with one click of a button. Plus, if he opens my snail mail, there's good reason to suspect he's not above snooping through my hard drive in search of deleted messages.

So there I sit for, like, thirty solid minutes trying to decide if it's worth the risk.

Finally I hunt for, and find, Arye's original e-mail. My fingers hover, hover, and then I hit REPLY: **I talked to my dad.** True. **I didn't get a straight answer.** Lie. **I'm sorry.** True. **But there's nothing I can do.** Also true.

And no, I can't fix it. I wish I could.

35

Nonny, Poppy, Aunt Colleen, and Uncle Dieter stop by after church the following Sunday. I endure the usual dysfunctional family madness, topped off by Poppy, who takes a dump in his pants at the table. So much for our cozy family dinner.

Aunt Colleen freaks. Klara hides; the time and a half Dad pays her for weekends doesn't include combat duty. Nonny withers with humiliation. Dad, who evidently considers this a "woman's problem," makes no attempt to assist. Instead, he takes this golden opportunity to inform Nonny that it's time to throw Poppy in a nursing home or hire a full-time nurse.

Maybe he's right. But how could he say this in front of Poppy?

It's up to me and Uncle Dieter to drag Poppy into the bathroom while Aunt Colleen zooms to the drugstore for a bag of Depends. Uncle Dieter holds him up while I, um, wipe. I am beyond grossed out. I'm not used to other people's bodily functions—heck, I don't even babysit—and now I'm scrubbing diarrhea off an eighty-five-year-old man. A man who can't stand up by himself. A man who may not even remember that I'm his granddaughter, which might be a blessing.

Perfect Shawna diligently performs the task, keeping in mind that this is the same grandfather who used to be a brilliant physician, who taught her to play chess, who once took her to Ireland.

Pathetic Shawna gags as she tries not to stare at his wrinkled butt and dangling scrotum.

And Evil Shawna wants to shriek at her dad: *He's your father! Why aren't YOU scrubbing his shitty ass?*

Later, I share these scenes with LeeLee as we wander through Macy's in search of the perfect dress for the Snow Ball.

"How're you gonna be a doctor if somebody's butt grosses you out?" she asks.

"You're missing the point. This was my grandfather's butt."

"Seen one, seen 'em all. Ya know, old lady Pfeiffer's right," she adds fiercely. "You ought to go to MassArt. Then you won't have to look at *anyone's* balls. Unless you want to, ha-ha."

I sigh. "LeeLee . . ."

"I know, I know. Med school. The Peace Corps. Saving lives, blah, blah. I can't believe you're letting your dad twist your arm like this."

"Nobody's twisting my arm. This is—my—choice! How many times do I have to say it?"

LeeLee glances heavenward. "Whatever. Let's go buy you a dress."

Two hours later I've tried on a total of sixteen formals, all of which end up back on the racks. Dress number seventeen is sexy and vivid red, but LeeLee insists it makes me look like a firecracker. Number eighteen I can't zip, although it *says* it's a six—and I'm not moving up to an eight. Number nineteen: stunning on the hanger, hideous on me.

Finally I get to number twenty. A strapless and silky midnight blue, it swishes snugly against my legs with a delicious rustle, though I'm not so sure about this no-strap thing.

LeeLee squeals, "Perfect!"

I pluck at the bodice. "I don't have a strapless bra."

"So? What do you have to hold up?"

"And the skirt's kind of tight . . ."

"That's a safety feature."

I pitch number nineteen at her head. She catches it with a grin. Then her smile kind of fades as she stares at my dress. Is she sorry she's not going?

"It's not too late to change your mind," I remind her.

LeeLee wrinkles her nose. "I'd rather stay home and scrape jam out of my toenails. Hey, what's up with Devon? Did he call you yet?"

I hesitate. No, he hasn't. You'd think after inviting me to this shindig, Devon might pay a bit more attention to me. No phone calls, no notes in class, and the dance is next *week*.

"No," I admit.

"Don't you wonder why not? Or why he barely talks to you in school?"

"He talks." Well, he asks me for pencils.

"Bull. Look, don't get mad," LeeLee warns, "but I have to ask you something. Why do you feel you deserve to be treated like a piece of crap?"

"He's not treating me like crap."

"Yes, he is. He asks you to this dance, then he doesn't call you a single time? Something's fishy here, *chica*. And I mean it reeeeks of fishiness."

Stomach in knots—why does she want to ruin this for me?—I snarl back, "You're full of it. Nothing's fishy. Maybe I'll just call him myself."

LeeLee points to my cell phone on the fitting room chair. "Go for it."

"What, now?" I bristle when she nods. "Maybe I'd like some privacy?"

"What do you need privacy for? You're not phoning the White House."

"I don't know, LeeLee. Maybe for the same reason you had to call *Tovah* in the middle of the night?"

LeeLee stiffens. "Fine. Call him." Out of the dressing room she storms.

Omigod, she is *so* on my last nerve. I yank off the gown, pull on my jeans and sweater, then sit down on the padded bench with my phone in hand.

Yes, I do it. And yes, Devon answers. I hear music in the background and a slew of chatter. "Hi, it's me. Shawna."

Pause. "Oh! Hey, 'sup, Gallagher?"

"Are you busy?"

"No, ya know, just hangin' out." The music fades. "I, um, we have some relatives over, so I'm kinda tied up now, so-o . . . 'Sup?" he repeats idiotically.

I say slowly, "Well, I haven't heard from you. We're still on for the dance, right?" Do I sound like a groveling loser?

"Yeah we are! I've just been, you know, busy and all. In fact, I was gonna call you tonight. Wow. You must be psychic."

I can smell the fish. In fact, I smell the whole ocean. "You were?"

"Yeah, I, um, I wanted to know what color your dress is. For the corsage."

Thank God I found one tonight. "Midnight blue."

"Oh. Okay. That's, like, dark blue, right?" Is he even paying attention? "Okay, cool. What time should I pick you up next Saturday?"

He doesn't mention a limo. I wonder if he plans to take me to the Snow Ball in his Jeep Wrangler. "Well, it starts at seven."

"Okay. See you at seven."

"No, I said it *starts*—"

"Hey, gotta go. Sorry! See you Monday, Gallagher."

"Shawna," I say, but he's already hung up.

Now I'm really having visions of *Carrie*: a bucket of pig's blood slopped over my head in front of a belly-laughing audience. Not only do I smell the whole Atlantic Ocean, I sense fish gills springing out all over my body.

As much as I hate to admit it, LeeLee might be right. Maybe he is a phony and a loser and a total horn dog . . . but no, no, no, I am going to this dance! What's the worst that could happen? I won't have a good time? Dad hurls Devon to the ground and frisks his pockets for condoms?

Oh-h, God. Think positive! And the positive part is that Devon could've asked anyone, but no—he asked *me*.

I snatch up the dress and march out of the fitting room.

36

A last-minute inventory of Shawna Patrice Gallagher:

- Skin: not bad, after quick dose of bronzing spray.
- Hair: squeaky clean, newly trimmed, and sprayed into shape.
- Jewelry: sapphire earrings and necklace.
- Makeup and nails: perfect.
- Perfume: a spritz of D&G Light Blue.
- Purse: black-sequined Marc Jacobs clutch.
- Shoes: black stilettos with a rhinestone-studded ankle strap.
- Underwear: a lacy black thong, and nothing else.
- The dress itself: breathtaking!

As I sit primly on the edge of my bed and watch the clock, Dad raps on my door. "So where is this young man?"

"It's not seven yet." Three whole minutes to go.

"Well, let's see the dress."

I drag myself up and twirl, faking delight as Dad examines the goods. "Wow! Very, very *nice*—"

I break into a relieved grin. "Thanks, Dad."

"—but don't you think it's a bit snug?"

Can't he just toss me a compliment and leave it at that?

I twitch one shoulder and pretend to fuss with my hair in the mirror. Dad, with a funny look at my reflection, adds casually, "Julie's right, you know? You do look like your mother." He turns before

I can tell if this pleases him or not. "Make sure he comes to the door, Shawna. I don't want him honking the horn."

Devon doesn't honk. At one minute past seven, through the triangular panes of my bedroom window I see an elegant white limo pull up in front of the house.

"Surprise!" Devon greets me when I fling open the door. He slips a blue carnation onto my wrist—and then, unexpectedly, kisses my lips. "Wow, Gallagher. You look amazing!"

I reel with joy. "So do you." No, he looks *more* than amazing in a regal black tux with a dark blue cummerbund the same shade as my dress. "Wait, my dad wants to say hi."

Holding my breath, I drag Dad out of his office. He extends a surprisingly friendly hand. "Nice to see you again, Devon."

"You too, sir." Devon drips with respect.

"How are your mom and dad?"

"Fine, thanks."

"Still playing hockey? Season should start pretty soon, eh? I remember when you were this big, running around the neighborhood with a stick and your bicycle helmet . . ."

Devon and I squirm in unison, and Devon masterfully interrupts with, "Yes, sir. Um, what time would you like me to have Shawna home?"

Well, damn. He does know my name after all.

"At a reasonable hour," Dad says genially, without any mention of sex or condoms. "You two have a good time."

I hustle Devon out of the house while we're ahead of the game, then stop in dismay. Looks like we won't be going to this big bash alone. Guess who's waiting in the limo?

Susan Connolly and Jake Fletcher.

And Paige Berry, with her own date, Brad Kilbane.

Oh. My. God. *Devon brought his sister on our date?*

Everyone chirps hi, and Susan adds, "Surprise, Shawna!"

"Surprise" isn't the word.

"Oh. Hi." I climb in with leaden feet.

"Your dress is *gor*-geous," Paige declares with a serpentine smile.

Brad scooches over to make room for me. "Yeah, baby. You look hot!"

"Hey!" Paige digs him with an elbow. "You're *my* date tonight. No drooling over the competition."

Competition? As if. Brad's IQ borders right around room temperature.

"She does look hot," Jake says, though Susan's elbow is within striking distance as well.

Susan Connolly and Jake Fletcher. Paige Berry and Brad Kilbane. What the hell am I doing in a limo with them? More important, why didn't Devon warn me?

Brad slides a silver flask out of his jacket. Waggling his brows, he passes it to me. "One for the road?"

Maybe I should be glad it's not a joint, or a line of coke. It's jarringly surreal to see everyone out of their school uniforms, and I can tell they're already more than a bit lit. I shiver as the liquor burns my esophagus. Teeny sips, Shawna, teeny sips. Still, by the time we reach the country club, I'm enjoying a comfy, well-deserved buzz of my own.

The chaperones include Mr. Twohig, in tweed, and Miss Pfeiffer in one of her less frumpy getups. Twohig's dentures almost drop out of his mouth, and Miss Pfeiffer demands, "Why, Shawna, is that you?" They're either astonished by my attire, or astonished I'm here. Both, no doubt.

Yes, we look stunning: the guys in tuxes, Susan in bubble gum pink, and Paige in white, with obviously no underwear. I spy Danielle and Melanie, who approach me with the caution of a couple of zookeepers.

"What're you doing with *them?*" Melanie whispers in horror.

"It just happened," I confess.

"I thought you hated her. That one, I mean." She points to Susan.

"I never said that."

Did I? Well, even if I did, I don't. Besides, by the end of tonight we might be friends again. Now, as for the winged monkey . . . I eye Brad's squat hand, fingering Paige's curvy butt through her sausage-casing gown. Well, Paige Berry may very well be knocked up by midnight.

Danielle chimes in, "Devon looks hot, and so do you." She spins me around. "Gawd, is this really our Shawna? Where's your lab coat, ha-ha?"

I see Devon gesturing madly, almost possessively, so I hug them both. "Have fun, you guys." If that's possible, considering they came without dates.

After a few closer-than-close dances in the swanky ballroom, Devon hauls me outside to meet up with the rest of our group. Brad's flask reappears. With a cautious eye we pass it in a circle, huddled on the slushy pavement in the shadow of the building. Strangely enough I'm, yes, having fun! We laugh. We flirt. We crack jokes. We alternate between dancing inside and sneaking back out to take a hit off the flask. Repeated layers of snow on my skimpy pumps turn my feet into Popsicles. My ear canals fill with spit, thanks to Devon's persistent tongue.

On our fourth trip out, Miss Pfeiffer goose-steps around the corner. Just like in school we lapse into immediate silence.

"Are you drinking out here?" Her beady eyes dart like a radar beam.

"Us?" Jake squeaks in such a funny way that I double over with laughter.

Miss Pfeiffer hammers me with a look. "Well, well. You, of all people." She points to Paige's hastily discarded cigarette. "Is that yours?"

"Of course not," I say indignantly. Devon splutters. I give his hand a warning squeeze.

"Actually, Miss Pfeiffer," Susan interrupts, "we were all just leaving, so . . ." Taking this cue, we dash through the snow toward the still-waiting limo.

"God, she's *soo* lame," Paige squeals, landing half on top of me.

"She likes Shawna, though," Susan says. "Shawna's, like, her pet."

"I am not," I argue, though I probably am.

Brad yanks Paige into his lap. "Better watch out. I swear she's a dyke."

My buzz fades a degree. "That's not true."

"I can spot 'em a mile away." Brad spits when he talks. I never noticed that before. All this liquor must have elevated me to a heightened state of awareness. "You can tell 'em by their shoes. Nuns, too," he says as an afterthought.

A weird, tiny silence. Suddenly I'm glad I shelled out beaucoup bucks for my gorgeous, ultra-feminine footwear. Glad I left my ancient Frye boots at home.

Susan kicks Brad's shin. "Shut up, retard." She aims a lighter kick at her brother, who's busy nuzzling my neck. "Hey, Dev? Since Mom and Dad'll be gone all weekend, let's all go back to our place." Leaning back into Jake, she notices my surreptitious glance at Devon's watch. "What's the matter, Shawna? Don't tell me you have a curfew."

"C'mon, babe," Devon whispers. I shiver as his lips move urgently toward my collarbone. "It's early yet."

I think for a moment, feeling pressured, but can't come up with a good reason not to go to the Connollys'. So I nod, and settle back to enjoy Devon's kisses.

37

"We're done with you." Jake thrusts bills at the sullen driver. As Susan, Paige, and I start down the walk, he pulls the other guys aside. "Wait, I need you to come with me to, um, pick up the stuff."

"What stuff?" I yelp, nearly losing my spiky footing.

Devon says hastily, "It's a surprise. We'll be right back," and sprints off with the others toward Jake's Mustang.

Outraged, I lag back. "I am so *not* doing any drugs tonight."

Paige titters. "Who said anything about drugs?"

I deliver her a *duh* look as Susan pushes me toward the door. "Get real. Jake's brother works in a bar and he promised us a keg. God, what a party pooper *you* turned out to be."

Smarting, I shake her off, then follow them inside. Up in Susan's room, Paige halts. "Oh, no. I don't feel so good." She flees to the adjoining bathroom and slams the door. I hear dainty retching, followed by multiple flushes.

Susan rolls her eyes. "I knew she'd do that. She does it every time."

With an exaggerated sigh, she draws a slender book out of her bookcase. She holds it up, flashing a familiar cover:

SUSIE AND SHAWNA AND THE HALLOWEEN HORROR
by Deborah Connolly
Photographs by Sonia Sorenson

"Remember," she says dreamily, stroking the title, "when we used to be best friends? What the hell happened, Shawna?"

Aside from the fact that she called me a lesbian? That she chose Paige over me? That she, inexplicably, turned into a self-centered bitch?

So why do I still miss her?

Susan sets the book down on the bedspread. "It's so weird. I mean, we were, like, *famous*. If our moms had stayed friends, they could've written a thousand more books." She giggles. "Can you picture it? *Susie and Shawna at the Snow Ball. Susie and Shawna Get Blitzed in a Limo. Susie and Shawna—*"

I marvel that Susan, like me, makes up these silly titles, too. "Why do you get top billing?"

"Well, my mom wrote the book."

"There wouldn't be a book if my mom hadn't taken the pictures."

"Who *cares*? It's like, so over."

"I do," I say softly.

Paige pokes her blotchy face out of the bathroom, and moans, "Oh-h, God. I'm soooo sick. Can I, like, just take a nap?"

She stumbles toward the bed, but Susan whirls her back around. "Oh, no, no, no. You're not gonna puke on *my* bed again." With an apologetic glance, she propels Paige toward the door. "Let's go downstairs and find some safe little hole for you. God, I wish those guys'd get back!"

I wave them off, smiling at Paige's twisted feet and flailing arms. Poor Paige. Looks like the winged monkey's grounded for the rest of the night.

While I freshen up in Susan's bathroom, I hear the guys come back. Music drifts up from downstairs, and I hear Susan and Jake laughing about something, and then—

"Hey."

I whirl around as Devon steps close to the bathroom door. "You scared me." My heart whaps the back of my throat like hummingbird wings.

"Sorry."

"So, did you guys get a keg?"

"Yep. Brad and Jake are cracking it open even as we speak." He smiles, moves closer, and pulls me back into the bedroom. Cupping the back of my head, he breathes into my ear, "So, you wanna see my room next?"

My brain spins with possibilities as his mouth descends over mine, his tongue thrusting dangerously close to my windpipe. One hand traces my neck, my shoulder, the top of my breast. The other one presses insistently at the small of my back.

"Wait!" I attempt to say around a mouthful of tongue.

Okay, it's not smart to speak with someone's tongue in your mouth, on the off chance you might bite off a significant chunk. Luckily, this doesn't happen; Devon retracts his tongue at the same time he pulls down the top of my dress. Instantly I curse myself for not springing for that strapless bra.

Speechless, yet oddly detached, I watch him stare at my breasts. Only LeeLee, my gym class, and my female pediatrician have ever seen these in all their so-called glory.

"Wow, Gallagher. You, you, you're really . . ."

Small? I think bleakly.

"Pretty," he finishes. I think he has trouble believing it himself.

I melt back to life by tiny degrees. "Shawna."

"Huh?"

"My name is *Shawna.*"

"Yeah, I know . . . Shawna."

He kisses me again, harder than ever, grasping my breasts like he's weighing them before purchase. He flops me onto Susan's bed and tugs my dress down farther, the weight of his body crushing me into his sister's mattress. For a while I kiss him back, trying to enjoy it, because isn't this what I'd wanted? How I'd secretly hoped the evening to end?

But there's nothing to enjoy.

Yes, it's exciting. Thrilling, too, in a dangerous way. I've imagined this moment a thousand times, so . . . why, why am I not having a good time?

Why do I want to jump up, all of a sudden, and run like hell?

"Susan—," I begin helplessly, twisting my face toward the door.

"It's okay," he whispers. "She's knows I'm here. She won't come in."

"But—"

But nothing. Devon tries to finagle a knee between my legs. My tight skirt, luckily, stops him at the gate. That's when I decide that enough is enough, that sex with Devon Connolly is no longer a part of tonight's plan. "Stop."

"What?"

"Just stop it, okay?"

Devon stops. And waits. And keeps his hands on my breasts in case I change my mind.

Breathing hard, I say it out loud. "I don't think I want to do this."

"You're kidding. Why not?"

". . . I guess I'm not ready?"

"What do you mean, not ready? I have a condom, I swear. I'd never do it without."

"It's not that. I'm just not ready," I repeat helplessly.

"When? *When* will you be ready?"

"I don't know, but . . ." I sigh. "It's not gonna be tonight."

I dreamed of this moment, of having somebody want me like this. But now I can't do it, because I don't want *him*. I feel nothing. Just sweaty, and yes, scared.

Devon rolls off me. His fly gapes open. I have to force myself not to look. "I knew it."

"Knew what?"

"That you weren't gonna let me."

"Well, that's funny. I didn't know it myself till, like, one second ago."

Devon gazes down longingly at my breasts. "Man, what a waste."

I yank the top of my dress up, annoyance blossoming into full-blown anger. "Trust me, Devon. They'll never go to waste."

"Ri-ight. I bet you and that girlfriend of yours put them to *very* good use." He smiles as I freeze. "Oh, don't look so shocked. I mean, it's no secret about your mom, so, whatever."

"What," I whisper, "are you talking about?"

"You and that Velez chick? Feeling each other up at the mall? Everybody knows how you two hang all over each other."

"You're crazy!"

"Then prove me wrong." He smiles that slow sexy smile that

used to melt my insides. "Take your clothes off. You want to, right?"

Oh. My. God.

"Not with you," I squeak out. "Not if you put a gun to my head."

Unceremoniously, he stuffs his package back into his perfectly creased pants. "Huh, Sue was right about you. You're a lez. Like your mom."

Out he charges, leaving me rigid and stunned, with what feels like a burning rash creeping from my chest to my face. I snatch up my coat and my purse with shaky hands, and stumble downstairs. Halfway there, I catch a pointy heel on the carpet and almost land on my head. Gritting my teeth, I hop the rest of the way down, then halt awkwardly at the bottom as fire shoots through my left ankle.

I see Paige sprawled across a chair, bare legs dangling limply over the arm. Susan, Jake, and Brad, lined up elbow to elbow on the sofa, stare at me with three pairs of knowing eyes. Devon's nowhere in sight. I'm not even sure he came downstairs.

Susan jumps up, a flurry of cotton candy pink. "Omigod, what? What happened?"

If this were anyone but Susan, I'd suspect they really cared.

I kick open the front door with my one good foot—"Ask your brother!"—and lunge into the cold night. Dark houses pass in a hazy blur as I limp home on my throbbing ankle.

Why did he have to ruin it?

Why did I have to ruin it? Of *course* he thought I'd have sex with him. I've been lusting over him for weeks. So why didn't I just do it?

I don't know, I don't know. Because he turned me off?

How could Devon Connolly turn me off?

Dad, buried in his study, doesn't hear me come in. Charles, never a barker, doesn't give me away. I let him out quietly, then wipe his paws and carry him upstairs, where I shed dress number twenty and leave it in an obnoxious blue pile. Then I roll up under the covers and cry into Charles's fur.

Tonight, Pathetic Shawna wins.

38

"Get up!"

I scream into the pillow when LeeLee rips off my comforter. It's after three p.m. and my room smells like dog pee. Poor Charles.

"I've been calling you all day! Are you hungover?" She bounces onto the bed. "Well, how'd it go? ¡Dígame!"

"It was . . ." A nightmare. "It was . . ." Worse than a nightmare. Because it really happened.

"What?"

I hug my sheet to my chin. "You were right. I should've stayed home."

"Oh, God. They didn't do the pig blood thing, did they?"

"No!" I shriek.

"Well, what happened?"

"He just wanted to have sex. He like, *expected* it." I rub my eyes hard. My fingertips come away caked with mascara and sleep guck.

"And you're surprised because . . . ?" When I fling an arm over my forehead, LeeLee asks in alarm, "You, um, didn't do it, did you?"

"No, LeeLee. I didn't do it."

"Why not?" When I snort, she adds, "You're hot for him, right? I thought you *wanted* to have sex with him."

"I did. I mean, I thought I did. But when he . . ." I try to remember how I felt last night when Devon tried to shove his knee between my legs. "Well, when he tried it, it was . . . I don't know. Gross or something."

"Gross?"

"No, gross is the wrong word. I can't explain it. I just wanted him off of me. So of course now he thinks I'm a lesbian, right? Because what other reason could I have *not* to have sex with him?"

LeeLee blinks. "He said that?"

"Yes, and that's not all. You're gay, too, didn't you know? Yep. We're a couple."

"Oh, c'mon. He just wanted to piss you off."

"He was serious," I say miserably. "They *all* think we're gay."

"Who 'all'—Paige and Susan? Who cares what those skanks think?"

"Maybe *you* don't. But I do not want to finish up high school with everyone thinking I'm gay."

"Why?" she asks evenly. "Because it's not true?"

"Yes! Because it's—not—true."

"So if it *were* true, would that make it any better?"

"Stop it, LeeLee. Stop analyzing everything. I'm not a dyke and neither are you. So what's the point in discussing ifs?"

"You sure like to throw that word around lately," she notes after a moment.

"Sorry you're offended by my politically incorrect choice of words," I snap back. "But I'm having a meltdown here, okay?"

LeeLee makes a face and pats my knee. "Look, why don't you get up and, ya know, break down and wash your face? We can go to the movies or something. My treat for a change."

"No. I just want to stay here and . . ." Sigh. Be depressed.

"Okay. Well . . . sorry the ball was such a bust." She chortles at that. "Busted ball! Get it?"

I get it. "Watch the puddle," I say loudly as she almost plants a foot into Charles's mistake. LeeLee steers around it and dashes off with a wave.

Charles flaps his tail, his expression a mix of hope and resent-ment as I haul myself out of bed. I scrub up the mess off the rug and the mess off my face and lug him downstairs to let him out for the first time in sixteen hours.

39

Monday morning, I dread school. Happily, it's a short week because Thanksgiving is Thursday.

Devon smirks as I slip into A&P five minutes late. Head down, I slide into my seat. A folded piece of paper waits on my table.

"What's this?" I ask Mary Therese Montgomery, who's scouring her tape recorder buttons with a toothbrush.

She shrugs. "It was there when I got here."

As Mr. Twohig yanks down the projector screen, I unfold the paper. A crude drawing of a naked female, a red arrow pointed to her crotch. The printed caption: EAT ME, BABY.

Swallowing the not-so-tasty surge of my thankfully light breakfast, I crumple the paper and turn around. Devon, mouth twitching, stares at Mr. Twohig with convincing fascination. I thrust the note into my bookbag, and then, behind my back, I flip Devon the finger. If anyone notices, I'll plead insanity. Poor Shawna Gallagher, insane with grief over her dead lesbian mother, has undoubtedly lost her last grip on reality.

"Right." Devon raps my hand, with one of my own pencils, no doubt. "You had your chance."

Forget my perfect GPA. Forget that I aced my SATs. Forget the fact that with "MD" after my name I'll be raking in seven figures if I join Dad's practice.

The question is, how smart can I be for crushing on the demented twin brother of the demented Susan Connolly? Same genetic makeup. Same poisonous blood coursing through their veins.

I remember his words: *Sue's right about you. You're a lez. Like your mom.*

Suddenly I hate Susan Connolly more than I'll ever hate Devon, no matter what he does to me, no matter what he says. How humiliating to wait for three long years, secretly hoping to become friends with her again.

Three. Stupid. Utterly Wasted Years.

40

A few days into December, as I'm IM'ing LeeLee, Mel, and Danielle all at the same time, Arye's screen name magically reappears. Wow, he unblocked me.

Sorry for what I wrote a while back. I was bummed.

Can IMs be traced by nosy parents? My fingers falter as I write: **No biggie. Did you move yet?**

Him: **Yeah.**

He types his great-aunt Rina's address in Cleveland Heights. I jot it down absently. It's only a couple miles away. I could walk there if I wanted to, not that I'd want to.

Him: **I'm at Heights High now.**

Me: **Do you like it?**

Him: **Duh. What do you THINK? My whole senior year is F***** up!**

Sensing he's about to go off on me again, I type in my cell phone number: **Call me sometime, but DO NOT CALL MY HOUSE EVER!** Unless, I think, you're in the mood for another funeral.

Him: **OK.**

A short lag. I can't think of anything intelligent to say because I'm distracted by the relentless pinging of my three other IMs.

Him: **Mom wants to know if you can come for dinner tomorrow.**

Dinner? With Fran? Tomorrow?

Me, obviously not thinking straight: **What time?**

Him: **Five?**

My fingers poise an inch above the keys. Dad'll never let me. How do I get out of it? Admit my father's a tyrant and beg for understanding?

Do I want to go?

Weirdly enough, I do. I'd like to see Schmule again, at least.

Me, rapidly, before I can change my mind: **OK. Thanks.**

Meantime, LeeLee, puzzled by my silence, invites me into a private room with Mel and Danielle. I plead exhaustion and sign off.

I need to think about this.

41

So, do I want to see Fran?

Probably not.

Do I want to see Arye?

I'm not sure.

But then I think again about Schmule, and the decision is made.

After school I shower, change into a nice dress, and toss a batch of cookies into the oven. Nonny's rule: never go anywhere empty-handed. Dad pops in, home early for once—just my luck—and sniffs the air. "Who's baking cookies?"

"Me."

"What's the occasion?" He surveys the so-not-my-usual-after-school attire, then ambles into the den to mix a martini. I follow slowly. "Are you going out tonight?"

"Actually, yes."

"Where?"

My brain revs into turbo. I could lie and say I'm headed over to LeeLee's. But Dad's penetrating expression stops me. I can't lie to my dad.

Grow up, dammit. You're seventeen years old!

Wow, Mom. I'm surprised you remember.

"Fran's," I say finally. "She invited me to dinner."

A blood vessel in Dad's temple threatens to blow. "Well, you can just call her back this instant and tell her you have other plans. You have homework, I imagine."

"Dad, it's Friday. And I really do want to go." The words surprise even me.

"Haven't we had enough trouble out of that woman already? Isn't it bad enough she chose to move two miles away from us?"

She didn't choose, Dad. You nailed Mom's bank account, her insurance, the brownstone, and the gallery. It's not like she had anywhere else to go.

Omigod, can this be true? I'm mentally sticking up for Fran?

"You are *not* going to socialize with her, Shawna. I absolutely forbid it."

I hear Mom's mirthless chuckle. *Don't you love it when he uses the word "forbid"? What was that you called him? A tyrant?*

I have two choices: shut my mouth, chill out, and sneak away anyway, or defer to my higher power. Namely Dad.

Dad then shocks me with an abrupt about-face. "Never mind. You can go."

I close my dangling jaw. "What?"

"I said you can go. But I want you to do something for me."

"Kill her?" I quip.

My smile shrinks as he snarls, "Don't be stupid, Shawna. Just listen." Steaming, I wait. "When your mother left, she took some things with her. Things that now, rightly, belong to you. I want them back."

"What things?"

"Some jewelry, for one. Your grandmother Sorenson's wedding set. Your mother's wedding set, too, assuming that woman hasn't hocked it yet." Pause. "That was a three-and-a-half-carat diamond, if I remember correctly."

Three and a half? He couldn't spring for an even four?

"And photo albums," he adds. "All the ones she took when she left. These should belong to you now and I want them *back*."

Oh, God. I've been hearing about these albums for years. When Mom cleaned out her office that night, she left nothing behind. Literally hundreds of pictures of me from birth to age seven, plus who knows how many others, vanished overnight. "Why didn't you ask for them back when Mom was *alive?*"

Dad huffs at my total lack of comprehension. "I tried. Multiple times, I might add. But since your mother was smart enough to move out of state, there wasn't much I could do."

"Well," I begin, not wanting to be dragged into this. "Since she took the pictures herself, maybe she assumed they were hers?"

"I don't know what she assumed, but Fran has no business keeping them. *You* are not her child." Dad tosses back a deep swallow, but the liquor doesn't mellow him; in fact, he grows crabbier. "Now, either you get them back or I'll have to do it myself. Legally, of course."

Good thing he added that disclaimer, because I can picture him with a crowbar, prying his way, in the dead of night, into Fran's aunt's house. "So, you want me to go over there and ask—"

Dad clicks his teeth in annoyance. "Not ask, Shawna—insist. Do you think you can manage that?"

Maybe. But do I want to? NO.

Wisely I avoid a straight-armed salute.

42

The cookies turn out crispier than planned; I didn't notice the timer go off during Dad's rant. I park in front of Fran's and skittle up the icy walk.

WHOMP! *"Sha-awn-ahh!"* Schmule plows into me, squeezing me hard.

"Hey, Schmule." Wow, I hardly expected a greeting like this. I hug him back, patting his long wild curls. "Long time no see, dude."

"Did you bring your dog?"

"My dog? No. I didn't know he was invited," I tease.

"Rats." With a forgiving grin, Schmule pushes me out of the foyer. "C'mon, I'll show you my new room."

"Wait, where's everyone else?"

"Right here." Arye saunters, unsmiling, into the living room, takes my jacket, and throws it in a closet. Although he doesn't look thrilled to see me, at least he didn't greet me with a butcher knife. "Shabbat shalom," he adds with a challenging gleam.

Oh-h, right. Friday night, the Jewish Sabbath. *Grrr!* Why didn't he warn me?

Fran emerges from the dining room, wiping her hands on the ruffled apron Arye wore in New York. Same dowdy clothes, same straggly gray hair. Fuzzy purple slippers adorn her feet instead of her brown clogs.

"Hi, Shawna." She air kisses my cheek. "I'm so glad you could make it."

Awkwardly, I thrust my foil-covered tray into her hands. "I brought cookies."

"Oh. Thank you."

She retreats back to the dining room, and Arye says, with half a smile this time, "There you go again trying to *treyf* up our kitchen."

"What do you mean, *treyf*?"

"Your cookies. Are they kosher?"

Double *grrr*. "They're Toll House."

"If you made 'em, they're *treyf*."

Schmule tugs me to his room before I can get into it with his brother. This house is smaller, crampier, than the New York brownstone, but warm and comfortable in the same cluttered way. Arye and Schmule apparently share this bedroom, boundaries defined by a bookcase in the center. Schmule's side appears obsessively tidy. DVDs and video games in alphabetical order. Bed perfectly made up with a Harry Potter comforter. No stray books, papers, toys, anything. Dad would love this kid.

Schmule points to an old Nintendo player. "Wanna play Yoshi?"

"What's Yoshi?"

"It's a game! You never heard of *Yoshi's Island*?"

"Not everyone plays video games," Arye says behind us. "Anyway, Mom says we're ready to eat."

The cookies stagnate off to one side, so I guess Arye was right. I stare in awe at the beautifully made-up table as Fran places a scarf over her head. She lights a total of four candles and makes circling motions with her hands. My stomach gurgles. I shift nervously, listening to the Hebrew words Fran recites with her hands now over her eyes. Why didn't she invite me over on, say, a Tuesday or something? If Nonny finds out about this, she'll drag me to confession, wailing Hail Marys the entire way.

The prayers end, we sit, and I eat slowly, rolling the delicious chicken around on my tongue. How do I ask for the pictures back? Drop hints? Ask her right out?

I take the plunge after a helping of warm cherry pie. "Uh, Fran, I was wondering. Do you have any old pictures of me or my mom around?"

"I'm sure we do."

Tell her you want them. Tell her! But instead I ask politely, "Do you mind if I look at them?"

"Of course not." Fran jumps right up, disappears, and returns with an armload of photo albums. I follow her to the living room, where she drops the books onto a braided rug. "As a matter of fact I just unpacked these today."

Choosing an album, I flip slowly through cellophane pages crackly with age. Wow, pictures of Mom when she was a kid: baby pictures, school pictures, and family outings with my Swedish grandparents. A prom picture, too: Mom in a ravishing black formal dress and hugely feathered hair, hanging on to some goo-goo-eyed dork.

Then it dawns on me that this dork is—"My dad? Holy shit." I clap a hand over my mouth.

Fran laughs. "Never mind. I said the same thing."

"They went to school together?"

"No, your father's a few years older. They met when they both took riding lessons. Your mom loved horses when she was a kid."

Mom, maybe, though it's news to me. But my dad? On a horse?

"Penny never dated anyone else after she met your dad," she adds.

Except you, I think. The discovery of this previously unknown part of my mother's life stuns me. More than that, I'm severely ticked off. This is my history, too. Something every kid knows: how their mom and dad met. I hate that I've been left out of this.

You never asked me, Shawna. You weren't interested anyway. Your father poisoned your mind for ten years.

I shake the voice out of my head. I can't tell if these messages are memories, or if I'm making them up myself. I trace Mom's face, wondering how much Aqua Net it took to cement her hair into that mile-high, utterly impossible position. Like me, she wore bangs. For some reason this makes me smile.

"And here are some of you." Fran pushes another album over.

Some? Try hundreds. Birthday pictures. Christmas pictures. Pictures of me with Nonny and Poppy, back when Nonny's hair was red, not white, and Poppy played with a full deck. Me, boarding a school bus. Flying on a sled down a snowy hill. Bouncing in a wading pool. My unabridged life for the first seven years, bound in plastic, captioned in Mom's handwriting.

I start to ask Fran if I can keep these albums. How can she say no? These pictures of me, the ones of Mom and her family . . . this is my history, not Fran's. Just as Dad said, I'm nothing to her and she has no reason to hang on to them, other than spite.

But I notice the way she pores over these pictures, as if she, too, were seeing them for the first time. Her hands caress each page, lingering on Mom's face.

With a sigh, I flip open the next album, one with a blue and white checkered cover. Several loose photos drop to the rug. I giggle at the sight of myself as a toddler, laughing on Mom's lap, hugging a stuffed blue bunny. "Omigod, this is—so—darling! Can I have it?"

A shutter smacks closed over Fran's face. She shakes her head.

What's her problem? "Well, can I scan it at least?"

"No."

Did she just say no, or am I imagining things? I honestly think she's joking around—but then she pries the snapshot out of my fingers. Scooping up the rest of the loose pictures, she stuffs them back between the pages. Then she closes the album and sets it aside on the sofa.

"Take these if you like." She offers two of the first albums, and adds, more kindly, "I'm sure there are others I haven't had a chance to unpack. That one, though . . ." Her eyes swivel toward the sofa. "It's kind of special to me."

Special how? She didn't know me back then. She didn't even know Mom.

I fume silently. Why *can't* I scan them? It'd take two minutes. I'd give them right back!

"Well, thanks," I say belatedly, trying to hide my irritation. "And thanks for dinner, but I'd better get going." No point in contaminating the kitchen by helping with the dishes.

Fran climbs to her feet, stretches, and knuckles the base of her spine. "There are plenty of leftovers. Do you want to take some home?"

"Sure. Thanks."

I gather up my purse as she scurries out—and then, casually, flip open the forbidden checkered album. One quick glance reveals more baby pictures of me, along with some older ones of Mom and the Goodmans. Impulsively, as Fran's footsteps approach, I snatch a handful of the loose snapshots and shove them into my purse. I hope the bunny one is there. I'll scan these tomorrow and get them back to her . . . but how? Crap. Too bad I didn't think of that first.

Fran breezes back with a brown grocery bag. I force a smile, she smiles back, and I see how haggard she looks. Haggard, and weary, and, in spite of the smile, very sad.

She misses Mom. I bet she misses Mom more than *I* miss Mom. All evening I noticed how cheery she pretends to be. How, the moment she thinks no one is watching, her face dissolves back into a dull mask.

"Fran?" I say softly.

She stares, trancelike, at the sofa. Does she already suspect what I did?

"Are you okay?"

"Oh, everything's fine." Fran, back to normal, thrusts the bag at me. She bellows over her shoulder, "Arye! Schmule! Come say good-bye to Shawna."

Schmule wrestles his way ahead of his brother. "Hey, I thought we were gonna play *Yoshi*. I can teach you, ya know, in like two seconds flat."

"Next time, sweetie," Fran assures him. Then, to me, "We're having some friends in from out of town over the holidays. We'd love to have you back."

Schmule smacks me a high five. "Yay! And bring your dog next time. Mom, can I have a dog? You said when we get a backyard, we can—"

Fran interrupts, "This is not the time to talk about this, sweetie. Say good-bye and go put on your pj's."

I wave to Arye around Schmule's quick hug. He waves back, unenthusiastically.

"Thanks for dinner," I say again. At least now I'll have a chance to return the photos. I only hope she doesn't miss them in the meantime. "Thanks for the pictures, too."

I bolt out of the house before she can pat me down.

43

I can't even wait till I get home. Car engine idling, dome light on, I thumb through the photos. Yes, here's the one with the blue bunny. Passing over a couple of shots of Arye and Schmule, I find another one of me, propped up in front of an autumn-themed backdrop, head covered with pale fuzz. Then another one of me, toddling through the snow. My blond hair fluffs out of my hood as I watch Fran twist a green scarf around a glistening snowman.

Wait.

Just.

One.

Freaking.

Minute.

Me and Fran?

How long has Fran been a part of Mom's life? At least since I was a baby, if you can go by these pictures. *All these years?* I can't— believe—it.

Did Dad know all along? Or did he not even suspect?

Oh, my God.

No wonder Fran didn't want me to see that album!

44

Over lunch with Julie and me on Saturday afternoon, Dad asks, "Did you get the rings back?"

Damn. The rings! I never thought of them again. "Sorry. I forgot."

"You *forgot?*" Silent, I poke at a tomato rolling around in my salad. "Well, what about the photo albums?"

On one hand, I'd like nothing more than to heave those pictures in his face. *See? See? Mom cheated on you for years! How does THAT make you feel?*

On the other hand, I'm scared of how'll he react. How he'll undoubtedly blame me, the bearer of bad news.

"Shawna?" Dad's impatience mounts.

Reluctantly I admit, "Uh, she did give me a couple of albums."

"Only a couple? Let's see them."

"Jack, let her eat." Julie tosses her flippy hair and winks as if to say *let's stick together, kiddo.*

As if, Julie. You're not my nanny anymore.

Dad smiles thinly. "Of course. That's what I meant."

It's not that I don't like Julie. What's not to like? She's sweet and she's cute, except for that mole. She doesn't slobber over Dad like his previous army of bimbos. And I'll always be grateful to her for one thing: she's the one who brought Charles to me soon after Mom left.

But I get the impression she wants to take up right where we left off, as if she weren't the second person in my life to dump me without notice.

I eat rapidly, barely tasting my salad. No point trying to converse; Dad rambles about his job and his latest miracle deliveries and semi-immaculate conceptions. Julie listens with rapt attention. How long will it take her to realize how boring he can be?

After lunch, Julie and Dad head to the den for a drink. I jump when Dad barks, "Shawna! The pictures!"

I hear Julie's hushed admonishment, which sounds something like: "Do you have to be so rough with her?" I miss Dad's reply. But he doesn't sound apologetic.

Fine! I haul out the albums from Fran, stalk to the den, and drop them down. Dad, oblivious to my mood, leafs through one with minimal interest. "Is this all she had?"

"I guess," I lie, remembering the checkered one she wouldn't give me.

"You guess?"

"Well, she gave me some loose ones, too."

"Good. Hang on to them. And next time ask about the jewelry."

"Where are they?" Julie sips her merlot as she peeks into the second album. "The other pictures. I'd love to see them."

"Oh, they're just baby pictures," I say, rapidly losing my nerve. "One of me in front of some tacky fall backdrop, and—"

Dad's glass pauses, midair. "A backdrop? Your mother never used commercial backdrops."

"I'm telling you, it's a backdrop." The fact that he's arguing with me whittles away at my indecision. "And there's another one of me, too, sitting on Mom's lap. I'm holding a blue bunny. I'm, like, one or two."

Dad does this quirky thing with one heavy eyebrow when he thinks I'm not being one hundred percent truthful. He's doing it now. "You never had a blue bunny."

"Oh, Jack, how can you remember?" Julie says with a small laugh.

Dad points at me. "Let's see those other pictures."

With a kind of grim satisfaction, I fetch them from my purse. Dad and Julie shuffle through them together, heads disturbingly close. Julie rests one hand on Dad's hairy arm. I wonder if they're sleeping together yet . . .

Dad finally pronounces, "Shawna. These pictures aren't even you."

"Well, some are of Fran's kids," I admit, squinting over his shoulder. "But these two—"

"Are not you." Dad slaps them down. "Your mother didn't even know Fran when you were that age."

"Well, Dad. Obviously she *did*."

I wait for the planet to explode. Instead, Julie says cautiously, "No, she didn't. I remember when they met, at a book signing, in Cleveland. You were in first grade or so." She waves a hand over the skimpy stack of photos. "*None* of these are of you."

Flabbergasted, I peer at the snowman picture. Blond hair, snowsuit . . . a boy's snowsuit?

Dad picks up the bunny one and compares it to a picture of the "real" me in one of the albums. Julie grips his arm again, slowly shaking her head. "Shawna's hair was never that curly. But the resemblance is eerie. Jack, you don't suppose Penny . . ." She glances my way.

"What?" I'm confused.

Cheeks coloring, she finishes, "Well, maybe she had an affair? And this little boy—"

I stare at the child in the snowsuit, grinning up at Fran.

Schmule?

Of course. Why didn't I see it?

"That's ridiculous," Dad says, and I know what he's thinking: why would Mom leave him for Fran, and then have an affair with a *man*? He pops the album shut. "How old is Fran's son? The younger one."

"I'm not sure," I hedge. "Nine, I think?"

"When's his birthday?"

"Why?"

"When—is—his—birthday—Shawna?"

"I don't know! What difference does it make?"

"Christ. Just find out his birth date. You're so chummy with them now, it shouldn't be that difficult." Dad whips the photographs out of range as I reach swiftly across the table. "No, I'll hold on to these."

"Da-ad!"

"Jack, you don't think . . . ?" Julie sends me an odd glance. "Well, wouldn't Penny have told you?"

"No," he says gruffly. "It'd be just like her *not* to tell me."

Okay, my mind at this moment isn't precisely a steel trap. Now it dawns on me what he's trying to say. "Dad, you are so off base. *Fran* is Schmule's mom."

Dad smacks the album. "Then why are his baby pictures identical to yours?"

"It can't be him. Schmule's hair is *brown*." Then I look at Dad's curly dark hair and realize how stupid that sounds.

"I was blond as a baby," Julie says unhelpfully. "Mine turned darker later."

Dad fixes his attention solely on me. "Find out his date of birth. It's a long shot, but—" He shoves the photo albums aside. "We need to find out."

Wait, wait. *If* by some miracle Schmule belonged to Mom, and presumably to Dad, wouldn't Schmule know? He calls Fran "Mom." He called *my* mom Penny.

Defeated, I jump up. "I'm going out. I'm taking Charles for a walk."

"Don't forget," Dad warns as I flounce off for the leash. "And get those rings back, too."

How can I forget? He's already been hounding me, like, every five minutes.

I never should've let him suck me into this drama.

But can it be true? Is Schmule my *brother*?

45

"So . . ." Paige Berry's artificially tanned arm snakes past my face as she places a hand against my locker. "Is it true?"

Shouldering her aside, I spin the wheel of my lock. "What?"

She leans close, the spiral ends of her hair bobbing in my face. "Are you really gay?"

If this were a movie, my character would haul off and punch her in the mouth. Good-bye, perfect porcelain veneers! But this isn't a movie and I've never hit anyone in my life. And Pathetic Shawna is in such a state of shock, she can only stand there, open-mouthed.

Susan sidles up. Her apologetic expression strikes me as genuine. "Paige, stop it."

"If you are gay," Paige continues, "why don't you admit it? Why go chasing after guys if you don't even like them? It's, like, no big deal anymore, right? Being gay?" she clarifies, in case I didn't get it the first time.

"I'm not—" My throat closes up. I can't even say the word.

Susan tugs Paige's arm. "I said *quit* it, Paige."

Paige gleams as Susan pulls her back. "Fine. But keep away from Devon, or you know what? The whole school's gonna hear about you, if they haven't already. Got it?"

Paige and Devon? Of course. How absolutely predictable.

Evil Shawna springs to life, battering her pathetic twin into a quivering mass. "Hear what? Hear how that limp-dick moron couldn't get it up?" I smile at their shocked expressions, never mind I just spit out one of the biggest lies of my life.

LeeLee barges in before Paige can go for my throat. "Excu-use me," she sings, elbowing the rats out of her way. "Don't you two sluts have someplace else to be? Somebody's backseat? The vomitorium, perhaps?"

"You think you're so funny," Paige says with a bitter edge of ice. She whirls on her heel. "Keep laughing, bitches."

She stalks off. Susan lags back uncertainly, and meets my hard gaze as if she has something important to say. Then she, too, sashays off down the hall.

LeeLee puckers her lips in my locker door mirror, adding another layer of scarlet gloss. "So, how'd your dinner go Friday night?" I hesitate too long. Her eyes meet mine in the glass. "Well?"

"I found some pictures of Schmule when he was a baby. I thought it was me. We look exactly alike."

"So?"

"So Dad thinks my mom pulled a fast one on him. He thinks Schmule's my brother."

"Shut UP!"

"Swear to God."

"And the father is—?"

"I think Dad thinks it's him."

LeeLee says something in Spanish that's beyond my comprehension. Then, "And she passed him off as Fran's? How'd she think she'd get away with it?"

I slam my locker and jam the lock into place. "She did get away with it for, like, ten damn years. So now Dad wants me to find out when Schmule's birthday is so he can figure out a time line, I guess."

"Are you gonna do it?"

"Wouldn't you? Wouldn't you want to know if you had a brother or not?"

Without answering directly, she warns, "You better think about this, *chica*. I mean, all *hell* will break loose."

"I know," I whimper.

"Maybe you should stay out of it. Tell your old man to hire a lawyer if he's so worried."

"But if he is my brother, I *have* to know."

"Why? Do you have any idea how lucky you are being an only child? No competition. No responsibilities. Look, if you want one so much," she teases, "why don't you take one of mine off my hands?"

"No, you try being an only child and having a father who's, like, obsessed with every detail of your life. Don't you think he has the right to know if he has a son?" I rage on when she doesn't answer, "Don't *I* have the right? I've *always* wanted a brother or a sister. Why wouldn't she tell me? Why pretend all these years?"

My mom once said after she ran off with Fran: *As ugly as it is, Shawna, sometimes you have to do the right thing. And sometimes people get hurt.* Did she think the "right" thing included hiding my brother? Lying to me?

No wonder Dad's obsessed with this infertility business. My parents waited ten years for me to be born, and I turned out to be a girl. If they'd had another baby—the son Dad wanted, and expected—would it have made any difference in their lives, or in mine? Would Dad be a happier person in general?

Would he be any happier with me?

46

The Friday before winter break I find another note on my science table. When I toss it in the trash without opening it, Devon whispers, "Change your mind about guys yet, Gallagher?"

I whisper back, "Not if they're all like you."

"She doesn't even deny it," Devon says to the atmosphere.

"Shut up," Melanie snarls from her own table.

Danielle drawls, "You're such a loser, Connolly."

Twohig's timely grand entrance prevents a full-blown riot. But my day is ruined. I simmer through every class, knowing, intellectually, I shouldn't let his idiocy get to me. But it's hard. Nobody has bothered to bring up my mom for a very long time. What if Devon starts telling people he "knows" I'm gay? Worse, what if people believe him?

What kills me is this: if Devon wants to spread gay rumors around, aren't there enough gay kids at Wade Prep for him to abuse? Like Jonas Dunn, from art, not that I'd ever wish that on Jonas. And what about Rosemary Wong, also in my art class, with her shaved temples and men's yellow rubber rain boots? If Devon's dying to gay-bash, why not bash the real gays?

Why bash anyone? How can he be so fucking ignorant?

In art, Miss Pfeiffer proudly announces a new project: "Your Life as a Collage: a Visual Autobiography." We can choose our own medium and we have till the end of next semester. All projects will be displayed in the annual art show in May.

Great. As much as I love art, I don't want to spend the rest of my senior year drudging over some juvenile collage. How about a papier-mâché bust of myself with a sword through my head?

"I'm doing charcoal," LeeLee announces, peering into her bookbag.

"Charcoal's depressing," Jonas argues, doodling hearts on his sketchpad. "I need color. Anyway, it smudges."

"*Life* smudges." Miss Pfeiffer's tiny wrinkled hands sweep the air for emphasis. Omigod, leave it to Jonas to throw Miss Pfeiffer into an artsy roll. "Art is all about challenge, people. I want you to challenge your audience, to make them see things in a new way. To make them *think*! But I also want you to challenge yourselves by—*Ophelia Velez*! What do you think you're doing?"

LeeLee, fumbling with her cell under the table, nearly tumbles out of her chair. Luckily the bell rings. She scrambles out ahead of me. "Guess who just texted me?"

I don't have to guess. "Tovah."

"Yep. She and her dads are coming to town over winter break"—she doesn't even stumble over the word "dads"—"and she wants to get together. They're staying with Fran through the New Year. Didn't you know?"

When, I wonder, did "Frankfurter" become Fran? "Well. Whoop-di-do."

She follows me outside, across the cold, slippery parking lot. "What's with you today?"

"Um, I'm in a crappy mood?"

"You've been in a crappy mood, like, forever."

"Tell me about it." I knock ice off my car door with my foot, and we climb into the cold leather seats. "My day sucked. Devon's back on his 'Shawna's a lesbian' kick."

"Shawna, trust me. *Nobody—cares*."

"Whose side are you on?"

"Please, this is so third grade. You act like being called a lesbian's the most god-awful thing in the world. It's not, okay? So stop playing into that *maricon's* hands and ignore him already. God, you slay me sometimes."

I'm too hurt, too furious, to respond. If she weren't already in my car, I'd tell her to walk home. I peel the car out of the lot, seething over the fact that LeeLee, my best friend, cannot comprehend my misery.

Not only is she clueless. It's like she doesn't even care.

47

Fran calls me the first day of winter break—luckily, on my cell phone—to invite me over, as promised. Yes, she mentions that Tovah will be there. "You remember Tovah, don't you?"

As if I could forget. "Yes."

"Anyway, she asked me to invite your friend Lia."

"LeeLee," I correct her. I wait, half expecting her to bring up those photos. Has she missed them yet? But Fran only adds that she hopes I can make it. And to be sure to pass the invitation on to LeeLee, which I do.

"Dinner next Sunday, at two," I tell her on the phone. Maybe this time I'll remember to ask about Mom's rings.

"What're you gonna wear?" LeeLee asks anxiously. "Should I dress up?"

"Why, you gonna be cruising for guys? Hey, Arye's free as far as I know," I add wickedly.

"Nah, he's cute, but too short. And not exactly my type."

"So what is your type?" LeeLee dates less than I do. She's picky as hell.

LeeLee sighs. "Good question. I'll get back to you on that."

48

No further word from Dad about Schmule. He doesn't even ask if I found out his birthday. This strikes me as strange, after he made such a stink.

On one hand I'm tempted to bring up the subject myself.

On the other hand I'm happy for the reprieve.

Because I don't like to procrastinate, I spend the week before Christmas working on my so-called "visual autobiography." I've decided to make a mosaic collage of pencil drawings, all scenes from my life, past and present. Fran's photo albums have totally inspired me, plus I'm taking a lot more with own digital camera.

"Can I get one of you?" I ask Dad after I explain my project.

Dad waggles a finger after I snap the picture. "Don't be posting pictures of your family all over the Internet, now."

Post them where? He knows I don't have a MySpace page. And I don't dare keep a blog.

By Christmas morning I have dozens of new pictures, mostly of Charles, my favorite subject. But also my house, the front of my school, my church, and my favorite places around the city. When Aunt Colleen, Uncle Dieter, and Nanny and Poppy stop by to open gifts—*I get a laptop from Dad!*—I snap a few of them, too. Poppy refuses to open his eyes, and drools into his necktie, but I don't care. He's still my Poppy.

But something is missing from my collection. Arye and Schmule?

Funny how I feel they should be part of this, too. Even if Schmule doesn't turn out to be my brother. And Arye, thank God, isn't related to me at all.

I use my project as an excuse to get those loose pictures back from Dad. Dad frowns. "You don't need any pictures of Fran's kids in your project."

"This is my project, right?" I say as patiently as possible. "I think it should be up to me to decide which pictures to use." He folds his arms, perturbed, as I cleverly add, "Anyway, those are *Fran's* pictures. They don't even belong to us."

The significance of my words isn't lost on him. He digs them up and reluctantly hands them over.

He doesn't say a word about Schmule and neither do I.

49

Sunday afternoon, the day before New Year's Eve, I dress in a brown pleated skirt and brown sweater, and fluff out my long hair with a handful of mousse.

"Where are you off to?" Dad asks, materializing out of nowhere.

I don't want to tell him I'm having dinner with Fran. All he'll do is harp about that jewelry. "I'm meeting LeeLee," I say, which is true. "We're just going to hang out." Also true. "Oh, and I'm taking Charles." For Schmule, of course.

"Got your phone?" he asks absently. Yes, I have my phone. Yes, he always asks me. "Drive carefully, and don't stay out too late."

Charles and I swing by to pick up LeeLee. Fran's house, when we get there, is flooded with people. Most are strangers, but I recognize a few people from Mom's funeral. Fran introduces us as, "Shawna, Penny's daughter, and her friend Lia."

LeeLee doesn't correct her. In fact, she looks pleased.

Schmule, thrilled, drags Charles away from me. "Oh, he's awesome! Look at those funny fat feet!" Charles, equally thrilled, slobbers Schmule's face. "Can I play with him in my room?"

"Okay. But be careful when you put him down, because he's really old, right, and he has a delicate back, and—"

"I'll be careful!"

LeeLee, overdressed in a *very* low-cut, maroon velvet dress, receives her own share of attention. Particularly from Arye, who, after he says hi, tries hard not to gawk at her stupendous cleavage. Since she rarely wears anything besides pants and sweatshirts, I wonder if LeeLee dressed up for him after all.

Tovah glides over, shining in layers of colorful, mismatched patterns, chopsticks poking out of the mind-boggling mass of curls piled on top of her head. On anyone else this might induce shrieks of horror. On Tovah, it's perfect.

"Hi, guys!" she greets us.

"Hi," LeeLee and I say at the same time. Whatever possessed me to choose brown on brown? I feel like a nun next to Tovah. Next to LeeLee, too.

Tovah hugs me first, then LeeLee. "I'm so glad to see you two! You know, Lia and I have been talking for ages," she tells me. "I honestly never thought we'd get to see each other again." She appraises LeeLee with glowing eyes. "What a gorgeous dress, Lia! You look nice, too," she adds belatedly to me.

I narrow my eyes. "Lia?"

LeeLee's smile spreads, engulfing her face. "Short for Ophelia. Isn't 'LeeLee' kind of juvenile? I might give it up."

Suddenly I'm cranky, and irritated, and—yes, I admit it!—ragingly jealous of this beautiful, radiant stranger who calls my best friend by a new name, who makes her smile in a new way. My head begins to throb directly above my right ear.

"We have so-o much to catch up on," Tovah insists, pulling LeeLee, aka Lia, away by her wrist. "Listen, I just *have* to tell you this . . ." LeeLee, enraptured, never glances back as she allows Tovah to whisk her away.

I forgot about Arye till he says, "Man, she's a trip." When I don't respond, he adds, "You hungry? We're not eating for a while, but there's munchies and stuff."

I stare longingly at the hall door that just swung shut behind my best friend.

I've been deserted.

"Knock, knock." Arye waves a hand in front of my face. "Uh, you can go with them, you know."

I don't recall being invited.

"Actually, I kind of have a headache . . ." I follow him to the kitchen, where he hands me some Tylenol. I down the pills, take a breath, and haul my camera out of my purse. No point in wasting an opportunity. "Do you mind if I take a picture of you? For a school project?"

He stares suspiciously. "You want a picture of *me* for your school project?"

"God, I'm not gonna cut off your head and paste it on a porn star. I just want some pictures of you and Schmule." And your mom, too, if she'll let me.

I still sense distrust, but he leads the way to his room, where Schmule has buried his nose in a book, and Charles snores on a pillow.

I peer over Schmule's bony shoulder. Botanical poisons? "So who're you planning to murder?" Evil Shawna hopes it's Tovah.

"Nobody," Schmule says, scribbling down scientific names. "I might write a murder mystery, though."

"A murder mystery? Aren't you, like, nine?"

"Ten. I just had a birthday."

I'm stunned by this timely revelation. "Really? When?"

"On the second," Schmule answers, oblivious to my delight. "I got two new video games and, yuck, some underwear, and double yuck, some crummy pajamas."

I study him as discreetly as possible. He has freckles on his nose. Dad and I don't have freckles, and neither did Mom. But Fran does. He could very well be Fran's.

On the other hand, Schmule has Dad's curly hair and square jaw, and dimples like me and Mom. He could just as easily be Mom and Dad's.

Then again, he has blue eyes. Fran and Dad have brown. Mom had blue.

All that time Mr. Twohig spent on genomes and alleles? Worthless. I'm completely mystified.

"Take a picture! It'll last longer!" Schmule quips.

"Actually"—I wave my camera—"that's exactly what I want to do."

Schmule mugs obligingly, first alone, then with Arye, who's much less eager to be immortalized by yours truly. When Fran pokes her head in to let us know dinner is ready, I draw her into the act, too. She poses gamely—her heart, I notice, doesn't seem to be in it—and then herds us to the dining room.

This time it's Rina who solemnly leads the table in prayer. I sit awkwardly between Arye and Schmule, resisting the urge to cross myself.

"What are the candles for?" I whisper to Arye after the prayer.

"One for each person in the family."

I count them. Fran . . . Arye . . . Schmule . . . and my mom, I guess. I sigh. Across the table, LeeLee smiles at me, then leans closer to Tovah to resume their conversation.

I eat slowly, examining each guest. The tattooed woman intrigues me when I find out she plays the flute for the Cleveland Orchestra. Her more feminine companion teaches Russian at Case Western Reserve. Tovah's "dads"—Leo, bald and flashy, and beefy Will, the guy who wore the lavender scarf to Mom's funeral—crack me up with their endless political arguments.

Over strawberry blintzes, I ask Arye, "Are any of these people related to you?"

"Only Aunt Rina. I have grandparents in Wisconsin, and my mom has three sisters, but . . ." He shrugs. "I never met any of them. I guess they like it that way."

I get it. I glance at Fran with a tweak of sympathy. Her whole family hates her because she's gay. Then I think of Aunt Colleen and all the nasty things she's said about Mom and Fran for the past ten years. Would she treat me the same way if I were gay?

Would Dad? Anyone? Surely not Nonny or Uncle Dieter.

But what if they did? How would I feel?

How did Mom feel when I cut her off? Not because she was gay, though that didn't help. I'm sorry, but yes, that was embarrassing. But, worse, she left *me* behind. And the last time I visited, she almost let me die.

Did she *care* when I stopped visiting? When I stopped returning her calls?

I squirm, wishing away the unsettling memories. Trying to picture myself without a family to fall back on. All because I chose to love the wrong person.

A jet-propelled strawberry lands on my plate. Lucky for LeeLee, nobody else notices.

"Behave!" I mouth as she winks at me.

Well, one thing I know: *LeeLee* wouldn't write me off, no matter what I did. So why am I acting like this because she found a new friend?

Ashamed of myself, I pop the strawberry into my mouth and suck the sweet juice.

Grow up, Shawna.

I'm trying. I really am.

50

Arye can be pretty good company when he's not acting like a jerk. As he, Schmule, and I walk Charles through the snowy streets, he announces, "My mom found a job."

"Doing what?"

"Teaching. Yeah," he adds at my curious look. "She hasn't done it for years. Plus it's a Catholic school, and it's in a real crappy neighborhood. But then she'll be home for Schmule so he won't, you know, get kidnapped by some weirdo."

"No way." Schmule waits while Charles whizzes on a snow-crusted bush. "Only, like, twenty-five percent of all kidnappings are done by perfect strangers. The rest I think are like custody battles and stuff."

Thanks for cluing me in, I think dejectedly.

It's after nine by the time we get back. LeeLee, Tovah, Leo, and Will are playing a rowdy game of Uno. Everyone else has left. Fran is nowhere around.

"Where's Mom?" Arye interrupts Will, who just called Leo a bonehead for voting Republican.

Will's fleshy neck ripples. "Lying down, poor darling. I think we wore her out."

Well, I'm worn out, too. "We'd better go," I suggest to LeeLee, who then launches into a thousand good-byes with Tovah.

Yes, I remembered to bring back those pictures. But the blue-checkered album is not in sight and I can't exactly scavenge the house. Instead, with no one else apparently paying attention, I slip the photos under the sofa. Maybe Fran will think they simply fell out.

I sneak back to the boys' room to retrieve a thoroughly spoiled Charles, and say good-bye to Schmule. Amazingly, Schmule and Charles are both asleep, exhausted from our twenty-block trek. Schmule's bare feet, uncovered, dangle off the mattress.

Now I have something else to add to my list: *I sleep with my feet hanging off the edge of the bed, too. And so did Mom.*

Secretly I snap one last picture before I tuck a drowsy Charles under my arm and tiptoe out. There, I stop dead when I hear someone crying across the hall. Another door stands open an inch or two, and I can't control the urge to peek in.

Fran, slumped on the side of the bed, sniffles into one hand, holding something else in the other. Even in the semi-dark I recognize the heart-shaped picture of Mom and Fran, on their wedding day, holding hands, beaming into the camera.

"I miss you," Fran whispers into dripping fingers. "Oh, God, I miss you! I miss you, I miss you, I mi—"

Although I swear I haven't made a sound, her damp face whips in my direction. Our eyes meet for a guilty microsecond—and then I spin, rush back to the living room with Charles, and drag LeeLee, mid-sentence, away from Tovah.

Of course I hear *Tovah-Tovah-Tovah* all the way home in the car. I barely listen. Because I'm remembering another time I peeked into a room.

That other night, the night my mom left, I wandered to their bedroom and this is what I saw: Dad, groaning and lunging, and Mom's kicking legs. At the time I didn't know what was going on. I only knew I was witnessing something not meant to be seen by anyone's eyes.

I felt sick. I felt betrayed. And that's how I feel now. If I wasn't meant to see it, then why did Fran *let* me?

I hate her for that.

LeeLee infiltrates my jumbled thoughts. "I invited Tovah over tomorrow to spend the night with us."

"Tomorrow? New Year's Eve?" LeeLee and I always spend New Year's Eve together. We watch DVDs, play Yahtzee, and stay up till dawn. It's a tradition with us, since we never have dates.

"Well, Tovah's leaving on New Year's Day, so I thought it'd be fun. You don't mind, do you?" she adds worriedly.

Do I mind? I tell myself no.

"Okay," I say lightly. "That'll be fine."

51

By the stroke of midnight, after a couple games of Yahtzee and countless bowls of buttered popcorn, I feel myself relax, sprawled on LeeLee's bed. LeeLee, without looking—another ritual of ours—runs her fingers through a stack of DVDs and randomly selects two. "Okay, *chicas*. *Muriel's Wedding* or *The Devil Wears Prada?*"

"*Muriel*," I say, not wanting to watch Meryl Streep and be reminded of Susan and the Snow Ball.

Tovah flips her long braid. "Fine with me. I've seen them both anyway." She tosses a kernel of popcorn into the air, catching it neatly with a silver-studded tongue.

"Doesn't that hurt?" I waggle my own tongue so she'll know what I mean.

Tovah taps the stud against her front teeth. "Only when I first got it. I couldn't talk for a week and it, like, bled for-*ever*."

LeeLee pokes me. "I'm thinking of doing mine. Wanna go together?"

"Ri-ight." I grimace. "A doctor with a tongue stud? How professional."

"You don't have to wear it to work," Tovah points out.

"I won't wear it anywhere because I'm not mutilating my body."

"It's not mutilation, it's self-expression. Anyway, Lia has a nose stud. *You* have pierced ears."

"Piercing your tongue is morbid," I insist. "Don't you know your tongue is the most vascular part of your body? Plus your mouth is full of bacteria, and—"

Tovah holds out a palm. "Don't lecture us, doc."

"Who's lecturing? I'm self-expressing." At LeeLee's thin look, I add pleasantly, "Hey, it's up to you if you want to risk your life."

"Well, thanks for your permission. Not that I asked for it. Jeez!"

Disgruntled, I settle back to watch the movie, wondering why I care if LeeLee shoves an ice pick through her tongue. *Muriel's Wedding* turns out to be about a weird, homely outcast whose lifelong dream is to have the perfect wedding. How lame is that? Plus, LeeLee and Tovah chatter nonstop, so I miss half the dialogue.

After the movie, LeeLee jumps up, checks the lock on her door—the sisters she shares her room with have been banished to the basement for the night—and hauls out, yes, a huge jug of sangria. "Party time!" I shush her, but she blows me off. "Those kids can sleep through a hurricane. And my folks," she explains to Tovah, "sleep downstairs on a pull-out. They won't hear a thing."

Tovah blinks. "They sleep in the living room?"

"Well, that's what happens when you run out of bedrooms."

We toast the New Year, and then Tovah marvels, "Damn, Lia. Your folks. So, when do they ever, you know—do it?"

LeeLee laughs. "Beats me. I never caught 'em at it, though."

Not in the mood to hear about Mr. and Mrs. Velez's sex life, I bleakly take a sip of wine. Then another. Then two more. Then I refill my glass. Finally I'm feeling a little less bleak.

Tovah admits, "I've seen people do it, like, three times."

"No way!" LeeLee screeches.

"I swear. I stayed overnight at a friend's house once, and I walked into the john while her folks were doing it in the shower. The mom broke the soap dish right off the wall. I was never invited back."

Okay, either this is really, really funny or I'm way more blitzed than I thought. LeeLee and I fall into each other, laughing our heads off.

"And then these friends of my dads? They're gay, too, right? So they're staying with us, and I walk in after school and one of them was—" She makes jerking motions with her fist in front of her mouth.

This is sick, this is sick! So why am I laughing so hard?

"So what's the third one?" LeeLee demands, convulsed with snorts.

Tovah's giggles fizzle out. She glances at me. "Never mind."

I stop laughing, too. Because I think I know.

Clueless LeeLee pushes her playfully. "Come on! You started this."

Tovah scrambles off the bed. "I forgot. Hey, we're out of popcorn! Who wants to—?"

LeeLee continues to beg. She doesn't get it. But I do. I didn't even sober up this fast that night with Devon.

Slowly I ask, "So who was it, Tovah? Fran? And my mom?"

Tovah looks away. "It's not important."

"Shit." LeeLee's mental lightbulb blinks on.

"Yes, it is," I persist, though it's the last thing I need to know. "So what were they doing? Tell me. Exactly! I really want to know."

"Shawna," LeeLee begins.

I sneer at Tovah. "What are you, anyway? One of those weirdos who like to watch?"

"Stop it! Now!" LeeLee points to the wine. "Man, I am cutting you off before you go *psycho* on us."

I wrench away. Tovah stares, her luscious lips transformed into a pink line. "I didn't do it on purpose," she says softly. "My dad sent me over for some books. We have a key."

It's too late to stop it. Paralyzed, I listen.

"I knew the books were in their room. And when I came down the hall, I heard them in there, and—"

"Forget it. Don't tell me." Why the hell did I ask?

"You wanted details," she says icily. "Like you think they're freaks or something."

Enough! I swing my legs off the bed. Alarmed, LeeLee asks, "Where are you going?"

"I have to pee. Do you mind?"

I stomp to the john, do what I have to do, and wander downstairs to the living room, where, yes, I see LeeLee's parents bundled under the covers on the sleeper sofa. Please don't let them be doing it! I've had enough twisted visions of sex for one night.

But I only hear snoring. I tiptoe to the kitchen, pour a glass of water, and sit at the table taking nervous little sips. Two separate pictures flash through my brain—first one, then the other, over and over.

Mom and Fran, together in bed.

Then Fran, sitting alone on the side of that same bed. Crying over that heart-shaped picture frame. Whispering, over and over, *I miss you! I miss you!*

I miss her, too.

And I've missed her longer than Fran.

LeeLee, behind me, touches my shoulder. "Um, are you coming to bed?"

"No."

"Well, what're you gonna do?"

"I don't know. I just want to sit here for a while."

LeeLee reaches an arm around to pull me against her. "She shouldn't have told you that. That was just, well, wrong. I told her that, too."

"Whatever. I don't care." Like, what, I didn't know? Of course I knew. I thought about it for years, wondering and imagining. I've seen movies, right? I've read stuff in books. But it was always so much easier to pretend Mom and Fran were just regular roommates.

I can't blame Tovah. I dragged it out of her.

LeeLee steps back when I shake her off. "We can talk about it when you come back up. Okay?"

"There's nothing to talk about," I whisper. "It's just, well, weird, hearing about it." Silence. "I'll be up in a bit. I promise. I just have to . . ."

Think.

52

When I finally straighten up from the table, the clock on the microwave says 4:45. My neck hurts and my temples vibrate. Rising gingerly, I make another trip to the bathroom and return to LeeLee's room. I hope I can crawl in, go back to sleep, and not wake up with this headache.

First, in the silvery moonlight shining through the window, I notice the empty wine jug on LeeLee's nightstand.

Second, I see LeeLee and Tovah curled up together on one side of the double bed.

So together, in fact, I can't tell where one ends and the other one begins. Both fast asleep. Tovah has her arms wrapped around LeeLee, one hand resting inside LeeLee's nightshirt.

Not resting there like it landed by accident. Resting there on purpose. Touching LeeLee's breast. Holding it deliberately. No question about it.

Now I know what I think my heart tried to tell me the first time I saw LeeLee flip open her cell phone and scream Tovah's name.

Heart hammering in my aching skull, I grope around for my clothes and pull them on over my nightshirt. I find my purse, coat, and boots, and head for the front door, closing it softly so as not to wake LeeLee's parents.

What does LeeLee expect me to do? Crawl into bed with them?

My nostrils ice up in the unbelievable chill. The streetlights shine painfully on the snow while the black sky shimmers with twinkling pinpoints.

I drive home in a semi-daze, wondering if I'm dreaming.

 **53**

I don't turn on my cell phone till after dinner the next day. I knew LeeLee would call and I don't know what to say to her.

Eight messages waiting. Well, five, actually:

1. "Hey, *chica*, where'd you go? I was flipping out! Anyway, call me later."
2. "Hey, I said CALL ME!"
3. "Why the hell do you have your phone turned off?"
4. "Um, Shawna, are you, like, pissed about . . ." Pause. "Look. Just *call* me."
5. "Okay, fine, whatever. Be a bitch. See you in school tomorrow. If you're alive."

The last three are hang-ups from her number. I guess she got tired of talking to dead air.

If I call her back, do I tell her what I saw? Or should I act like nothing happened?

I can't think about this now.

54

I swear I don't know how I make it to school the first day after vacation.

LeeLee doesn't make it at all.

Miraculously, I ace a pop quiz in A&P, breeze through a Spanish test, get back an A on my latest English paper, and survive economics without lapsing into a coma. No "dyke" comments from Devon, Susan and Paige ignore me, so all in all it's a decent day.

Too bad I can't stop thinking about LeeLee and Tovah.

Last period Miss Pfeiffer drags me aside. "Shawna, by any chance did you get a surprise in the mail a while back?" I draw a blank. "A brochure from MassArt?" she prompts, noticeably disappointed at my lack of enthusiasm.

I never got a brochure from MassArt. Why would she send it to me anyway?

"MassArt? I'm going to Kenyon, remember? Then med school, and—"

"Then the Peace Corps." Yes, Miss Pfeiffer knows the drill. "I understand. And I'm proud of you, Shawna, if that's what you want to do." She waves dramatically. "Granted, I'm not scientifically inclined. And medicine *is* a noble profession. I'm sure you'll excel at Kenyon. I just wish you wouldn't give up your art so easily."

"I'm not giving it up." How can I give something up that was never a part of my plan?

"Well, I'm glad to hear it, because"—Miss Pfeiffer whips an envelope out of a torn pocket in her skirt—"I've been a bad girl, I'm happy to say."

"What's this?"

"Take it home and read it. It's from my friend at MassArt." I open my mouth, but she hustles me to the door. "I'll see you tomorrow, Shawna. Run along! I have some cleaning up to do. Honestly, for a bunch of soon-to-be-graduates, this is the sloppiest class!"

I yank out the letter and read it in the hall.

Dear Agnes, So nice to hear from you! Things have been hectic to say the least—Blab, blab. I scroll down till I find my name.

—want to thank you for the portfolio you sent. Yes, I have to agree, this student has talent. I found her pen- and-ink drawings particularly breathtaking and I've taken the liberty of sharing them with my colleagues. All of us agree that Miss Gallagher shows great promise. I believe, based on this work of hers alone, she has an excellent chance of being accepted. Please ask her, if she decides to change her major, to submit an application and an updated portfolio. I'll be more than happy to put in a good word for her . . .

Oh. My. God. That crazy woman submitted my eleventh-grade make-believe portfolio to her buddy at MassArt? Is she crazy? Senile?

Okay, I should be thrilled. But this is so not my plan! Why would I go to MassArt? So I can sleep on the sidewalk and beg for change while I wait for the world to appreciate my so-called talent?

Worse, if Dad suspects I've had *any* second thoughts about med school . . . well, Mom won't be the only member of the family to end up on life support.

Still, what this means is: somebody other than Miss Pfeiffer thinks I have talent! Not in science. Not in math. Not in designing floral centerpieces or coordinating china. But talent in what I love to do *best*. This revelation alone should make me ecstatic.

It doesn't. I can't enjoy it, because of the two other thoughts knocking through my brain.

Schmule, for one. Who, I know, has no idea that Dad suspects he's my brother.

And LeeLee, my best friend. No, my *gay* best friend.

How the hell am I supposed to deal with everything at once?

55

LeeLee, red-eyed, waits at my locker the next morning. Either she hasn't been sleeping or she's been crying. Crying because Tovah flew back to New York?

"Hi. Did you get my messages?"

I nod, my slippery fingers working the combination.

"So why didn't you call me?"

32-16-33 . . . 32-16-33 . . . This sucker won't open. I jerk on the lock, snapping a nail. Blood wells up in a crimson crescent. "Crap."

"Shawna. Are you not speaking to me?"

I suck my injured thumb. And then—thinking that this is something Perfect Shawna wouldn't do because it's rude and immature, and Pathetic Shawna wouldn't do because she's too much of a wimp, and Evil Shawna wouldn't do without one parting bitch-zinger—I walk away from her without a word.

So who is this new, nameless Shawna who can't look her BFF in the face?

Whoever she is, she barely makes it through the morning. At lunch I spot LeeLee with Danielle and Melanie. My usual carton of yogurt, even unopened, suddenly turns my stomach. I toss it into the trash, slink back toward the door—

And a hand grabs the back of my jacket, which, yes, I'm still wearing.

"How long do you plan to keep this up?" LeeLee asks.

"What?"

"Not talking to me."

"I'm talking to you now."

"Shawna, what's your problem?"

"I have no problem." I hesitate, glance around, and then it falls out of my mouth. "Why don't you ask Tovah what my problem is? I'm sure she'll tell you all about it."

LeeLee pushes me out of the cafeteria. "What're you talking about?"

"You know what I'm talking about. I saw you, LeeLee. I saw you and—" Tovah, Tovah, Tovah. I can't even say her name.

LeeLee draws back, her face blooming redder than the blood around my nail.

"When I went back to your room, I saw you two—*together*." My neck prickles under the collar of my jacket. I can only imagine the parts I missed.

LeeLee stands there, at a loss for words. A door slams. I hear approaching chatter from the opposite end of the hall. I hoist my bookbag and rake my hair off my blazing neck. "See ya."

I'm ten feet away by the time she calls, "Shawna, you're my best friend. You don't have to be jealous."

I'm not jealous. I'm—

What? *What?*

There's no word in the English language for what I am.

I walk faster. Best friend? Ha! Ask Susan Connolly what "best friends" means.

How can LeeLee imagine we can be *any* kind of friends? She's gay. I'm straight. Can a straight person be friends with someone who's gay?

Please. It doesn't happen, at least not in this school. Jonas Dunn has no male friends at all. Guys either avoid him or rag on him, so he hangs out with the girls. It makes no difference how nice he is. Guys know if they hang out with him, they risk being called a "fag." Most likely by Devon, or some other dumb-ass jock.

Rosemary Wong, with the yellow boots? Once she started buzzing her temples and wearing knit caps and men's jackets, all her female friends drifted away. Now she hangs out with nobody in particular. I wonder if she prefers it that way.

Maybe this is why Mom and Fran moved to New York. Maybe people there are more tolerant or whatever.

I remember Susan's and Paige's funny looks when LeeLee and I hugged at the mall. A hug between friends, nothing else. Can we ever hug each other again without people wondering? If I'm not strong enough to lie and simply say "I don't care," how can I be strong enough to change the way I feel?

Or even know how I feel.

 56

LeeLee either walks home from school now or takes a bus. In art, she mysteriously ends up at Rosemary Wong's table, while Jonas and I wind up with an Arabic boy whose name I can never remember. He's in trig with me, too. He never speaks, but he watches me all the time. And he's desperately handsome in a scary kind of way. Ha. Just imagine Dad's reaction if I ever bring *this* dude home.

LeeLee has officially abandoned our lunch table, too.

"Did you two have a fight?" Melanie asks.

I lick blueberry yogurt off my plastic spoon. "Not really."

"What do you mean, not really? And why is she suddenly hanging out with *them*?" Mel points her vegan pita sandwich toward LeeLee, who's sharing a pizza with Jonas and Rosemary.

"Maybe she's working on a research project," Danielle says optimistically.

Mel scoffs. "What research project?"

"Hell if I know. It sounds good, right?"

They look at me, awaiting explanation. I study my yogurt label. I'm staying out of this.

Devon deliberately bumps my chair. "Lovers' spat?" he inquires loudly, nodding at LeeLee's new table.

Those who hear this titter, except for Mel and Danielle. LeeLee flips him off without looking over.

"Must be serious," Devon drawls. "Maybe you oughta kiss and make up?"

Being a mature and responsible adult, I ignore him even as Melanie and Danielle hammer him with insults. This is when I realize something else: if the Snow Ball had gone differently, if I'd had sex with Devon, I'd be in the same position—only he'd be calling me a slut now, instead of a lesbian.

Either way I'd lose. But I think "slut" I could live with.

57

"One—two—*three!*" Uncle Dieter shouts.

Both of us barrel hard against the back of Poppy's wheelchair. Five inches of snow last night ended my miserable week, and nobody—meaning me—remembered to call the plowing service. Poor Poppy's mummified expression never changes, but his swiveling eyes show he fully expects to be dropped on his head. Aunt Colleen flits uselessly. Nonny fans her face.

"This is ridiculous!" Dad explodes once the wheelchair thumps safely over the threshold.

"*You're* the one who doesn't seem to own a snow shovel," Aunt Colleen sniffs.

"He needs to be in a home. This is just too difficult."

I put an arm around Poppy and kiss his cheek, furious that Dad once again says this in front of him. Poppy smells exceptionally bad today. Not like diapers, or medicine, but a sick-old-man-who-can't-bathe-himself-anymore smell. I pat his hand. His faded eyes gaze past me and his thin shoulders tremble. I hope that's from the Parkinson's, and not from terror at the idea of a nursing home, of all places.

Dad adds, more nicely, "You can't take care of him anymore, Ma. Why can't you just admit it? You're killing yourself."

This, naturally, throws Nonny into a royal Highland snit. She snarls something in Gaelic that probably starts with an *F* in English, and knocks back three glasses of whisky during dinner. When Uncle Dieter tries to lighten the mood with a goofy joke, Aunt Colleen bites his head off and calls him "juvenile." Crestfallen, he stomps out and returns reeking of tobacco.

"Fine! Smoke!" Aunt Colleen huffs. "Won't Shawna be thrilled when *you* drop dead on her, too?"

Which, of course, launches us onto the subject of Mom. Between dainty bites, Aunt Colleen batters Dad with questions: why is Mom's estate still in probate? Why can't Dad's worthless lawyer, Mr. Weiss, speed up the process? How could Fran have imagined she'd end up with a single cent?

Then she starts on me. "Your father tells me you went over there for *dinner*?" I nod cautiously. "Well, what're they like? Fran and her *boys*?" She says "boys" with the same sneer she used for "dinner." As if they aren't really boys, and no, we didn't eat dinner—we drew pentagrams, sacrificed babies, and danced naked around a bonfire.

I take another bite and chew slowly . . . slo-owly . . .

Aunt Colleen smirks at my non-reply and brandishes her fork at Dad. "You see? So it begins."

Dad slices into his roast, nearly cracking the plate. "Shawna went over there for a reason. I asked her to get some of Penny's things back for me."

"What things?" Uncle Dieter looks surprised that, yes, I'm such a stooge.

"Some jewelry. All the pictures she took. In fact"—Dad crosses his silverware precisely on his plate—"that's the reason I wanted to get together with all of you." Obviously it's not for the pleasure of their company.

He pats his blazer and produces a paper. For one horrible moment I'm sure it's the letter from Miss Pfeiffer. Not only does he open my mail—now he rifles through my purse?

I stare at the document, first with disbelief. Then with amazing satisfaction.

Child's name: Samuel David Goodman.

Mother's name: Sonia Anne Sorenson.

Father's name:

No answer to that last one.

"His birthday," Dad proclaims, "is December second. Eight and a half months after Penny left."

Aunt Colleen snatches the birth certificate away. "How did you get this?"

"Why do you think I pay Weiss five hundred bucks an hour?"

Nonny stops shoveling sweet potatoes into Poppy's mouth long enough to take a peek. "Mother of God. She didn't know who the father was?"

"Of course she knew," Dad says impatiently. "She deliberately left it blank."

"Is that legal?"

"Yes, it's legal. Not that it matters now," he adds thoughtfully

Aunt Colleen slaps the table, a Gallagher trait. "Well. That bitch!"

Nobody speaks for a few seconds. Aside from the sound of Poppy's fingers scraping the arm of the wheelchair, I can almost taste the silence.

"She used the name Goodman," Uncle Dieter points out. "Is *that* legal?"

"Apparently so," Dad says shortly.

Schmule's name is Sam? And Mom gave him Fran's last name, and then passed him off as Fran's? How would any of us ever know that Sam was really Mom's? Schmule was born in New York. Until Mom's funeral, nobody but me had ever met him. Even Schmule might not know, since he shares the same last name as Fran.

"When Shawna showed me the boy's baby pictures"—Dad, unexpectedly, sends me a startling smile—"I knew it immediately. He looks just like Shawna."

"Well." Aunt Colleen strokes my hand. I try not to recoil. "Aren't *you* the little super sleuth? Maybe you should forget about medical school and join the CIA."

Unconvinced, Nonny protests, "Ah, Johnny, I dunno. I know the two of ye had your ups and downs. But what would possess her to do something so desperate?"

"Desperate?" Dad's fist rattles the china. "What's 'desperate' about it, Ma? She left me for no reason. I supported her. I gave her a child. I gave her everything she ever wanted, and what did she do? She ran off with that, that *person* without saying good-bye to her own daughter!"

Lips pursed, Nonny prods me with an arthritic knuckle. "Shawnie, dear, perhaps you should step out for a wee bit, seein' as how your father's so upset—"

"I'm not upset!" Dad thunders. "I'm mad as hell! She knew I wanted a son, and she doesn't tell me she's pregnant? She takes off?"

"Maybe she didn't know," Uncle Dieter suggests.

"She could have told me when she found out. I would've taken her back."

Chilled to the bone, I hear myself squeak, "Maybe she didn't want to come back."

Dad's gray matter nearly erupts through his hair follicles. "What do *you* know about it?"

"Well . . . nothing. I mean, it was just an idea." Carefully, I add, knowing I'm making things worse, "Maybe she thought if she told you about Schmule, you'd somehow *make* her come back. Maybe that's why she kept him a secret."

Dad views me with undisguised contempt. "Don't be stupid, Shawna. She had no reason to leave in the first place."

Don't be stupid, Shawna, don't be stupid. How many times have I heard those words? Why does he think I'm an idiot with no ideas of my own? Why does he dismiss everything I say? Always, always. Every single time.

A river of lava bubbles through my chest. "Maybe she did have a reason." I jab the prongs of my fork into my palm to keep from chickening out. "Maybe she left because you treated her like shit! The way you treat everyone. Did you ever think of that?"

Mouths gape as I throw down my fork, fly out of my chair, and slam out of the house.

58

Snow falls, hard and relentless, melting into my face as I trek clumsily to the garage. Nonny's black van with the custom wheelchair lift and Uncle Dieter's Lexus block the end of the drive. This doesn't stop me; I gun the motor, reel the car backward, and careen around the other cars, leaving snake trails in the lawn.

It's true.

I have a brother.

Heading nowhere, I circle through ice and snow for a couple of miles, waiting for Evil Shawna to simmer back into her wormhole. Evil Shawna, who screamed at her dad in front of the whole family.

But I have a brother—a brother!—and his name is Schmule.

No. It's *Sam*.

Nobody mentioned it, but Sam is Poppy's first name. Poppy loved my mom. Mom loved him back, and always asked how he was doing. Poppy, if he could, would've kicked Aunt Colleen's ass today.

I drop my forehead on the wheel, waiting for a light to change.

I have a brother . . . a brother!

Oh, God.

What'll Dad do now?

A horn blasts behind me. Green light! I step on the gas, but, unfortunately, the pickup truck ahead of me moves slower than I expected.

"Shit!" I mash my foot down two seconds too late. *Crunch.*

The driver climbs out, a hefty guy who spews out a tirade of colorful words as I roll the window halfway down. I clutch the steering wheel, tears squirting down my face, blubbering, "Sorry! I'm sorry, I'm—"

He stops yelling and peers into my car. "Okay, chill out. Ain't even a mark on mine, but your front end's kinda mashed. You wanna come out and take a look?" I shake my head. "Well, you're gonna tear up your tire, you try drivin' on that. You hurt?" He thumps hard on my roof. "Hey, quit bawling. I ain't gonna turn you in, even though it was, ya know—*your* fault."

"Thank you," I whisper, wiping my face as he stomps back to his truck.

Miserably, I yank my car back into gear and cautiously inch forward. Something scrapes my front tire, I hope I can drive it, and, oh, what if I'd hit a vanload of kids? A ninety-year-old lady? Or worse, a lawyer? Thank you, God. Thank you!

I putz along for a couple blocks, but the scraping grows louder. Terrified I'll blow out the front tire, I notice the street sign for Coventry and creep into the turn.

I didn't plan it, but now here I am. Will Fran be home? If so, what do I say? "I got into an accident and I can't drive my car. Oh, and by the way, we know all about Schmule." The secret weighs on my heart like a basket of dynamite.

My crunched bumper, smooshed against the tire, refuses to budge under my repeated tugs. Feet sopping, I slog up to Fran's porch, wishing I'd remembered my cell, or at least my boots.

Arye answers my halfhearted knock. "Surprise." Sheepishly I point to my car.

He squints toward the street. "Who'd you run over?"

"No one. I hit a truck. I don't think I can make it home. Can you do something?"

"I don't do cars. I'm from New York, remember? Just take it somewhere."

"Take it where? It's Sunday! Can't you, like, push the bumper up or something? Just to get me back home?"

With a put-upon sigh, Arye fetches his coat, a clothesline, and a roll of duct tape. After a few grunts, kicks, and pulls, he drags the bumper up, and ropes and tapes it away from the tire.

"You rock," I say sincerely, staring at my slushy shoes.

"What's the truck look like?"

"It's fine. The guy was nice about it, at least."

"Lucky you. Quit bawling."

I didn't realize I was. "I'm upset, okay?"

"Yeah, and you look like crap." He doesn't look so hot either with half his hair hanging out of his ponytail. "You might as well come in and warm up." Astonished at his generosity, I follow him in. "Mom and Schmule ran to the store. They'll be back any sec."

Schmule. My brother.

I sink into the sofa. Does Arye know? Are they all in on this together?

He hands me a cup of bottom-of-the-pot coffee. I hand it back. "I don't drink coffee."

"Well, it's all I have. You want some water? *Tap* water," he stresses, falling down beside me. "Not the fancy stuff in a bottle."

I ignore his sarcasm. "I need to ask you something." Arye blinks and waits. "I mean, did you know . . ." I sit there like a cretin, unable to find the right words.

"Know what?"

Ask him, Shawna. Ask him!

But what if he doesn't know? Should I be the one to break the news?

I catch sight of Mom and Fran's wedding picture, now placed prominently on the mantel.

Mom and Fran . . . now LeeLee and Tovah.

"Did you know Tovah's gay?" I blurt out instead.

Unperturbed, he shrugs. "She doesn't exactly keep it a secret."

She doesn't? "Why didn't you tell me?"

"Why would I tell *you*? It's not like we talk to each other. It's not up to me anyway."

"Well, did you know she and LeeLee are . . . you know . . . ?"

Arye nods.

I snatch up a sofa pillow, hugging it close in a lumpy ball. Digesting the fact that Arye knows about LeeLee and Tovah. And that he knew it before me. "Oh, God. It's a mess. My whole life's a mess!"

Arye is not impressed by my theatrics. "Why is *your* life a mess because of Tovah and Lia?"

"*LeeLee!*" Then I ask, more civilly, "So when did you know?"

"I figured it out at the funeral. I mean, didn't you see them together? I thought it was pretty obvious."

"Not to me. And I don't even think LeeLee's gay. I think she was, like, seduced?" I throw the pillow when he laughs in my face. "I'm serious! I mean, we were all together New Year's Eve and they drank all this wine, and the next thing you know they're, like, all over each other."

"In *front* of you?"

I shake my head. I know what I saw, but I'm not giving him the details. "So isn't it possible she just got carried away? People do stupid things when they're drunk."

"Maybe," he concedes. "Or maybe she's bi. Or maybe she's *gay*. Who cares?"

"I care! I don't want her to be gay. Anyway, why wouldn't she tell me, when we tell each other everything else?"

"Ri-ight." Arye heaves the pillow back hard. "Do you seriously think she'd come right out and tell you she's gay? *You?*"

"Why not me?"

"Please. I'm sure she knows what a homophobe you are." Before I can defend myself, he spits out, "Penny's friend? After the funeral? You called her a dyke in front of LeeLee. I heard it, too. Nice talk, Shawna."

For one awful moment I can't catch my breath. I had no idea he'd overheard that remark.

But he has no right to throw it back in my face.

"My mom," I say hotly, "left me for *yours*. I was seven years old! I had to hear about it my whole life. Do you think that was fun? It wasn't. So what do you want me to do now, wave some rainbow flag around?"

"Nobody's telling you to wave a flag." Arye's mottled face grows darker and darker. "I just couldn't believe you'd say something like that about someone you don't even know."

"She looked like a freak. People were staring."

"Ooh, what's the matter?" he taunts. "Were you embarrassed?"

"Yes!"

"God, you're too much. You think everyone should bend over backward just to make you happy. They weren't there for *you*. They were there for Penny. You're so ignorant," he finishes furiously. "Ignorant, and insulated, and, well, really pathetic."

Evil Shawna, flaming, springs back to life. "Right. I'm pathetic? You know what somebody at school is saying about me now? That I'm gay. You know why? Because I wouldn't screw around with him. So of course I'm gay, right? Everyone expects it. Because I'm Shawna Gallagher, the girl with the fucking dyke mom—who dumped me for *your* dyke mom!"

As I spew out the last words, I catch, too late, Arye's sharp glance and warning wave.

I never heard the back door open. I never heard Fran and Schmule come in.

"I think you should leave," Fran says quietly. Her nose is pink from the cold, the rest of her face the same shade as the winter sky. Schmule—yes, Schmule, my brother—leans into her, picking at his braces with a thumbnail.

I open my mouth.

"Now, Shawna. Get up. Get your things. And get out of my house."

The apology sticks like a wad of fresh tar. Arye won't meet my gaze. Fran doesn't take her eyes off me. And Schmule stares at the floor as I let myself out, leaving the silence behind.

59

I can't believe I said that. And I can't believe Fran heard me.

I drive home in a blur, heart throbbing in my throat, hands slippery and cold.

I swear I didn't mean it.

How could Perfect Shawna let something like this happen?

 **60**

Convinced Dad'll kill me when I get home, or at least demand an apology, I'm shocked when he does neither.

All he says is, "Your allowance is revoked. I don't have to explain why."

"For how long?"

"Indefinitely."

I consider apologizing. Then decide against it.

Next, I figure he'll blow a fuse when he sees the damage to my car. Or ask if I'm hurt.

He does neither. "Well, good luck paying for the repairs without any allowance."

Whatever. I'm in no mood to argue. Does he care that I could've been killed?

I don't care that he doesn't care. At least I tell myself that.

I spend the rest of the evening in my room, running my hands through my latest prints, trying not to think about anything else. I pause at the picture of Schmule's bare foot, noticing every detail: the creases in his skin, his neatly trimmed toenails, the way his anklebone throws an odd shadow.

Now, clear as day, I can picture this same photo blown up larger than life-size, hanging on a gallery wall. The gold metal strip reads:

"Foot, Unaware"
Shawna Gallagher

Entranced, I wonder—could this ever happen?

I flip it facedown, and concentrate instead on copying the best of my photos over in pencil. But I keep replaying, over and over, that scene at Fran's. Wondering how it might have turned out if I'd paid attention to Arye. If I'd kept my voice down. Better yet, kept my mouth shut completely.

If I hadn't rear-ended that guy. Or if I'd simply driven home.

I've always thought of myself as a good person. Yes, sometimes I say stupid things. Doesn't everyone?

It's bad enough Fran had to hear what I said. But Schmule, too?

Here I've finally gotten what I've wished for—a brother—and in the space of one hour I managed to destroy it. If Fran and Arye will never forgive me for what I said, how can I expect Schmule to? He's ten years old. My cruel words might stick with him for the rest of his life.

I flip the photograph of his foot back over and, sadly, begin my sketch. Less than a minute into it, my pencil point snaps. Taking this as a sign, I give up and bury my face in the crook of my arm.

61

Stuck without a car, I'm forced to get up an hour and a half earlier to ride a city bus to school. At lunch, Danielle and Melanie eye me like hungry puppies when LeeLee, again, sits with Rosemary and Jonas.

"Well, at least we know you're not fighting over a guy, because"—Melanie explodes into giggles—"we know you don't like them."

A fiery barb shoots through my spinal cord. "What's that supposed to mean?"

"Hello! It was a joke?" Embarrassed, Melanie rushes on, "That crap Devon's been saying? God, Shawna, nobody believes it. It was a *joke*," she stresses.

Danielle adds, "You remember jokes, right? Why do you take everything so personally?"

Because it is personal. Everything's personal.

LeeLee doesn't show up for art. Once, Arabic Boy touches my foot lightly under the table. A subtle signal, I'm sure. But I'm too depressed to care.

When I stumble off the bus and trudge back home, I notice the red blinking light on the message machine. I hit PLAY, and Fran's voice blasts from the speaker: "John. It's me. You know, I always knew what a bastard, what a son of a bitch you could be. But I had no *idea* you could be so, so *fucking devious*! My son has been traumatized! DNA? My ass! And I am telling you now, you'd better go find yourself a better lawyer because *mine*, goddamn it, is gonna eat this one alive. Do you hear me? *Do you hear me?*"

No, but I do. As Fran's venomous tirade cements me to the floor, I think of the expression about shit hitting the fan. Yes, it's fair to say that's what's going on here. Shit everywhere, dripping off the walls.

My hand springs to life and I hit ERASE. If Dad hears this message, he'll totally spaz out, maybe have her arrested—for what, cussing him out? Maybe they call that "menacing."

Then, to top off this crappy day, I go online and find a message from Arye: You think YOUR life is a mess? Maybe now you'll be happy. You fucking DESTROYED MINE.

62

"Why didn't you tell me?" I ask in the morning, when Dad stumbles back home from an all-night stint at the hospital.

He collapses into a chair and yanks off his tie. "Tell you what?"

"That you're trying to get Schmule."

I spent most of last night picturing how it might've gone down: Fran, calling Arye and Schmule together with that old "there's something I have to tell you" line. I pictured their reactions. And then I quickly blocked them out.

Dad works his jaw. "Who told you about that?"

I ignore this. "You never said anything about DNA. It's not true, right? You're not *really* going after him."

Dad adds Splenda to his coffee. He stirs it slowly, obviously stalling. "Drop it, Shawna. I'm tired. I've been up all night with a leaking placenta and a horrible surgery. The babies—"

"Dad, I don't care. How can you do this to Schmule?"

Dad whaps his spoon across the kitchen the same way, I'm sure, he throws instruments at nurses. "His name is *Sam*. Who the hell gives their kid a name like Schmule?"

Charles, watching this exchange with wary ears, shuffles over to lick the spoon. I bend down, pick it up, and hold it limply in my hand. Dad'll pitch a germophobic fit if I put it back on the table.

Dad's rock-hard gaze follows me. "He's my son, Shawna. Do you understand that at all? My son. Your mother had no right to keep him from me."

"You don't know he's yours," I whisper.

"Do *you* think he's mine? Do you think he's your brother? Of course you do. Why else would you bring me those pictures?"

I wince. "I thought they were pictures of me! And *you* made me *do* it. But you can't, you know, just take him away from his family."

Dad tilts his head, as if mildly confused. I believe it's genuine, that he truly doesn't understand what I'm trying to say. "What did you think I'd do, Shawna? Leave him there?"

I don't know, I don't know! Maybe I was so thrilled to find out that Schmule might be ours, I didn't think that far ahead.

Yes, you did, Shawna. As soon as you saw that birth certificate, you knew what would happen. Stop lying to yourself.

Okay, maybe I did think that far ahead. But I sure as hell didn't think it through.

"I don't know," I say at last. "I guess."

"You guess what?"

"I guessed *yes*, that you'd leave him with Fran! I mean, God, Dad. DNA? Like he's a criminal or something!"

Dad brushes this off. "You're overreacting. It's a simple test. All they do is—"

"Dad, you're totally not hearing me! How can you even *think* about taking Schmule away from Fran? I thought—"

"What? That we'd visit him on weekends? Take him to McDonald's?"

No. Yes.

"I don't know," I say softly. "But it sure wasn't this."

He lowers his voice, too. "How did you find out?"

"Fran left a message. I erased it," I say quickly as he starts to get up.

Dad falls back into his chair. "Why the hell did you erase my message? Oh, never mind," he says shortly, sparing me for once. "The last thing I need now is to listen to that woman's voice."

"Dad," I begin again, but he cuts me short.

"Drop it, I said. This conversation is over."

I throw the spoon in the sink and walk out.

 **63**

A presence looms near my locker after school. I stiffen in self-defense, thinking it's Devon.

LeeLee, a baggy CAVS sweatshirt covering her Wade Prep vest in direct violation of the dress code, asks, "Can we go somewhere and talk?"

I grapple inside my locker so she can't see my face. Talk to her, dummy, talk to her . . . "Um, about what?"

She moves close enough for me to smell her shampoo. "Come on, Shawna. Don't do this, okay?"

"Do what?" I say stupidly. "I'm putting my books away."

"Meet me by your car? I have to run to the john."

"I don't have a car."

"What happened?"

"I plowed into some guy."

"Loser," she says, but in a playful way. "So meet me by the door."

Five minutes later under a gunmetal gray sky, the wind socks our breath away as we head toward the bus stop.

"Guess what?" LeeLee kicks at a clump of muddy snow. "I'm sick of this."

"Me too," I agree. Relieved, but petrified.

"So what's up, *chica?*" She nudges me, throwing me off balance. "You never used to be like this. We'd tell each other everything, right?"

"That was before . . ." I clench my hands inside my jacket pockets.

"Before you knew I was gay?"

She said it. She said it. I flinch at the word. "I don't believe it."

That came out totally wrong, and LeeLee kind-of-but-not-quite laughs. "Oh. Well, I guess if *you* don't believe it, it can't be true."

"No, I mean . . . I think you . . ."

"You think I what?"

I'm not prepared for this. But I owe her something, I guess. I wish I knew how to start, how not to sound like a—what did Arye call me? A homophobe.

Inanely I ask, "So why did I think you liked guys?"

"I do like guys."

"But not for sex."

"I dunno. I never did it with a guy."

"Well, if you never did it, LeeLee, then how do you know?"

"You never did it with a guy, either. How do you know *you'll* like it?"

"I just know," I lie weakly, remembering how Devon's hands on my boobs turned me off.

"Well. Me too." LeeLee hesitates. "Shawna, I didn't plan this, you know, just to piss you off. And I did want to tell you way before this. Remember when Tovah and I were on the phone so late? At your house? That's what she was bugging me about."

"Well . . ." I hesitate, then rush on while I have the courage. "Maybe you just got caught up in it all. You were drinking that night, right, and I wasn't around, so . . . maybe you got carried away. Maybe it was a one-time thing. Kind of like me and Devon."

"Devon? Please. Don't compare Tovah with that scum bucket. And it's nothing like that anyway," she adds firmly. "Not one bit."

As always, it's useless to argue. We stroll in silence for a while, boots crunching in the snow. At the bus stop she says, "Look. Let me tell you this, okay? I always knew something was different, like, when we'd watch movies, okay? And you'd drool over the guys? I drooled over the girls."

"No, I remember you drooling over the guys," I object.

"Duh. I was faking. I thought you wouldn't be friends with me if you knew. That you'd think I was a freak." She nudges me again. "And I was right, wasn't I? Don't lie. I can tell."

"Bull." I nudge her back, less nicely.

"Please, Shawna, please. Just be honest with me and say it. The whole idea grosses you out and you can't wait to get away from me."

"No," I moan. "You don't gross me out. It's just, I don't know, all that stuff with my mom—"

LeeLee throws her hair back in irritation. "You've been saying that since I met you. So, like, your mom was gay, and she dumped you, so now you hate everybody who's gay?"

"I don't hate gay people."

"*You* can't believe I'm gay," she insists, "because you don't *want* to believe it. You're making up excuses and it ain't gonna fly. I'm gay, okay? Deal with it."

The bus roars to a halt in a cloud of black exhaust. We ride in silence all the way to her street. When LeeLee jumps out, I jump out, too. The wind blows my hood off and I have to yank it back on.

LeeLee tucks her hair under her earmuffs as the bus rumbles away. She stares at me stonily. "Just tell me now, before we waste any more time. Do you still want to be friends?"

"Yes! I do, but—"

"But what?"

"You're not going to, like, tell people, are you?" I ask shamefully. "That you're gay?"

She chills me with a look ten times colder than the wind. "If I say yes, then I guess *your* answer is no."

I close my eyes for an undecided moment. I do want to stay friends.

I love her. I miss her horribly.

I shake my head at last, but I took too long. When my eyes open, LeeLee's already fifty feet away, trudging home without a backward glance. She didn't even wait for my answer.

"LeeLee!" I shout, the wind whipping my voice into the bare trees.

I know she heard me. But she won't turn around.

 **64**

You get to a point in your life where you think nothing can get worse.

I'm there now.

The only "good" thing that's happened is that Nonny paid for my car repairs. I promised to pay her back by babysitting for Poppy every now and then.

LeeLee no longer acknowledges my existence. Worse, she told Melanie and Danielle the truth, and then asked them the same thing: did they still want to be friends? Danielle said yes, because nothing fazes Danielle. Mel, on the other hand, was too flabbergasted to answer. LeeLee, no doubt, counted that as a no.

Now that our foursome has permanently turned into a lopsided party of three, it hits me how few *real* friends I have. True, I "know" a lot of people. I talk to them all the time. But I'm so far down on the social food chain, I feel teeth snapping at my tail.

Next year it won't matter. College, everyone says, is nothing like high school. New people, new surroundings. A new chance to make friends. Next year at this time I won't even be thinking about Wade Prep. Hopefully I'll no longer feel like the biggest loser in the universe.

Every single person won't always like you. And if they're not "real" friends, then who needs them? Think about it, Shawna.

So is it better, or more noble, to spend your life in a vacuum instead of surrounding yourself with people who don't give a damn about you, Mom?

Then, of course, there's the stuff going on at home.

Dad's been on the phone every night with Mr. Weiss. I listen in whenever I can because dad tells me next to nothing. Yes, he got a court order for a DNA sample from Schmule.

Tonight, the results are in.

Mr. Weiss shows up late to deliver the news in person. Dad doesn't invite me down to share the moment. I hear the news from the top of the stairs.

A split second later, a champagne cork pops.

It's official. Shawna Gallagher is no longer an only child.

I hug myself, joy and relief pulsating through every vessel in my body. Then, slowly, inexplicably, both emotions trickle away. All that's left is a clawing sensation, the toenails of a rat scrabbling against the lining of my stomach.

I huddle on the staircase, my cheek pressed against a mahogany spoke, and listen to Dad and Mr. Weiss exchange good-byes.

I want the joy back. And I want to share it with my dad.

So I wait for Dad to call up: *Shawna! Great news! Come on down!*

Nothing.

Or maybe run upstairs and stop in surprise: *Oh, there you are! I suppose you heard? Well, let's celebrate!*

Still nothing.

The rat in my stomach scampers off, replaced by mounting fury. Now that Dad found his son, has he forgotten he has a daughter?

And how are the Goodmans "celebrating" this news?

Dad, back in the den, makes phone call after phone call. My anger at his silence dissolves into pain. With Charles squiggling in my arms, I escape the house without notice.

I have to see Fran. And Arye.

And my brother, Sam.

65

I sit in the dark with my cell phone, my car engine humming. The windows at Fran's house blaze like bonfires, shadows dancing in the motionless flame. Charles hops around, smearing doggy slime on the car window, wondering why we haven't climbed out yet.

Because I'm afraid to?

I want to see my brother. And I want to see him first, before Dad, before anyone. I toy with my phone, knowing I couldn't have picked a worse time. But if I can get to Schmule before Dad, maybe I can explain . . .

Explain what, Shawna? How you took those pictures you knew Fran didn't want you to see? How you showed them to your dad? How you planted the idea? And now what do you want to do? Apologize?

Why should I apologize for helping find my brother?

Yes, you found him. And you see how anxious your dear father was to share the news with you.

"Shut up!" I say out loud. Charles blinks at me.

After a few deep breaths I tap the number into my phone. I'll ask for Arye. Better he cusses me out than Fran.

Rina answers. I have to jump-start my vocal cords. "Can I speak to Arye, please?"

"Who's calling?"

"Shawna."

Click.

Maybe I should've lied.

Tossing the phone onto the dash, I jump out and quickly shut the door. Charles yaps in betrayal as I make my way, in utter dread, to the Goodmans' front door.

What the hell are you doing here, Shawna?

I don't know, Mom. And will you please, ple-ease shut up for one frickin' minute?

The door opens and Fran's aunt Rina eyes me coldly. "You're not welcome here, Shawna."

"I know. But I need to see—" She waits, and I add helplessly, "Arye." I'm afraid if I say Schmule she'll gun me down where I stand.

"Arye doesn't want to see you. Go home."

"But—"

Rina shakes her head and calmly shuts the door.

66

As I rush around gathering up my books in the morning, I hear Dad whistling merrily in the kitchen. Funny, I have no memory of him whistling before. I'm surprised he knows how. Plus, he's not dressed.

"Aren't you going to work?" I ask as I let Charles out to pee, placing mental bets on how long it'll take Dad to mention Schmule.

"Nope, not today, honey. I'm taking a well-deserved break."

"Where's Klara?"

"I gave her the day off, too."

Outside, Charles whimpers to come in. He shoots off through the house before I can wipe his damp paws, and Dad, still whistling, pays no attention. He tosses water into the coffeemaker and flips down the lid. I watch with astonishment.

Suddenly I find I have a whole list of "firsts":

1. Dad took the day off.
2. Dad's whistling.
3. Dad made his own coffee. Who taught him that?
4. Dad called me "honey" in his first sentence of the day.
5. Dad freed Klara from her chains for no particular reason.
6. Dad didn't freak out over Charles's dirty paws.

All this in less than ninety seconds.

"What'd you have for breakfast?" I ask. "Magic mushrooms?"

Dad chuckles instead of splattering me with a look. "Nothing, honey. This is a natural high!" Inhaling deeply as the aroma of coffee permeates the air, he turns around and clamps my shoulders. "And *you* are the one I have to thank for this!"

He crushes me to him, jamming my face into his fleecy robe. Too astonished to respond, I stand there and try to enjoy this shocking moment, because:

7. Dad just hugged me out of the blue.

I breathe in a waft of yesterday's aftershave—he didn't shower last night?—and a hint of old liquor. Plus one other, less familiar scent: a "Dad" scent, one I haven't noticed in years because we haven't been this close to each other in years. Feeling my own smile, I let him hug me another second; then, before I can lift my arms to return the hug, he holds me back out. Well, it was nice while it lasted.

"So, are you ready for the good news?" His grin illuminates the whole kitchen.

"I heard," I admit, stifling a renewed surge of resentment.

"You did?"

"You were, like, trumpeting it all over the universe." To everyone but me, that is.

"It was late. I thought you were in bed." He sounds ridiculously sincere. "Well, I apologize. I did want to give you the news myself."

"No, you didn't. You weren't even thinking about me."

Dad reddens. "That is not true. I was excited, dammit. My God, do you know what this means? You have a brother, Shawna!"

I step back as he reaches for me again. "Great. Now you can put me up for adoption and make your life complete."

"What the hell are you talking about?"

"Nothing!" I fling my arms up and stalk off. "I'm talking about nothing."

I'm shaking so hard, it's a miracle I make it to school in one piece. My day passes in a painful blur—and the pain skyrockets into agony when, after school, I spot LeeLee lounging around at Rosemary Wong's locker near the main doors, jabbering with her the way she used to jabber with me.

Crazed, I stumble toward the exit, reach for the metal bar—and find myself pushed flat into the door. Devon grinds his hips insinuatingly into my rear, and whispers, "Change your mind yet, Gallagher?"

Two simultaneous thoughts whiz through my brain:

1. I'm being sexually assaulted right here in plain sight.
2. I'm so sick of this crap. Who does he think he *is*?

I ram my elbow back, striking his ribs hard enough to send a bolt of lightning into my fingers. "Get off me!"

He grunts, recovers, and slides a steel arm around my waist to drag me closer. "Hey, c'mon . . . play nice . . ."

"Hey!" someone shouts.

Behind us, LeeLee and Rosemary descend like a pair of rabid Dobermans. Devon, outnumbered, releases me with a petulant shove. His nasty smirk, however, vanishes a split second before my seemingly disembodied hand whacks him hard in the face.

"You bitch!" he roars, but by then I'm well out of his range.

67

I drive maniacally, weaving in and out of traffic, queasy at the memory of Devon rubbing the back of my skirt. Yet the stinging of my palm makes me feel even sicker. Can he press charges? Have me arrested for assault?

Dear Miss Gallagher: We regret to inform you that because of your criminal record we cannot accept you into the medical program at Case Western Reserve University . . . or Duke . . . or Purdue . . . or . . . Yep, that's one letter Dad'll be sorry he opened.

No, I'm safe. Devon assaulted me first, in front of witnesses, no less.

But I don't feel safe. I feel alone, and hunted.

Betrayed.

Out of my mind.

I veer into the lot at Arye's school and watch a wagon train of yellow buses line up, one by one. A bell rings, sending kids spilling through doors in a raging exodus. I climb out of the car and tug my jacket closed over my vest with the gold Wade Prep emblem. Amid this laughing, jostling mob of baggy pants and ball caps, I look like a creature from outer space in my plaid skirt and knee socks. How I'd love to join in, to laugh and scream with them, just to shake this disturbing sense of not belonging anywhere, to anyone.

I almost spot him too late, and shout his name. Arye twists

around, openmouthed, and then approaches warily. "What're *you* doing here?"

"I have to talk to you."

"About?"

"Uh, can we talk in the car?"

"Are you stalking me?" he asks without humor.

"Please."

Silence. Then he nods and follows me to my car, where I find a pink warning slip already stuck to the windshield. Faculty space. I crumple it up and slide in. Arye joins me, but he doesn't look happy about it.

"I'm sorry," I say as the passenger door slams.

Arye scoffs. "Not as sorry as I am."

I nod miserably.

"I mean, it was bad enough when your old man made Mom sell the gallery. Penny *loved* that gallery. Mom put a lot of work into it, too. It should've gone to her."

". . . I know."

"Then you make us move, right? So then my mom has to take, like, the first crappy job that comes along so she won't have to live off Aunt Rina the rest of her life."

"My dad did that," I say. "That old will he had . . ."

"I know all about the will," Arye snaps. "Did *you* think it was fair?"

No. It wasn't. And Dad *easily* could've helped out Fran if he'd wanted to. It's not like we needed that stupid money.

"Now this," he finishes bitterly. "This is so fucked up. You know he's going after my mom for custody, right?"

I nod, twisting my fingers. "So now what?"

"We go to court, that's what, which is stupid. It'll cost money, it'll put Schmule through hell, and your dad's gonna *win*, Shawna. So what's the point?"

I don't trust myself to speak. Anything I say would be a lie. Of *course* I don't want Dad to lose. Schmule's my brother! Am I crazy for wanting him?

"You know what else? Did you ever think of *this*? All this lesbian stuff's gonna come out, too, and everyone'll know about our moms. My mom'll probably lose her job—who wants some lesbian in a Catholic school contaminating their kids? Never mind what your priests have been doing all these years." Arye kicks the bottom of my dash. "Your dad already said he'd go to the media if Mom gives him a hard time."

What? No. Dad would never do that, never make all this public!

Oh, yes he would, Shawna. Make no-o-o mistake about it.

I stir uncomfortably. Can Arye hear Mom, too? Maybe he senses it, because his gaze darts, left and right, without meeting mine.

I whisper, once again, "I am so, so sorry."

My hands fly up because I know I'm ready to cry, but Arye unexpectedly jerks them down. *Now* he looks at me. I shrink under his hot contempt.

"Sorry about what? That you took those pictures? That's what started it, right?" I twist one wrist away. He clenches the other one more tightly. "Mom knew what you did, before she even found them under the couch. I don't know why she didn't call you on it. She never even told me, till she heard what you said about her that day."

"I didn't mean that!" I plead. "I—I was upset about LeeLee."

He flings my arm aside. "Wow, you're just full of excuses."

"I'm not making excuses! Look, I don't know how this happened, and you're right, it's fucked up. But it's not just me, okay? You can't just blame *me*."

Arye takes a hard breath. At least he doesn't argue.

"I don't know why my mom did it, why she pretended Schmule wasn't hers. But *your* mom went along with it. Right?" No answer. "Arye, did you know? All along? Or did they lie to you, too?"

Ignoring my question, Arye scoffs again. I absolutely hate it when he makes that sound. "Don't pretend you're not happy about this. I'm not that stupid."

If I argue, he'll know I'm lying.

Hunched, rigid, he stares at the buses rolling out of the lot. "At Penny's funeral, all those things Schmule said? Yeah, they were true. But she wasn't all that hot. She always went off and did her own thing, and hardly saw us half the time. My mom," he adds gruffly, "was always Schmule's mom. Penny never even tried, so just remember that, okay? And tell it to your dad."

"You didn't answer my question," I remind him. "Did you know, too?"

"No," he says hoarsely. "I didn't know. Neither did Schmule. Not till the day they came and stuck a Q-tip in his mouth."

"Wait!" I catch his sleeve as he fumbles for the door latch. "Can I drive you home? Can I just stop in and see him?"

Arye whips away from me. His poisonous stare splinters my

thudding heart. "He doesn't *want* to see you. He hates you, okay? Can you, like, get that at *all?*"

"But if I can just see him for a second, and maybe explain—"

"Explain?" he shouts. "Explain *what?*" He wrenches open the door, and spits back, "Anyway, you'll get to see him soon enough. When the police come by and drag him out of our house!"

68

Up till this moment I'd forgotten about the last of LeeLee's sangria, tucked under my seat since Mom's funeral. I find it only after I've driven what feels like a hundred miles, around and around, no goal in mind. I drop my cell, which I forgot to turn on this morning, when I brake at the last second at a flashing red light. The bottle rolls out from under the seat and clanks into my cell. I squeal into a Wendy's lot, snatch up the bottle, pop the cork, and take a few grateful swallows. Yes, in public, in semi-daylight, with my engine running.

My cell rings the second I turn it on.

"Shawna!" Dad bellows. "Where are you? It's after six!"

Well, so much for his jolly mood this morning. "It is?"

"What the hell are you doing? I've been calling you for two hours!"

"Just driving around . . ."

"Well, drive your ass right back here, young lady. A friend of yours called to see if you're all right"—LeeLee, of course; why does he pretend not to know her name?—"because you got into an altercation with Deb Connolly's boy after school today?"

Thanks, LeeLee. "Sort of."

"Sort of?"

I nestle the phone between my ear and shoulder. How do I tell Dad what Devon did to me? I can't, I can't say it, and I don't know why. Partly, I'm embarrassed. After all, who made out with him after the Snow Ball? Who let him feel me up and see me half-naked? What Devon did this afternoon was nothing compared to that.

So what's the difference? I wasn't "asking" for it today?

"Shawna," Dad barks. "What happened?"

"Nothing. I'm just having some issues with him, and, um . . ."

"What issues?"

"It's personal, okay? I'm not giving you the details."

Good girl, Shawna! Don't let him push you around.

Dad roars all in one breath, "You don't bother to come home after school, or answer your phone, and you've been driving around for three hours, only God knows where, and you say it's because you have 'issues' with that Connolly kid—and you don't feel the need to give *me* the details?"

Evil Shawna pricks at my periphery. I take another long, delicious sip from the bottle. "No, Dad. I don't feel that need. I don't *feel* you have to know every fucking detail of my *life*."

"WHAT?" The phone practically shatters in my hand.

"If I wanted you to know, I'd tell you. But it's personal. Personal!" My voice rises and rises, paining my ears in the stuffy enclosure. "So leave me alone for once. You don't give a shit about me anyway!"

The cell phone cracks against my windshield, clatters off the dash, and lands back on the floor. I'm sobbing, sobbing, and I never felt it coming. Like stepping on a land mine, tears explode without warning. Blowing me to bits. Hurtling pieces of me everywhere.

I screech back onto the road, gulping wine as I drive. I don't care that people can see me or that I'm doing this in Cleveland Heights, a city renowned for a brutally efficient police force.

I don't care. I don't care. I just wish I could make everything right again. Cast a spell, wave a wand. Whatever it takes.

I want my mom back. I want the old LeeLee back.

I want Dad to love me and the Goodmans not to hate me.

I want Schmule to know who I really am. That I'm not the terrible person I feel like now.

69

Mrs. Velez opens the side door without a glimmer of surprise. *"Ella está arriba,"* she chirps as if I've never been away. I smile back, plod familiarly through the house, step over the kids sprawled in front of the TV, and stagger upstairs.

LeeLee's tackling homework. She shuts the book and stares at me, askance. "Where've you been? Didn't you get my messages? I was freaking out! I even called your *dad*."

Arms dead weight at my sides, I simply start crying again.

"What happened?" LeeLee jumps up. "Shawna, is somebody dead?"

"No-o," I moan.

She fans her face. "Omigod. You're drunk."

"Yes. I am. And it's your stuff, too."

"Well, damn. Did you save any for me?" When I can't smile at this, she slings her hair back, drags me to the bed, and forces me to sit. "What's the matter?"

"Sch-Schmule's definitely my brother. Dad found out. They tested his DNA and now Dad's taking Fran to court."

"God." She reflects a moment. "Well, you always said you wished you weren't an only child."

"I know, I know. But not like this. Plus I saw Arye today. He says Schmule's been traumatized, that he hates us, and if he comes to live with us . . ."

"Can you talk your dad out of it?"

"Yeah, right. You should hear him: *I got a son, I got a son, I got a—*" .

"Aw, man." LeeLee pulls me close. "Look, Shawna. Your dad's, well, just your dad. It's not like he doesn't love you. He just . . ." She trails off, obviously unwilling to say anything too unkind. But she knows my dad well.

"Your family's perfect," I say into her neck.

"You're so full of it. No family's perfect. I could tell you stuff that'd make your toenails curl up, *chica.*"

"*Your* parents don't talk to you like you're an idiot."

"Yes, they do. They just do it in Spanish."

"I understand Spanish, LeeLee. And no, they don't."

"Whatever. Forget it." She hugs me tighter. I hug her back, the room spinning in a way that makes me sorry I drank all that sangria. "Anyway, you sure did a number on Connolly. Wow, you of all people."

"I think I'm possessed. I never hit anyone in my life."

"I saw what he did. He deserved that."

"I can't take him anymore. I'm sick of his lies. Oh, just wait, LeeLee. Wait till he finds out about you, that you really *are*—" I shut my mouth.

"You can say it, ya know," she says gently.

Remembering, I blubber, "You sound like my mom."

"I'm not ashamed of it. It's who I am now, okay? I mean, yeah, it's hard. I haven't even told my folks, but—" She draws away so she can see me better. "It's harder to hide it. Besides, why should I have to?"

I'm crying too hard to answer. I have no answer to this anyway.

She hugs me again. "Look, picture it the other way around. Say it was, like, this totally *huge* stigma to like guys, okay? Say it was against the law, even. What would you do? Pretend? Or would you just say screw it and not care if people knew?"

I sniff hard, trying to keep my drippy nose out of her hair. "Oh, don't ask me that. It's a really dumb question."

"People live their whole frickin' lives pretending to be something they're not. I'm not gonna do it, *chica*. I like myself, okay? I just want to be me."

Blown away by her honesty, I lean back to stare into her blazing brown eyes. *Is* it so hard to pretend not to be gay? To act like everyone else, and hope no one picks up on it? How long did Mom pretend, before Fran came along?

I wish I could ask her. I wish I could ask her a thousand things.

Maybe figuring I'm about to argue, LeeLee holds me tighter. I relax in her arms. And then . . . something happens.

First I think of Tovah, and how she and LeeLee fell asleep in each other's arms.

Then I remember all the nights LeeLee and I've spent together. Cozied up in the same bed, holding hands, whispering. How we'd give each other back rubs and foot massages. How we'd undress in front of each other all the time without once imagining it might be weird, or wrong.

I never thought of her that way. Did she ever think of me?

You never did it with a guy, either, she'd said. *How do you know you'll like it?*

And I never did it with a girl. But, if I did, I think I'd want it to be LeeLee.

Blanking out in a crazy-weird way, I move forward and cover her mouth with mine. Strands of her hair float through my fingers, softer than baby powder. For the briefest of seconds LeeLee parts her lips, her warm tongue flickering against mine—

Then she shoves me away. "Jesus Christ. What—are—you—doing?"

I shut my eyes to block out her incredulous expression. "I want to know what it's like," I whisper. "I mean, why not me? Why does it have to be Tovah?"

"Because"—scarlet, but with cool, quaking fingers, LeeLee drags my hands out of her hair—"I love Tovah."

"But not me." I yank away to hide my streaming eyes. "It's okay. I get it."

"Shawna, it's not *right*. You and me, we're like sisters. It'd be . . . I dunno. Like incest or something. This so can't happen."

"I know, and I'm sorry," I say numbly. "It was a stupid thing to do." For once, "stupid" isn't a strong enough word. "Well. I love you, LeeLee."

LeeLee rubs away her own tears. "Me too. I love you to death."

70

February, a thunderbolt of activity.

Dad goes to work. I go to school. He never mentions the fact that I cussed him out over the phone. Either he's tucked the incident away for future reference, or face it, I scared him. I scared myself, that's for sure.

Dad's lawyer fights with Fran's lawyer. Social Services inspects our home, a violent affront to my father. They interview Dad, who maintains composure. They interview me, and seem pleased by my polite, correct answers. Dad beams his approval: I am such a good daughter.

LeeLee and I speak casually in the halls at school. Although I'm sure she's forgiven me, my humiliation clings to me like a sticky web.

Miss Pfeiffer's project keeps me occupied, thank goodness. Day after day, I'll select certain photos, toss others aside, and then sketch, sketch, sketch, till my hand-drawn picture evolves into a near-perfect replica of the original. Lately it's hard to choose one photo over another. I'll stare blankly at the familiar faces, each one silently begging: *pick me, pick me!* When I take a break, I cover my worktable with a sheet. Something tells me, if Dad peeks, he won't like what he sees.

Within two short weeks, workers transform our guest room into what Dad now calls "Sam's room": designer bedding, red wallpaper, a plasma TV, stereo, Xbox, PlayStation 3, Nintendo Wii, and a computer with a monitor nearly as big as the TV.

Julie, who seems to be popping in almost every day, joins me in the doorway of that room. "Wow. Isn't this a bit . . ."

"Overkill?"

"Exactly." When I glance at her glittery red dress and the fur jacket—from Dad?—slung over her arm, she explains, "Your dad and I are going out to dinner. Would you like to come along?"

"No, thanks." What I'd like is to get through an evening without hearing *Sam, Sam, Sam.*

"I was hoping we could, uh, talk." When I don't respond, Julie draws something out from under her arm. "Did you see this yet?"

She points to a page in the current issue of *Cleveland Moves*, the magazine she edits. I skim the words with growing alarm. The article names no names, but you'd have to live in a different solar system not to figure it out. Prominent Cleveland area obstetrician and infertility expert. Renowned photographer, cocreator of popular picture book series.

The article ends with: "Now a child may be torn away from the woman who nurtured him all his life, and flung into a family of strangers who have publicly denigrated the only 'mother' he has left—the same woman who is not only mourning the loss of her partner, but who has lost her home, her share of a business, and her most recent job as a substitute teacher in a local Catholic school. Now, sadly, she may lose her child as well."

I swallow hard. "Did you write this?"

"Of course not!"

"Fran lost her job?" Arye predicted that weeks ago.

Julie touches my shoulder. "How do you feel about all this? Honestly?"

"I don't know how I feel. Except I'm sick of talking about it."

A minor lie. I do know how I feel—like someone sliced me in half with a sword. Part of me is so happy to have a brother. Happy that Dad's been mysteriously transformed into someone who calls me "honey" instead of "stupid" and who whistles around the house. Someone who not only gave me back my allowance but doubled it as well.

Selfishly, yes, that part of me is happy.

The other half wants to stop it all from happening.

71

The phone rings after Dad and Julie leave for their date. "Shawna?"

I can't believe I'm hearing this voice on the phone. I ask, just to be sure, "Who is this?"

"Susan." She must've dialed wrong. "I, um, heard about your brother. My mom saw your dad at a benefit last week, and he told her all about it." Probably the rest of the world, too. "So you had a brother all these years? And you never knew? Omigod. Isn't that bizarre?"

No. What's bizarre is that I'm speaking to Susan Connolly on the phone.

"Are you writing an article for the school paper?" I ask coolly. "Or are you going to announce it over the PA? Am I on a three-way by any chance? Paige! You there? Hel-*loooo?*"

"Knock it off," Susan begs. "I'm not even speaking to her anymore. Can you stop acting like a stuck-up bitch just this once?"

"I'm a stuck-up bitch?" I loosen my grip on the phone to keep from crushing the signal. Then it dawns on me what she said. I ask, morbidly curious, "Why aren't you speaking to Paige?"

Susan releases a diva-worthy sigh. "She hooked up with Jake. He dumped me. For *her.*"

So Paige dumped Devon for Jake. Then Jake dumped Susan for Paige. Maybe there's justice in this world after all. "That's nice. But what do you *really* want?"

Another sigh. I picture her resting her chin, studying her nails, considering each careful word. "I was just wondering how you were doing with all this."

"I'm fine with it," I say breezily. "'Bye, Susan."

"Remember how we used to let people think we were sisters? How you hated not having a real brother or sister? And how we'd dress alike, and—"

"Why'd you call me again? I forgot."

"Because we used to be friends," Susan says forcefully. "And now we're almost out of high school, and we never talk to each other, we never hang out anymore—"

"We hung out at the Snow Ball. Or did you forget?"

"And we had *fun*, didn't we? I mean, until . . ."

She falters, and I finished the sentence. "Until your brother tried to get in my pants."

"Sorry about that. But I thought you liked him."

"Well, I hope you guys had a good laugh over that. What'd you do? Place bets?"

"No! It was nothing like that. I mean, Devon liked you, and I knew you liked him, so . . . well, we thought we'd leave you guys alone for a while."

The last thing I want to discuss is the Snow Ball. And the longer she talks, the angrier I get. "Right, Susan. And you know what he said to me? He said, 'Sue's right, you're a lez.' That's a direct quote. So *that's* how much your brother liked me, okay? And this lesbian business, by the way, is really getting stale. Can't you cretins come up with something new?"

"That was years ago. Eighth or ninth grade! I never called you that since. Maybe Paige did, and Devon. But not me. Never!"

I twist the phone cord, refusing to say anything that might make her feel better.

Susan sighs again. "Look, I admit it—I sucked as a friend. I treated you like crap because I wanted to hang out with Paige."

"Why?"

"I don't know! Who remembers? I guess I wanted to be popular, and Paige didn't like you. She *still* doesn't like you. You intimidate the hell out of her."

I snort. "Intimidate her how?"

"Uh, because you have a brain?" Susan giggles nervously. "Anyway, it's all so, so stupid. But we're older now. I've grown up a lot. Haven't you?"

I refuse to answer. But I don't hang up.

Susan hesitates. "I'm sorry I said those things about your mom. I told you back then I was sorry. I meant it. I mean it now, too."

I play with the phone cord again, unsure of what to say.

"We're graduating soon," she says quietly. "So maybe it's time we, ya know, bury the axe?"

"Hatchet," I correct her.

"Whatever."

I don't trust her. I can't tell if she's sincere, or merely sucking up so she can glean more information about Schmule for the gossip mill. Plus she'd just lost her number one stooge, which means Susan, possibly, might have fewer friends than me.

When I don't reply, she says sadly, "Well, think about it. Okay?"

I'm already thinking, and yes, it's true—I can't remember Susan calling me any names. True, she hasn't exactly been "nice" to me. But the worst abuse always came from Paige.

I remember when she asked me to hang out with them at the mall Halloween night, and Paige's negative, icy reaction.

Paige, at my locker, asking me if I'm gay. Susan, trying to intervene.

How Susan jumped in alarm when I ran out of her room, away from Devon. How I refused to consider the idea she might be sincerely concerned.

"You there?" she asks tentatively.

"Yes. I'm here."

"Well, anyway. Good luck with your brother, okay?"

"Thanks," I say, surprising myself.

"'Bye."

"'Bye."

If I'm not in shock, I don't know what you would call it.

72

Oh-my-God: Julie slept over.

I didn't hear them come in from their dinner date last night. I do, however, find her in the kitchen wrestling with an egg poacher. One of Dad's white undershirts dangles mid-thigh.

"Oops," I observe.

"Shawna! You're up early."

"No-o, it's, like, nine o'clock?" I watch her blush, curling plump pink toes into the cool tiles. "Where's my dad?"

"He must have gone to the office. I didn't see him this morning."

I don't know why I'm so blown away. I'm not naive enough to believe my dad never does the dirty deed. I don't know *where* he does it, but I know it's never in this house. Unless he hustles them out in the dead of night.

Julie scratches a bare thigh. "Are you okay with this? Because if you're not . . ."

"No, it's no biggie." I grab Charles's leash off the hook. "See you later. I have to go help my grandmother."

Today isn't one of my Poppy days. I usually stop by once or twice a week after school so Nonny can shop, or play bingo with her cronies. But who wants to hang around and entertain an ex-nanny? Especially an ex-nanny who had sex with my dad last night.

I escape with Charles, take him on a short hike through the park, and arrive at my grandparents', sweaty and exhausted. Over a cup of Irish tea and a box of shortbread cookies, Nonny asks the same thing Julie asked yesterday: how do I feel about bringing my "wee brother" into the family?

When I shrug noncommittally, she brushes back my bangs. "Try not to squint, dearie. You'll get wrinkles, aye?" She sighs, then picks up a crisp linen towel to dry a couple of dishes. Nonny can't simply talk; she has to be moving. "Mother of God, I just pray this won't turn out like those terrrrrr-ible cases on TV. The cameras, the news-people . . ."

I stifle a groan by stuffing two cookies into my mouth.

"Well, 'twill be interesting, for sure. How nice to have a wee one around for a change. Your father's delighted! Why, even your grandda's pleased."

How can she tell? I glance around. "Isn't Poppy up yet?"

Nonny flashes a look toward his room, which used to be the dining room. "I haven't been able to get him in his chair yet this mornin'. I'm afraid he's becoming a wee bit much to manage. Can ye give me a hand, Shawnie?"

Poppy looks clean enough, already bathed and shaved. The dining room, however, reeks of stale urine—and worse. Trying not to inhale, I lift his bony shoulders as Nonny swings his legs over the side of the bed. Somehow, between the two of us, we drag him into the wheelchair. Face masklike, he still watches my moves with eerily alert eyes. I park him in front of the History Channel, peck his cheek, then race back to the kitchen and collapse.

"I don't think I can do this anymore," I burst out. "I know, I promised you, but—"

Nonny wipes her sweaty neck with the dishtowel, yuck. "Try doin' it twenty-four hours a day, dearie. Oh, I know what your father says. Hire a nurse! Put him in a home! Well, that auld laddie and I've been married over sixty years, and—"

"It's not just Poppy. I don't think I can do it at all."

"Do what, Shawnie?"

Unable to believe I'm saying this to another human being, I confess, "Take care of sick people. All day, every day. Nonny, when I saw my mom in the hospital? I almost threw up."

"Well, 'tisn't easy seeing a loved one like that. Besides," she adds gently, "it's not like you're plannin' to be a nurse, dearie. Nurses do the dirty work, God bless their souls."

True. But I'd only walked into Mom's room. Would it have been easier if it'd been a stranger, not my mother, in that bed?

Nonny, all of a sudden, understands. "Shawnie. You're not thinkin' of not going to medical school, are ye? Why, what else would ye do?"

Be an artist. Create beauty. Avoid blood and gore at all costs.

Surround myself with passionate, creative people. Not starchy eggheads with calculators for brains and some twisted desire to control life and death. Even obstetricians can't avoid death. Dad, I know, sees his share of dead babies.

The words dissolve on my tongue, unspoken. I trust Nonny, true. But not enough to trust that this whole conversation won't find its way back to Dad.

Charles yips and dances, his signal to go potty. I rise and

gratefully kiss Nonny good-bye. "Don't worry. I'm cool. Maybe I'm having, you know, an identity crisis or something."

I snap on Charles's leash and lead him outside. Nonny's gaze follows me, slit-eyed and unconvinced.

73

Dad's home. Julie has clothes on. Both of them wait for me at the door.

"What?" I stop dead, half expecting to see Schmule gagged and duct taped to a chair.

Dad ruffles my hair the way he used to do. "Two pieces of news, honey."

Julie extends her left hand, palm down, wrist arched. An almond-shaped, and yes, almond-sized diamond sparkles on her finger. "You guys are engaged?"

Julie nods blissfully. "Are you surprised?"

Dad's marrying my ex-nanny?

"When?" I ask feebly.

"As soon as possible," Dad says—just as Julie says, "Next year, we hope."

They look at each another.

Uh-oh, I think.

"What do you mean, next year?" Dad uses his trying-so-very-hard-to-be-pleasant voice.

"What do *you* mean, as soon as possible? Jack, we have to plan this—"

"What's to plan? I asked you to marry me and you said yes, so . . ." He slings a cozy arm around Julie's noticeably taut shoulders. "Let's do it!"

"Jack, this is my first wedding! It's not something we can do on a moment's notice. We have to find a church, and a hall. The hall alone might take months. And I have so many relatives I'd like to invite—"

Dad forces a chuckle. "I know you want a nice wedding. But can't we do the church thing later?"

Dead silence.

"Later than what?" Julie asks coldly.

Oh, man, Dad. You blew it.

"Yeah, Dad. What's the rush?" I know what the rush is. But I want to hear it from him.

Dad realizes I'm still in the room. He cuts his eyes at me in a way that would normally make me flinch. It doesn't work this time. "Maybe you'd better go upstairs."

"I'm not rushing this," Julie says before I can argue my civil rights. "Jack, you know I love you—but I do not want two weddings!" She notices Dad glaring at me and steps in front of him. "Forget Shawna. Talk to *me*."

Dad looks from me, to Julie, to me, and back to Julie. At last, he admits, "Yes, I'd like us to be married as soon as possible. Weiss thinks it'll look better if this whole, uh, situation gets dragged out in court. He says a two-parent family stands a much better chance. Not that I'm worried we won't win," he clarifies. "Julie, I *love* you. And yes, I want to marry you. So if we're going to do this, let's do this now."

I'm sorry I'm here. I'm sorry I have to witness Julie's rapidly changing expressions. Confusion, disbelief, hurt, anger—an emotional kaleidoscope—and then, unbelievably, understanding.

She slides her arms around Dad. "He means so much to you. Doesn't he, Jack?"

I can't see Dad's face. But I see his nod.

Your father's a user, Shawna. He uses people the way bakers use dough. Pumping them up and then smashing them down. Twisting. Shaping. Mashing them into a ball. Then he leaves them alone in the dark to rise up on their own. Or not.

Dad notices as I move in disgust toward the door. "Wait, honey. There's something else. There's a hearing next week, but I'm hoping it's just a formality." As he kisses Julie's temple, Julie sends me a beatific smile. "If everything goes according to plan, Sam will be coming home."

Something ripples inside me. Maybe excitement, maybe dread, or a combination of both.

"Schmule," I say quietly. At Dad's bewildered look, I add, "His name is Schmule, Dad."

 74

Dad asks me to stay home from school on the day of the hearing. "We have to stand together as family," he insists when I remind him about a trig exam. "How could you miss this? It's unacceptable, Shawna."

Unacceptable? Deal with it. I'm not sitting in the same court-room as Fran so I can see her face when the judge tells her Schmule's going home with the Gallaghers. Arye, no doubt, will be there, too. If someone tried to steal my brother, *I'd* be there.

Then again, is it stealing if Mom stole Schmule first?

Who *does* he belong to? Us? Or Fran?

Both, I guess.

So, in that case, can't Schmule decide?

75

All through trig I count the minutes till eleven, the time of the hearing. Then I count every minute that ticks by after. I'm so busy imagining what might be going on that I forget to work the problems on the back of the page. I notice too late, after Mr. Clancy announces, "Time's up, people."

How, how could I have blown this test? I stare helplessly at the rows of unmarked circles, and then reluctantly zing it into Mr. Clancy's basket. It lands backside up, and Arabic Guy—whose own paper, I'm certain, is perfectly filled in—lifts his brows in disbelief.

Yeah, dude. Shawna blew a test. Bummer.

At lunch, Susan slips up beside me as I'm studying the yogurt section. Only cookies and cream? No fruit? "Hi."

"Hi."

"You take that trig exam yet?" I nod. "How'd it go?"

"Don't ask."

"Damn! I have it after lunch. Hey, you know"—Susan reaches for a yogurt, too—"I was wondering, maybe we could—"

"Diarrhea alert," LeeLee warns behind us. She rips the yogurt cup from my hand and squints at the label. "Do you ever, like, look at these dates?"

"Excuse me," Susan snipes, "but Shawna and I are having a conversa—"

LeeLee barks one of her more graphic Spanish insults. Susan, who takes French, not Spanish, gets the basic gist. She glares as LeeLee prods me across the cafeteria with her own junk-food-loaded tray. I notice Rosemary Wong's perplexed look as we pass her table. LeeLee answers her with a cryptic nod, then drops her tray on another table and rips into her milk with her teeth.

"I didn't buy anything," I point out.

LeeLee points to her monumental pile of fat, carbs, and chemicals. I select the least offensive item in sight—a soft brown banana—and peel it diligently. We haven't said much to each other since that day in her room. My skin prickles as I remember how that ended.

"Are you friends with her again?" She nods toward Susan, now plunked between Alyssa Hunt and Brittany Giannelli. Paige Berry's new place of honor is at Devon's table, planted happily in Jake Fletcher's lap. Devon, cuddling with a ditzy, redheaded junior whose name I don't know, shows no signs of heartbreak over Paige's defection. I watch Jake pop a potato chip into Paige's mouth while Susan, two tables away, smolders into her outdated yogurt.

I refocus my attention. "No, but she called me a while back."

"What for?"

"Oh, you know. Life's short, blah, blah, let's make up."

LeeLee sucks milk through her straw. "Kind of the same thing I was just gonna say myself."

Wonderment washes over me. She should hate me for what I did that day.

"I guess we kind of misunderstood each other," she goes on. "I don't feel bad about it. Do you feel bad about it?"

I pick a yellow string off my banana. "Yes."

"Well, maybe it's good we get this out in the open, then."

I shrug. "I got drunk. What can I say?"

"I know." She mashes a Dorito with her thumb. "But I didn't mean to hurt your feelings."

"You didn't," I lie.

"Yeah I did."

She touches my fingers. One second later a balled-up brown bag almost knocks the banana out of my other hand. A chorus of howls floats over from Devon's table.

"Dykes!" Devon whoops through cupped hands. Jake slaps him on the back. Paige shrills with laughter.

LeeLee, typically the one who can't resist the bait, yanks me back as I start to rise. "Not worth it, *chica*. Screw him. Sit down." Knees watery, I sit. "And screw that sister of his, too."

"She had nothing to do with that." I can't believe I'm defending Susan, of all people.

"Are you going to make up with her?"

". . . I don't know."

LeeLee snorts. "Great. She treats you like shit for years, you've been mooning over her forever, and now that *she* wants to make up, you—"

"I don't moon over girls," I snap. "You moon over girls."

"Sor-ry. Wrong word."

"Are you jealous that I might give Susan another chance?"

"Jealous?" she hisses. Ha, how does *she* like that word? "Are you out of your skull?"

I hunch forward. "Then what's your problem?"

"My problem is, I was never your first choice for a best friend. It was always Susie and Shawna, Susie and Shawna. You were only civil to me *after* Susan dumped you for that bitch. And yes"—she steamrolls over my interruption—"I do know the difference between loving a friend, like you, and loving someone like—" Clamping her mouth shut, she fumbles savagely at a Ho Ho wrapper.

A lo-o-ong silence, and then I finish the sentence. "Like Tovah."

Nodding, LeeLee spits out a fragment of cellophane. "I meant to tell you, I got accepted at NYU. I'm moving to New York after graduation."

"You are?"

"Yeah. And I'm moving in with her."

"Oh." I pick up a napkin and, finger by finger, wipe the banana slime. "Wow." She watches me twist the napkin into a knot. "Well, that's good, right?"

She smiles a tiny smile. "Yeah." Her smile explodes, lighting up her face like a thousand candles. "God. I'm so happy."

"Me too." How could I not be? Just *look* at her!

The relief on her face almost makes me want to cry. "Thanks, *chica.*"

I hesitate. "So are you, you know . . . ready for all this?"

"Totally. I even broke down and told my family." LeeLee snickers. "My dad freaked out and busted a hole in the wall. Mom ran off to church. I don't think she's been home since." She inches her hand closer to mine; then, changing her mind, she lets it fall. "The point is, my life didn't come to an end. Everyone's pissed. But they'll get over it."

I hope so. I picture Fran at her lavish holiday dinner, surrounded by friends—but, other than her aunt Rina and the boys, not one member of her family. Arye said he never met his grandparents, or his aunts. "I think they like it that way" is what he'd told me.

I don't want this to be LeeLee. I don't want LeeLee's family to hate her.

"Okay. Be honest." She pops half a Ho Ho into her mouth and asks around crumbs, "Are we friends again? Or will you be, like, too embarrassed to talk to me, in case anyone around here thinks you're my girlfriend?"

"Yes, we're friends. And, no, I won't be embarrassed. Then again," I add sternly, pointing at scattered bits of her Ho Ho, "there's this issue about your table manners, LeeLee . . ."

LeeLee loses it, spewing more crumbs than ever. I laugh with her, not caring who sees.

76

Cars jam the driveway when I get home, so I park on the street. As soon as I open the back door, I see it's party time at the Gallaghers'. Apprehensive, I drop my books and wander to the living room. Dad, beaming in a joyfully deranged way, shoots me a thumbs-up and thrusts me a glass of champagne.

"We did it!" he declares. Then he hugs me—hard! Champagne sloshes out of my glass. "Sam's here. He's upstairs."

The yammering adults—my handful of relatives, and dozens of Dad and Julie's friends—pat me, hug me, and deliver congratulations as I ease toward the stairs.

Happy, I tell myself. You're supposed to be happy.

I ditch the champagne—I've had enough alcohol this year to last me the rest of my life—and trot upstairs. The door to what-used-to-be-called-the-guest-room stands open, and yes, there's Schmule. Poised in front of the TV, he aims an uncannily realistic gun at his Xbox, or Wii, or whatever it is. *POW! POW! POW!* Swinging the gun muzzle back and forth, he effectively destroys every monster on the screen.

"Hi, Schmule."

Beep, beep, beep! Game over. How apt is that?

Without acknowledging me, he drops the gun and reaches for the TV remote.

"I haven't seen you for so long. You got, well, big." Oh-h, is this the best I can do? My Nonny imitation?

"Most male Homo sapiens reach seventy-five percent of their

adult height by the time they're ten," Schmule intones, zipping through channels. "I'm four feet nine and a half inches tall. I'm in the upper end of the fiftieth percentile on the growth rate chart. So if I continue to grow at an average rate, how tall will I be by the time I'm eighteen?"

"Male Homo sapiens?"

"Guys, duh."

"I know what it means."

"Well?"

I fidget, revving up my mental calculator. "Um, what's the average growth rate?"

Schmule's mouth pulls down. "You're not so smart."

What did I expect? That he'd jump into my arms?

I take one uneasy step in. "Schmule. Are you okay?"

He faces me for the first time. I've seen that look before. It's the same expression I saw on Fran that day she heard me call her a dyke. "The name is Sa-am."

"No, it's not," I assure him.

"Huh. Tell that to my *dad*."

I want to hug him. I want him to know I love him, that I want him to love me back. But Schmule, aka Sam, punches a button, and Harrison Ford swings across the screen at the end of a rope.

"Schmule?" I begin, praying he'll understand, though I have no idea how to explain what I'm feeling. "Listen, I'm really sor—"

Music thunders as Schmule presses the volume control, bruising my eardrums, drowning out my voice.

I take the hint and reluctantly back out again.

77

The party lasts all evening. I hide in my room, alternately memorizing the Krebs cycle for Mr. Twohig and sketching more pictures for my collage. Charles drools into my comforter, emitting snores. At midnight, jittery from nerves and hunger, I go back downstairs, where the crowd has thinned and nobody sees me sneak by.

Julie's loading the dishwasher. "Where've *you* been hiding?"

"I wasn't hiding." I think of Schmule's hateful expression. "I don't feel much like celebrating."

"Aw. Everything will work out." Julie stacks another greasy plate into the rack. "Sam'll get used to us and hopefully open up. Your dad thinks we should leave him alone for a while."

"Really? Is that why he invited a zillion people over tonight?"

"Can you blame him for wanting to celebrate?" she counters.

I counter her back with, "Did Schmule *know* he was coming here today? Or did you guys, like, drag him out of the courthouse kicking and screaming?"

"If you'd been there," she says snippily, "you'd have seen it was *nothing* like that."

"I had a test." Which I flunked.

"Well, your father was pretty disappointed in you."

"So what else is new?"

This stops her cold. "Shawna. What's happened to you lately?"

Oh, Julie, do you have a few hours? Pull up a chair. I'll spill my guts.

As I shake honey-wheat pretzels into a bowl and dig up a bottle of mineral water, Evil Shawna asks slyly, "So when's the wedding? Or *is* there a wedding? I mean, he got what he wanted, right? Maybe he doesn't need you anymore."

Julie pales. "Is that what you think?"

Another idea occurs to me. "On the other hand, maybe you'd better hurry up and do it, in case Fran decides to take it to the Supreme Court or something."

"Your father and I had already *planned* to get married." But her eyes bounce nervously toward the sound of Dad's laughter. "Whether or not Sam stays here has nothing to do with it."

"If you say so." I'm egging her on, and helpless to stop.

"Look, Shawna. I know you're probably feeling a little left out now—"

"Actually, I'm glad everyone's leaving me alone for a change." Except her, of course.

"—but you have to understand what this means to your dad. For a while he'll be very wrapped up with Sam. Getting acquainted, helping him adjust. But he loves you, Shawna. You're so moody lately." She bumps the dishwasher shut with her knee and cranks the knob. "I think he's afraid you're having second thoughts about med school."

"Who told him *that?*" Nonny? I'll kill her.

Julie's round cheeks pink up. "Well, you know how he opens the mail. And I guess some art school sent you a brochure."

Calmly I say, "I get stuff like that all the time. If he was so bent out of shape, why didn't he say something to me?"

"I asked him not to. I know how he can—" She stops. I nibble a pretzel, feigning nonchalance. "*Are* you thinking about art school?"

"If I were, do you think I'd tell you? So you can run right back to Dad?"

Trancelike, she asks, "Is that what you think of me?"

Honestly? I don't know what to think of her. Her or anyone else in this house.

All I know is, in the past four months, my life has changed so much it hurts to breathe.

78

It takes me a couple of days to pry Schmule out of his room and away from his Wii. Yes, he's speaking to me. But not to anyone else.

Unsurprisingly, he's being a pill.

"I don't want to go that stupid school and wear that stupid uniform." He drills his red plastic spoon into his Dairy Queen sundae with the chocolate syrup and peanuts and a truckload of whipped cream. "Why can't I stay at my old school? I was just getting used to it."

Because it's a Hebrew school and Dad won't stand for it? "You'll get used to this one, too," I promise lamely.

"No, I won't. It's too late to make friends. I bet *nobody* talks to me." He adds in an undertone, "You guys suck."

I wish I could say what I'm secretly thinking. That yes, we suck. That he has every right to be mad at us.

Louder, he asks, "Why can't I go to the same school as you?"

"Because the waiting list is too long." Six months to a year for the lower school. The fact that I, myself, have been there for twelve years didn't cut any ice with the dean.

I watch him duck his newly clipped head and slurp noisily from the dish. I'd like to take those clippers to the throat of that barber who whacked Schmule's long, gorgeous curls right down to his scalp. I'm only surprised Schmule didn't put up more of a fight when Dad insisted he get a decent haircut for his first day of school tomorrow.

He sucks on a peanut, then spits it into the bowl. "Who's gonna take me to school?"

"Me. Klara will pick you up after." For a hefty raise, of course.

"I'm not wearing that crappy shirt," he warns again.

"What's wrong with it?"

"Stripes are for prisoners. It looks like an Auschwitz uniform."

"Don't say that in front of Klara. She lost relatives in the Holocaust."

A spark of interest. "Is she Jewish?"

"No. But it wasn't only Jews who died, you know."

"Reeeally?" Schmule drawls. "Duh. Who knew?"

This is so not going the way I'd intended.

"Are you finished?" I ask as he flicks a spoonful of soupy ice cream in my general direction. "Or do you just want to hang around and make a bigger mess?"

Schmule drops the spoon on the floor and cracks it under the heel of his brand-new sneakers. "I want to go home."

"Well, let's go, then."

By the time I realize what he means by "home," it's too late. Schmule, dodging tables, flies outside. I see him pound madly cross the street, against the light, and disappear in a flash.

Damn, damn! Do I call 911? Dad? Julie? Who?

I grab his coat, rush to my car, and circle the block frantically. Where the hell did he go? I can't find him anywhere. Without a coat, he'll probably freeze to death.

The Dairy Queen is closer to Fran's street than it is to mine. I cruise nervously past Rina's house, terrified Fran will spot me and race after my car with a chain saw. I know he couldn't have made it this far already. But what if Fran met him somewhere? What if they'd planned this whole thing? Whose idea had it been to go to DQ in the first place?

Yours, you idiot.

Swearing, I drive up and down nearby streets for twenty minutes. Finally I head home with a sense of dread, knowing Dad'll find a way to blame me for whatever happens.

I find Schmule, shivering at the back door.

He came back! Why, when he had the chance to escape? He easily could've done it.

Because he knows, I think grimly, we'd set the hounds on him in a second.

"I don't have a k-key," he chatters through bluish lips.

"That's okay," I say, limp with relief, though I'd like to choke his skinny neck. "I have an extra one you can have."

I unlock the door and hold out the key. Schmule flips it sharply out of my hand and it lands in the snowy bushes.

"Keep it!" he snarls, and pushes ahead of me inside.

79

I jiggle on one foot as Schmule toys with the buttons of his shirt. "Do you want to be late *again*?"

His fingers slow deliberately. "Ask me if I care."

It's been exactly two weeks since Schmule Goodman officially became Samuel Gallagher.

"I'm ready!" he screams in my ear. Charles wakes up in his wicker bed with a startled yip. Schmule pats his thigh, a signal for Charles to come. "C'mon, Charles! Go for a ride? Go for a ride?"

"Stop teasing him," I say as Charles dances excitedly. "I thought you *liked* Charles."

"I hate that ugly dog."

He saunters to the door. I grind my teeth. I have a huge, huge exam this morning on the vascular system. Twohig will not be happy if I fly in late yet again.

Ten blocks from home, Schmule decides to mention, "I forgot my books."

"Well, you'll just have to do without them."

"I can't! Mr. Gorski will kill me!"

"Schmule, I have a *test*."

"I don't care. Turn arou-ound!"

Okay, deep breath. Hold it. Count to ten and slo-owly release. Executing a U-turn with amazing aplomb, I'm gunned down by flashing lights thirty seconds later. Here's your ticket, thank you, have a good day, drive carefully.

"Hee-hee," Schmule titters as we pull back into traffic.

"It's not funny, Schmoo."

He giggles harder. My nerves are shot by the time I drop him off. Too shell-shocked to speed, I meander to school, park, and race to A&P. I've barely touched my trusty mechanical pencil to the paper when my cell phone vibrates. I ignore it at first—nobody calls me at school—but it buzzes and buzzes. When a perturbed Mary Therese Montgomery gives me a dirty look, I break down and peek under the table: Dad's office.

I raise my hand. "Can I be excused?"

Displeased, Mr. Twohig asks, "Running on warp speed today, are we? Did you finish the test?"

"No, but it's an emergency."

"Are you ill?"

"No, but—"

"Finish your exam and then you may be excused."

Ignoring Devon's infantile snicker, I scribble through the exam, praying I'm right about the differences between lymphocytes and erythrocytes. What if Nonny had a heart attack dragging Poppy to the toilet? I fling my test at Mr. Twohig, duck into a restroom, and punch in Dad's number.

His secretary answers. "What took you so long?"

"I'm in school!"

"Well, your father needs you to pick your brother up."

"Why? I just dropped him *off*."

"I don't know, but it's an emergency. Your father's tied up."

I explain at the school office. Of course they let me go. I, Shawna Gallagher, would never skip out without a good reason.

At Schmule's school, I find him in the principal's office. He sits quietly in a chair, hands folded on his navy blue Dockers. Blood splatters the front of his Auschwitz shirt.

"What happened?" I shriek.

The principal, with gray goatee and furry black toupee, asks for ID. "I'm his sister," I say as I hand him my driver's license.

"No, she's not." Schmule, unhelpfully, addresses the wall.

"Sam," the principal says, "you may wait outside." Schmule, with a poisonous glare in my direction, slides off the bench and marches out.

If I were in a better mood, I'd laugh at the principal's name: Mr. Dickerhoof. "Did he get into a fight?"

He studies me over laced fingers. "Not exactly. What started all this is that Sam referred to his teacher as a Nazi. In fact, he repeated it several times."

Maybe it's the shirt? Maybe he's role-playing? "Why?"

"I have no idea. According to Mr. Gorski it was completely unprovoked."

"Then who hit him in the nose?"

"Sam did that to himself."

The word "bullshit" nearly escapes my lips.

"When Mr. Gorski confronted him, Sam deliberately slammed his face into his desk."

"Why?" I ask around my bucking esophagus.

"Good question. I'm very concerned. I do understand the circumstances, however. And I know it's a difficult time for Sam. So, for that reason, I won't be taking any disciplinary action at this time."

"Disciplinary action for what? For smashing his own face?"

His furry black toupee quivers. "No, for what he said to Mr. Gorski. Now, you may take him home today to give him a bit of a break. But I'll need your father to contact me *personally*."

Good luck, Dickerhoof.

In the car, I face Schmule. "Okay, I give up. Why'd you call him a Nazi?"

Schmule kicks the glove compartment. I remember Arye doing the same thing. "I didn't call him a Nazi."

"Your principal said you did."

"So who you gonna believe, me or him?"

"Well, what *did* you say?"

Schmule blows out a mouthful of air and picks at a bloodstain on his shirt. "Okay, so like, the whole class is acting up, right? And Gorski goes, 'You guys start behaving or you're all staying after school!' And I go, 'You can't do that, that's a Nazi tactic.' He's like, huh? So I tell him about prisoners in the death camps. Like when they did something, like refused to work, the guards would beat up a whole bunch of 'em. And that's true," he adds defiantly.

"I'm not arguing, Schmoo. But why'd you hit your nose?"

"Because Mr. Gorski says you can't compare school to a Nazi death camp. And I'm like, well, pain is pain, right? And it's not fair to make people suffer for what other people do. So he goes, 'This isn't pain, this is *school*. You guys are, like, ten years old. Wait'll you grow up, blah, blah, and find out what real pain is.' So that's when I rammed my face into my desk. To show him I already do."

I'd like to turn this car around, march back to that school, and slam Mr. Gorski into a desk.

Instead, I say, with caution, "Schmule, you can't do stuff like that. People'll think you're . . ."

"Yeah, I know. Crazy." He scratches harder at the dried blood dotting his shirt, then blows on his fingertips. "You know what they did to crazy people during the Holocaust?"

"Yes, they murdered them."

Schmule nods. "Maybe they had the right idea."

80

I barge into Dad's office after Schmule goes to bed, to talk to him about Schmule and how worried I am—and Dad says, barely tearing his eyes from his computer, "I'm on it, Shawna. I spoke to his principal this afternoon."

"You're on it?"

"I am. I made an appointment for him for tomorrow morning."

"What appointment?"

"A psychiatrist. Isn't that what you're getting at?"

Half-relieved, half-outraged, I ask, "Oh, do you want me to cut school tomorrow and take him to that, too?"

"No. I have it covered."

"I was in the middle of an *exam* when your secretary called me."

"And I was in the middle of monitoring a very sick patient! Am I supposed to drop what I'm doing every time my child acts up in school?" Dad swings around in his enormous leather chair to lacerate me with a glare. "In case you haven't noticed, our family has changed. The universe no longer revolves entirely around you."

"No," I spit out. "It revolves around you and *Schmule*." I dare him to argue.

All he says, quite calmly, is, "Jealousy doesn't become you," and wheels back to his keyboard. "I said I have it covered, and I do. Now, do you mind?" *Tap, tap, tap.* "I need to finish something here."

That *J* word again. Well, why not? I mean, Dad does a lot of things for Schmule that he's never done for me. Gifts. Outings. Extravagant spending sprees. Dad's never bought me a present for no reason in my life. He never suggests we go anywhere, not even out to dinner. Unless something needs to be done, or I screw up somehow, he pays no attention to me.

But when Schmule walks into a room, Dad falls all over himself.

Am I jealous? Maybe a bit. But one thing I know—I'd never change places with Schmule.

"He misses Fran," I tell him.

"I'm sure he does." *Tap, tap, tap-tap-tap* . . .

"So, maybe we could let him visit her sometime?" *Tap, tap.* "Dad?"

The tapping slows almost imperceptibly. "I heard you, Shawna."

"I mean, did the judge, or whoever, order visits or something? You know, so Schmule can keep in touch with them—"

Chair wheels grind savagely into the carpet. "Are you out of your mind? That woman has no legal right to my son what-so-ev-er." Each syllable splinters the air. "Of course she asked for visitation. I said no, Weiss said no, and the judge agreed. She's free to appeal. End of story."

"But don't you think it'd be better if Schmule could *see* her?"

"Don't be stupid, Shawna. *Sa-am*"—he deliberately draws out the name to remind me—"is better off without her. He'll be fine. Now drop it!"

You know that expression "I was so mad I saw red"?

I see it now. Pure red, burning and visceral, like buckets of fresh blood splashed across my vision. "I am so—*sick*—of you calling me stupid all the time!"

The chair spins, but I'm gone before he leaps up. I rush upstairs on thundering soles, imagining the heat of his fury scorching my back. I slam my door as hard as humanly possible.

Your dad doesn't listen to half of what he says. He's bitter, Shawna. Bitter and unlovable.

I try not to listen, but I can't block out her voice.

Lucky you. In a couple months you'll graduate and then you'll be out of that house. Med school, art school—it makes no difference. Just get the hell out of there and never go back.

Like you did, Mom?

No answer.

"Did you love him?" I croak out loud.

Do you? she asks.

81

The psychiatrist, Dr. Silverberg, says Schmule's depressed. Give the dude an award for Most Brilliant Observation of the Millennium.

Schmule barely eats. Klara can't prepare his favorite foods because he won't tell her what they are. Then I wonder if it's the kosher thing, but there's not much I can do about that.

Aside from school, he spends every waking moment playing video games. He speaks when he's spoken to. Sometimes not even then. He's marginally polite to Nonny, outright rude to Aunt Colleen—can't blame him for that—and barely civil to poor Uncle Dieter.

He likes Poppy, though. When I take him along to babysit, he'll sit with Poppy for hours watching history and science shows. Funny, but I swear they share a kind of mental telepathy. When Schmule gets up to leave, Poppy grows so agitated he rattles his whole wheelchair. When Schmule hugs him good-bye, he settles back down, but he won't take his eyes off Schmule till the door closes behind us.

Schmule's shrink appointments are on Tuesday evenings. Because Dad never knows when he'll have to work late, I've been elected to drive him there and back. Tonight Schmule storms out, red-faced, after his session. He won't say what upset him. Neither will Dr. Silverberg, thanks to confidentially laws. I bet he'd tell Dad fast enough if he thought he might not get paid.

"It's private," Schmule grumbles in the car. "It's none of your bus-i-ness. And I'm not going back there."

"You have to go back. Dad'll have a cow."

"Let him." He blows an impressive five-second raspberry. "Maybe I'll just run away."

"Don't say that," I say nervously. "I'd be sad if you left."

This he ignores. "I could go to Jerusalem, maybe, and live with Arye's dad."

"Arye's dad's in Jerusalem?" I know when Mom and Fran first moved in together, Arye lived with his dad. I never asked, or cared, how he ended up back with Fran.

"Yeah, he's writing a book or something." Impatiently, Schmule persists, "I could do it, ya know. I know some Hebrew. Well, sayings and stuff."

"Really? Like what?"

"*Ein Somshin Al Haness.*"

"And that means—?"

" 'Don't hope for any miracles.' "

To distract him from his running-away idea, not that I think he'll get as far as Israel, I ask, "Do you want to stop at the mall and get some ice cream?"

"I don't care. Beats going back *there*." Meaning home, of course.

At the mall we load up with treats—a giant chocolate cone for Schmule, a soy mango shake for me—and sit on opposite ends of a bench. Schmule swirls ice cream with his tongue as he watches a group of kids line up for a chance to bungee jump, right in the center of the mall. Creamy brown rivulets drip through his fingers. He licks his messy hands, daring me to challenge his manners.

"Gross" is my only comment.

Schmule's eyes widen. He gestures broadly with his cone. "Hey, look! There's your friend."

LeeLee waves from her perch by the marble fountain. With her are Rosemary Wong, Jonas Dunn, and a couple people I don't recognize. Definitely not from Wade Prep.

She lopes over alone and rubs Schmule's buzzed head. "Yo, *chico*. Remember me?"

"You're Tovah's girlfriend."

I take a quick suck of my soy shake, cringing with brain freeze. I hope, someday soon, I'll get used to hearing that.

"So how ya doing, Schmoo?"

Schmule studies what's left of his dripping cone. "I'm clinically depressed. I might have a borderline personality disorder, too, with, um, suicide ideations. But no suicidal impulses."

I spit out my straw and shriek, "Did that doctor tell you that?"

"Nah-h." He stares longingly at the death-defying teenagers waiting their turn to be dropped from the ceiling. "Poppy and I watched a special on mental illness. I kinda diagnosed myself."

"Jesus," I breathe. I slap LeeLee's arm when she bursts out laughing. "It's not funny!"

"I'm sorry!" LeeLee gasps. "Ho-ly shit, Schmule, how old are you again?"

Schmule pops the last sticky crumb in his mouth. "Why do people keep asking me that?"

"Um, because you sound like a freakin' college professor? Are you a midget by any chance?"

"Midget is derogatory," he admonishes, gaze glued to the excited, jostling kids. "You should say dwarf or little person."

LeeLee digs money out of her purse. "Here, go jump. You know you want to."

He recoils. "Didn't you just hear me say I have *no-o-o* suicidal impulses?"

"It's not a good idea," I add hastily.

"Why not?" LeeLee nudges him playfully. "You chicken? *Bra-a-awk, brawk, brawk!*"

"No!" he yells, but with a funny, intense kind of hunger in his eyes.

"It's perfectly safe."

She shoves the money at him. He looks at it, comes to a decision, and asks me anxiously, "Will you watch?" Taken aback, I nod. LeeLee brandishes a fist of triumph. "Will you call 911 if something happens?"

"Nothing'll happen," I say without much assurance. "Go, already."

"Yeah," LeeLee adds. "Be a kid for once."

Schmule slides off the bench and wanders away. "Why did you laugh?" I demand. "He *is* depressed."

"So what're you doing about it?"

I falter. "Well, he's on medication—"

"Oh, goody. Drugs."

"—and he's seeing a psychiatrist."

LeeLee flutters a hand. "You guys are wa-ay off base."

I know what she's getting at. "My dad won't *let* him see Fran. We already talked about it." I look away. "It's not up to me, anyway. I'm not his mom."

"Right. His mom's dead. Well, one of 'em, anyway."

Wordlessly I get up, gather the trash, and toss it into a bin. LeeLee follows me over to the bungee jumper line, where a zit-faced, gum-cracking guy straps Schmule into a harness.

Behind me, she whispers, "If you're so worried about him, Shawna, then *do* something."

"What, LeeLee? What can I do? My dad—"

"Do you have to do everything he says? What is he, like, God?"

I move away and watch apprehensively as Schmule rises by degrees closer to the ceiling. Face pinched, he clings to the sling with both fists, growing smaller and smaller by the second.

LeeLee's hand encircles my wrist. "What're you gonna do when you find him hanging from a rafter? Or dead in the garage with the motor running?" Her nails bore through my sweater sleeve. "I don't care about Fran. But tell me this: did he get to say good-bye?"

"I don't know," I whimper. "I wasn't there."

"It's wrong," she insists, as if I don't already know this.

Schmule, a tiny blur, reaches the mall ceiling after his momentous climb. For one breathtaking second he dangles, helpless, and then plunges downward with astonishing speed. I hear him scream as his impending death dawns on him with sickening finality, scrunch my eyes shut in terror—

And then he leaps on me, hooting with joy. "Did you see? Did you see me jump?" He hugs me hard, nearly dragging me to the floor. "Ha, Shawna, you, like, totally *freaked out*! Why'd you scream? Did I scare you? DAMN, that was a blast!"

LeeLee meets my burning eyes behind Schmule's head. She forces a smile. Dizzy and embarrassed, I manage a nod back, because I know why she's smiling.

82

A while later in the car, Schmule says, "Maybe I don't want to."

"Well, make up your mind." Sorry, but I'm losing patience. This is nerve-racking enough without all his hemming and hawing.

"Maybe I'm mad at her. Because she lied, okay? She says it's wrong to lie and then she does it herself. Like, my whole *life*!"

I just asked him how Fran told him the truth about our mom. He said she'd blurted it out and then abruptly left the house, leaving Arye to deal with Schmule's reaction. Schmule hit her when she came back. Then he cried so hard he threw up.

"Well," I say gently, ashamed of my snarkiness. "You have to decide, Schmoo."

He bites his lip. "I know."

I touch his knee. His clammy hand covers mine.

83

The next week, we do it.

"You remember what I told you."

Schmule nods.

"Say it," I command.

"I won't stay," he chants. "Even if she says no, I'll still come back out."

"And?"

"And I won't tell her anything that's going on in the house. Nothing personal, I mean. Can I tell her I have a Wii?"

"Yeah. But nothing about me and absolutely nothing about Dad. Got it?" He nods, making a face. "Okay, now tell me *why* you have to come back out."

"Because your dad might call the cops and Mom'll be arrested for kidnapping. You're not making that up, are you?" he adds suspiciously.

"Nope." Well, at least contempt of court.

"Oh, yeah," he goes on. "And your dad will, like, ser-i-ous-ly kill you." *Your* dad, Schmule says. Never "my dad," or simply "Dad."

"Right. So promise me."

"I already promised you a bajillion times! I won't say anything personal and I'll be out in, like, fifteen minutes. I'll even climb out a window if she locks me in." He seems intrigued at that idea.

"She won't." Though I'm not so sure.

Schmule glows with heart-wrenching happiness. "I'll come back, Shawna. I swear."

Now for the clincher. "So what're you going to do for *me?*"

"Be good. Don't act crazy in school. Go to the stupid shrink. And," he finishes reluctantly, "be part of the family. Be nice, even to, yuck, Aunt Colleen."

I pop the button to unlock his door. "Okay, go. See you in fifteen minutes. I'll park down the street and meet you over there."

He needs no encouragement. He jumps out of the car, races up to the porch, and lets himself into the house with the key he'd wisely never returned.

The illuminated numbers on my dash read 8:25 p.m.

I know they're not expecting him. I know they'll wonder how he got here. Sure enough, the front door flies open and Fran dashes out to the porch, startled, searching. Not wanting to answer any questions, or even face Fran after what we just put her through, I hit the accelerator and park halfway down the street. Hopefully she can't tell my car from the others parked at the curb.

Then I stare at the clock and wait.

84

8:28: *Well, Shawna. I hope you're happy. You just made everything worse.*

How could I make it worse?

8:30: *He won't come back. Why didn't you go in with him?*

I didn't want to go with him. I'm not part of that family.

8:33: *She'll keep him forever.*

He promised he'd come back.

8:37: *Promises mean nothing. He hates you. He hates Dad.*

Shut up, Mom. Or me. Whoever you are.

Plus you just blackmailed the poor kid. Aren't you the least bit ashamed?

La, la, I'm not *lis*-tening anymore . . .

8:39: *Do the right thing, do the right thing. Ha, ha, ha, you played right into your father's hands. You're Daddy's little girl, Daddy's STUPID little—!*

"SHUT UP!" I bash both hands on the wheel.

8:40.

85

8:42 . . . 8:43 . . .

And then my car door swings open and Schmule leaps back in.

"You're three minutes late!" Cold perspiration drips freely down my back.

"Sorry," he whispers, fastening his seat belt.

Breathe, Shawna, breathe. "Are you okay?"

He nods. "Mom wants to talk to you. She wants to ask you why."

"Why what?"

"Why you brought me here." He turns his face away. His breath fogs the window.

I glance fearfully into my mirror. No one in sight.

I can't believe Fran let him go. I can't believe she didn't barricade him in.

"Well?" he demands, glancing back at me.

It would be so easy to get out of the car, walk up those steps, and knock on the door.

But then what?

I peel away from the curb. "Maybe next time."

Schmule's face lights up like nothing I've ever seen. "There's gonna be a next time?"

"I hope so."

As long as Dad doesn't find out.

 **86**

The next two weeks in a row we do the same thing. Schmule suffers through his head-shrinking; then, instead of stopping by the mall—the excuse I give Dad so he won't wonder why we're late—I drop him off at Fran's, park down the street, and wait.

Thirty minutes the first week. An hour the second. No more than an hour, because the mall closes at nine.

I don't speak to Fran. I'm afraid she still hates me.

I'm more afraid that she doesn't. I deserve her hatred after everything that's happened.

After the second visit, Arye IM's me: **Thanks.**

Me, stupidly: **You're welcome.**

Arye: **Why don't you come in next time?**

Me: **It's better if I don't.**

Arye: **Can we TALK at least?**

Me: **Talk about what?**

Arye: **Stuff.**

Me, embarrassed: **You don't have to be nice to me.**

Arye: **LOL. Me, nice?**

I type nothing, unable to think of a reply.

Him: **Well, thanks. It means a lot.**

Me: **I know.**

87

The following week, Arye's waiting on the sidewalk. Schmule high-fives him, rockets inside, and Arye jumps into the front seat before I can zoom off.

"What're you doing?" I yelp.

"Let's go get some coffee."

"I don't drink coffee."

"Tea, then. What*ever*."

Bizarre ideas batter my brain: Arye sticks a gun to my head and forces me to drive a hundred miles. This gives Fran and Schmule a significant head start to the Canadian border. Dad, of course, kills me, dismembers me, and dumps me in a national forest. I make CNN. All of Wade Prep turns out for a candlelight vigil. Cadaver dogs discover my remains. Susan weeps over my casket: *how could you die without forgiving me?*

"You fly, I'll buy," Arye says, with no clear intention of getting out.

Too rattled to argue, I let him direct me to a coffee shop on Coventry. We sit together at a small table like boyfriend and girlfriend, only in abject silence. I watch him covertly. Arye's still stocky, though not fat, and shorter than me, but he lost the lame ponytail. Dark hair, as curly as Schmule's shorn locks, frames his sober face. I can't see his eyes through the glare on his glasses.

"So why *are* you doing this?" he asks me at last.

"Because I think it sucks what everyone's doing to him?"

Arye stirs his coffee before he speaks. "That first time Schmule ran into the house? I thought my mom was having a heart attack. She didn't want him to go. She totally spazzed out when he said he had to leave."

"Why'd she let him?" *I* wouldn't have.

"He said he promised you."

"Well. He did."

Arye shakes his head. "I can't figure you out."

"I can't figure me out, either." I sip my usual chai latte. I don't want to talk about me. "So, what's been going on?"

"Well . . . Mom hasn't found another job yet. Aunt Rina's letting us live here rent-free, but she can't afford that forever. I told Mom she can cash in my college fund if she wants to pay for a better lawyer. But she says enough's enough."

"Cash in your college fund?" I repeat in horror.

"You'd do the same thing if it'd bring back your brother, right?"

Yes. In a blink of an eye.

Arye looks straight at me. "So what're *you* risking by pulling this off every week?"

"My head." I giggle weakly. "If my dad finds out, you'll see me on *Forensic Files.*"

"Well, he won't find out from me." Inexplicably, he rests a finger on my wrist. I stare at it, mesmerized. "Not to make you feel worse, but . . . my mom's not the same. She hardly gets dressed. She won't take phone calls. Aunt Rina almost put her in the hospital a while back. But now . . ." He flushes. "Okay, this sounds dramatic. But now it's like she has something to look forward to, you know? Like, every Tuesday she comes back to life."

"I wasn't even thinking about you guys when I decided to do this," I confess. "I just want him to be happy. I'm only doing it for him."

Arye links his fingers through mine. "Yeah, I know. It's okay."

A peculiar energy passes between us. I study his hand. Square, like his mom's, with bitten-down nails and wisps of fine black hair—

I plunge ruthlessly back to reality. "What time is it?"

"We still have fifteen minutes."

"No. Let's go back."

He releases my hand and grabs lids for our cups, and we don't speak a word on the way back to his house. Schmule wanders out as soon as we pull up—proof once again that Fran didn't whisk him to the airport and abandon me to the wrath of the Gallagher wolf-clan.

"Maybe we can do this again?" Arye nudges me hopefully.

Something new prickles inside me. Something kind of nice. "Okay."

"And . . ." He hesitates. "I know it's a lot to ask. But do you think you could bring him for Shabbat one Friday? My mom would love it. I think he misses that stuff."

Maybe, but what excuse could I give Dad? This mall story won't hold up forever.

"You can come, too." With that, he touches my face. I'm utterly immobilized. "Seriously. My mom wants to talk to you."

"I know."

Arye waits. There seems to be no way out of it.

"Um, this Friday might work," I mumble, mind racing.

"Cool."

Sliding out of the car, he exchanges a friendly punch with Schmule before Schmule jumps in. On the way home I only half listen to his chatter, because I'm thinking, insanely, about that burst of electricity. That bizarre, totally out-of-the-freaking-blue attraction to: Arye Goodman? How is this possible? God must be laughing his ass off.

Then I notice the heart-shaped picture frame in Schmule's lap. The one Fran clutched to her chest when I found her crying in her room. "Did Fran give you that?"

"Yeah." Schmule extends it face out. Mom and Fran smile at me, their fingers intertwined, the single red rose brilliant against Mom's white gown.

"I like it," I croak.

He touches Fran's face. "Yeah. Me too."

88

LeeLee gawks at me after school on Friday. "You want me to lie for you so you can get Schmule over to Fran's?"

"Not lie. Just cover." I can't believe I'm doing this, let alone come up with another way.

LeeLee, true blue, agrees. "Say you're bringing him over to my house to play with the kids. Just keep your cell on you in case your dad calls me or something."

"Omigod. I totally love you."

"Sh-h!" LeeLee gleams wickedly. "We got enough rumors flying around."

"Shut up," I say around my smile.

I tell Dad the "plan" for tonight. He repeats, "Play *where?*" as if I just suggested Schmule take a leisurely swim in a crocodile-infested swamp. "Mm. I don't know."

"Come on, Dad. Schmu—Sam doesn't have that many friends of his own yet. It'll be fun for him. Maybe he'll pick up some Spanish." Not that this is much of a selling point with Dad.

"Well, I'm taking Julie out for her birthday tonight, so . . ." I wait. "Don't be too late, okay?"

"We won't. Tell Julie happy birthday." I kiss his cheek, and hug him an extra second. "Thank you, Daddy."

89

Schmule skips up Fran's steps ahead of me. "We're he-e-ere!" he shouts.

I lag back, not entirely convinced Fran won't disembowel me on sight. But she rushes to the living room, smiles when she sees us, and hooks an arm around Schmule's neck. "Hey, dude." She kisses his head with a loud smack. Her brown eyes meet mine. "Welcome, Shawna. Shabbat shalom."

"Shabbat shalom," I repeat, and accept a glass of wine as Schmule torpedoes to his room. "Um, where's Arye hiding?"

"He's here. But first I'd like to talk to you for a minute."

Crap, I think as she guides me to the sofa and sits beside me. Here goes.

"Thank you," she says.

I twirl the glass of purple liquid. "You don't have to thank me. Really."

"I think I do. I can't even guess how you've been getting away with this, and, well, I appreciate it. More than you can imagine." Fran's own glass trembles in her hands. "You can trust me, Shawna. Do you understand? I won't use this against you. Ever," she adds firmly.

I believe her. Suddenly, all my fears about her smuggling Schmule out of the country disappear just like that. She wouldn't do that to me. She'd never do it to Schmule.

"I'm sorry," I say. The same words I've repeated so many times over the past few weeks. "I'm sorry this whole thing happened."

"Me too. But . . ." She zones out. I wonder if she's thinking about my mom. Cursing Penny Sorenson for being stupid and selfish. Maybe cursing herself for playing along from the start. For living the past ten years of her life knowing that something, like this, could happen at any time.

Feeling jumpy, I finger my cell phone. I haven't planned any defense should Dad track me down, but that's not very likely. I bet he's whistling once again as he rolls back the bedsheets, elated at the chance to be alone with the birthday girl.

Ha, poor Julie. How long can Dad stay on his best behavior? How long till—?

Fran interrupts my thoughts. "I found a job. It's only for the summer, but it's better than nothing. I'll be temping for a receptionist at a law firm downtown. I'm hoping they'll like me and maybe hire me on full time."

"You're not going to teach?" As if any school would hire her after all the publicity.

"No. But I am going back to law school if I can get a loan, or a grant."

"Law school?"

"Well, I was never crazy about teaching. And I *was* in law school, back when I met your mom, but—" She stops.

"You dropped out? Why?"

Fran sighs. "I don't want to say anything that'll embarrass you, Shawna."

"Well. You guys already embarrassed me for years," I quip.

Her surprised smile fades almost immediately. "I know. We expected that. We talked about it a lot. That, and the way Penny left you."

I don't want to talk about this. "So why'd you drop out of law school?"

She waits a beat. Then, reluctantly, she says, "I was living here with Aunt Rina when your mom left your dad. She stayed here with us a few weeks, then she found out she was pregnant. She told me she hadn't, uh, been sleeping with your dad. But I thought it might be his. She wouldn't tell me one way or another. Just that she wanted an abortion."

"*What?*" My officially Catholic mom wanted an abortion?

"I know. That was my reaction, too. I was teaching at the time, and going to school at night. But I told her if she'd change her mind, if she had the baby, I'd quit working, quit school, and be the stay-at-home mom."

I'm still stuck on the abortion business. "An abortion. God! *Why?*"

"I guess she cared so much about her work, her goals, her life in the art world . . ." Fran chokes off, twisting a corner of her drab green shirt into a spiral. "A baby didn't figure into it. It doesn't make her a bad person, Shawna."

I fall back into the cushions. Schmule almost never existed. He came *that close.*

Maybe Fran didn't give birth to him. But she's the only reason he's here.

"So we moved to New York," Fran finishes.

"And Mom had Schmule and gave him your last name." It's true—Mom literally gave my baby brother away. "You pretended he was yours." What did Mom think would happen when Schmule finally saw her name on his birth certificate?

"He *is* mine. I loved him before he was born."

I stare at her round face, scrubbed shiny, free of makeup. Her gray hair, jammed in a big plastic clip. Her dowdy, functional clothes. So different from Mom with her chic outfits, her perfectly coiffed hair, her allure. How, how did these two ever hook up? Mom, crazy and artistic and self-centered as hell. Fran, so motherly, so grounded in reality. Maybe they saw, and envied, something inside of each other. Something neither of them could hope to be.

Opposites attract, Uncle Dieter told me at the funeral. First Dad. Then Fran. As if that's all Mom ever searched for. Somebody different from herself.

"She should've told us," I whisper. "How could she keep him a secret?"

Fran starts with the shirt-twisting thing again and I sense the words straining at her lips. Words she's afraid to say out loud.

"She hated him," I answer myself.

Fran shakes her head unconvincingly. "No, she didn't."

"Yes, she did. She wanted to punish him, right? He always wanted a son." I shrug helplessly and stare down at my hands. "What better revenge?"

Fran touches my knee. "Revenge for what? She was more scared of him, I think." When I shake my head hard, Fran leans closer, her voice tinged with suspicion. "Sweetie. How much do you know?"

"Enough," I say softly.

Arye speaks up from the archway, making us both jump. "Hey, Shawna."

Zapped back to Earth, Fran heaves herself to her feet. The corner of her blouse unravels into a rumpled tail. "There you are." With a glance out the window at the descending dusk, she claps a hand over her mouth. "Uh-oh, the candles. Hurry, hurry!"

"Wait!" My butt feels rooted to the sofa. "I have something to say." I shrivel under their curious stares, but I can't hold back. "What I said that day, when I was talking to Arye? When you walked in on us?" I squeeze out the words I wish I'd said months ago. "If I told you I never meant to say it, I'd be lying. Because I did mean it at the time. I just didn't mean for you to hear it."

Fran doesn't move. "And now?"

"It was the worst thing I ever said." I add miserably, to Arye, "Especially to you. Because it wasn't just my mom I was talking about."

My voice breaks. Fran's beside me in three quick strides, to draw me into a hug. "I know, sweetie. I know."

Did Mom ever hold me like this? I can't remember a single time.

"Candles, Mom," Arye prompts, with a peculiar smile for me. "Two minutes till sundown."

But Fran refuses to let go.

 90

We decide God will forgive Fran for lighting the candles after sundown. When she touches the match to the wicks, I notice the extra candle. Arye meets my questioning glance, and nods. That's how I know: this new candle is mine.

After dinner, Fran and I play Scrabble under a kerosene lamp while Arye and Schmule play Battleship on the floor. Fran's ahead by four points when I slyly turn the vertical "fox" into a horizontal "xero." The *e* lands on a triple word space.

"Don't you mean *z-e-r-o?*" Fran asks suspiciously.

"No. It's a medical prefix. It means 'dry.'" I refrain from gloating.

Schmule, sprawled at my feet, does that same twitchy thing with his eyebrow that Dad likes to do. "Better challenge her, Mom!"

My cell phone tinkles as Fran whips out the Scrabble dictionary. Okay, I'm not Jewish, and not subject to the same rules against using electricity on Shabbat. But it *is* their home.

I duck into the kitchen, flip open my phone, and hear LeeLee shrill, "Where are you?"

My heart plummets. "Still at Fran's. Why?"

"Well, get the hell out of there and get home!"

"Why? Did Dad call?"

"Worse. He came over."

I stifle my scream. "Why-y?"

"I don't know! He didn't call or anything, he just showed up and started yelling. And when I couldn't get you or Schmule to come out, he *knew*, Shawna. I'm sorry. I tried!"

"What?" Schmule asks hollowly from the kitchen door. I guess he sensed my panic.

I throw my phone into my purse. "We have to leave."

"I don't want to."

"Tough! Get your stuff. Dad's onto us."

His face blanks out. "Don't tell Mom."

"But—" Shouldn't I warn her? No, she'll freak. "Okay. Let's just go."

Shakily, I stammer to Fran that it's later than I thought, and we have to leave, like, *now*. She hugs Schmule and me together, and it takes a few seconds to disengage Schmule's arms.

"Be a good boy," she whispers to him.

"I will," he answers automatically.

Arye walks us out to the car and says through my window, "Thanks for coming" with his face so close to mine, I wonder . . . does he want to kiss me?

Like *that's* something I should be thinking about now!

"I'll e-mail you," I promise, rolling up the window.

"What're we gonna do?" Schmule asks through white lips.

"We're gonna lie, that's what we're gonna do."

"Lie?"

"Yes, lie. Dad knows we weren't at LeeLee's. We have to come up with something else." Something believable, dammit. ". . . Okay. I got it. We went to Mom's grave."

"Her *grave*?"

"Yes. And we said we'd be at LeeLee's because we knew he wouldn't approve."

"Why wouldn't he approve?" Schmule asks sensibly.

"Schmule, in case you haven't figured this out, Mom's not exactly Dad's favorite person in the world."

He scrunches his forehead. "Is this the best you can come up with?"

"Yeah, under the circumstances!"

All the house lights are on. Julie's car is in the drive. We wait a few minutes, prolonging the inevitable. Then I reach over to squeeze my brother's damp fingers.

"It'll be okay," I promise. But he doesn't squeeze my hand back. "Come on."

91

Dad's icy tone hits us like an arctic blast before we're fully into the kitchen. "Where the *hell* have you been?"

I feign surprise. "What's wrong?" Then casually, to Julie, "Oh, hi. Happy birthday."

"Thanks." Across from Dad, Julie taps a spoon around in her glass of iced tea. I note her remote tone, her oddly forced smile.

"I asked you a question," Dad growls at me.

Schmule shrinks. My arms creep around his small shoulders. "We were at LeeLee's, remember?"

"Try again. I went over there myself and you most certainly were *not* there."

Stifling my indignation, I calmly ask, "Why were you checking up on me?"

"I'm the one asking the questions here, Shawna. Where— were—you? I'm giving you ten seconds to answer."

Evil Shawna, who's been flying under the radar, pops out of nowhere. Yes, I'm happy to see her. "Then what, Dad? What're you gonna do? Kill me?"

Dad's face turns purple with rage and disbelief. He starts to rise, but Julie holds up a hand. "Jack, just let them tell the story."

Dad sinks back. Folds his arms. Waits.

I look him in the eye. "We went to visit Mom's grave."

"Her grave?" No answer required, so I wisely keep quiet. Dad turns his fiery glare to Schmule instead. "Sam? Is that true?"

Schmule, bones rigid under my arm, doesn't bat an eye. "Yes, sir."

"You went to your mother's grave."

"Yes, sir. We knew you wouldn't approve," he recites.

"You were there all evening?"

"Yes, sir."

"In the dark?"

". . . Yes, sir."

Exasperated, I break in. "He answered you already. I'm sorry, okay? But we wanted to see her grave and we knew you'd go postal. We're back now. Can we ple-ease be excused?"

Instead, Dad stands—I duck as he passes me—and sails out of the kitchen. Almost immediately, he returns. An indistinguishable blur flies through the air as he slams something on the corner of the kitchen table. Glass explodes. I slap a hand over my mouth. Schmule whimpers.

The picture of Mom and Fran, their wedding picture, lies on the floor in a twist of metal and shattered glass.

"Jack!" Julie cries, springing up.

Dad, oddly composed considering his performance, asks Schmule, "Would you like to explain this?" Schmule says nothing. "Where did you get that picture?"

"Leave him alone," I interrupt. "It's just a picture of Mom and—"

"I'm not blind. I know who's in the picture. I'm asking your brother where he got it, and *when* he got it."

When he got it? My heart thwacks. "He probably brought it with the rest of his stuff."

"Stop it, Shawna. You're only making it worse. I know he didn't bring it when he came here, because I went through all his things."

Why am I not surprised?

"You went through my stuff?" Schmule asks faintly. "You mean you looked at everything, like, to see what I had?"

"Exactly."

"That sucks!" Schmule shouts. "You had no right."

"I had every right, young man. This is my house. You did not have that picture when you got here, and frankly, I'm outraged that you'd bring such a thing into this house." Dad aims a halfhearted kick at the rubble on the tiles. I see a flash of Mom and Fran, faces ignited with happiness. "It's disgusting and offensive, and I can't believe you'd be so disrespectful."

Schmule smacks a fist into his palm. "I am not disrespectful. You're disrespectful! You went through my stuff," he repeats, as if unable to believe it. "Why were you even in my room? Even my mom never pokes around in my stuff. My real mom!" he shouts. "My real, *real* mom."

I watch Dad's hand move again, in slow motion this time, and land flat on the side of Schmule's head. Schmule stumbles into me and I have to catch him under the arms to keep him from falling. Julie stares, undoubtedly believing she's trapped in a sideshow.

Schmule shoves me roughly. *"Leave me alone!"* he screams, and bolts from the room.

"How could you hit him?" I shriek at Dad.

Dad wags a finger under my nose. "Don't you raise your voice to me. I know where Sam got that picture and I know where you two went tonight. Did you think I'd never figure it out? Did either of you think I could be that *stupid?*"

"No, Dad! I'm the stupid one, remember?"

"Well," he shoots back. "This just proves my point."

I face Dad. But it's Julie I'm speaking to. "Remember this, okay? This is who you're marrying. He hits people. He hits them, and he hurts them."

"I do no such thing!" Enraged, Dad advances. I pray he'll hit me, too, so I can prove *my* point. His hand, at the last second, flops to his side. "I never touched you, Shawna. I never hurt you in your life."

"No, Dad. You only hurt Mom."

92

He hurt me, Shawna. You saw him do it.

Yes, Mom.

Now you know why I couldn't stay.

You could've taken me with you. Why would you leave me behind?

I wanted to take you! He wouldn't let me. He said he'd drag me through court. He'd expose Fran and me. He'd never let me see you again.

You didn't want me anyway. You didn't even want Schmule. You never would've had him if Fran hadn't talked you into it.

I didn't know Schmule then. Schmule was the unknown. You, I always loved.

But you left me with him! How did you know he wouldn't hurt me?

Because he loves you.

He doesn't love me. He owns me. The same way he owns Schmule.

He loves you, Shawna. He loves you more than I could ever love you myself.

How do I know you're telling me the truth?

The answer never comes.

93

Unsurprisingly, my laptop is already gone by the time I get upstairs. So is my old PC. I dial Fran's number immediately from my cell. It'll show up if Dad checks, but hey, I'm already screwed. By tomorrow I probably won't have phone access, either.

Arye answers instantly. "LeeLee called and told me what happened. Is everything okay?"

"No." I burst into sobs. "Everything's not okay. It was just, well, just *horrible*!"

"Shit. I'm so sorry."

"Dad took my computers. I can't even e-mail you. So if I want to call you I'll have to sneak around, maybe use a pay phone, and—"

"Can we meet somewhere?" He whispers this, as if he's afraid Dad has magical powers and might overhear. That wouldn't surprise me.

"I don't know. Maybe when things settle down. Or . . . maybe never," I add hopelessly.

"Don't say that. Just call me when you can."

"Okay. I promise."

Promises mean nothing, Mom once said.

I tiptoe to Schmule's room. Door shut, room silent beyond. I hear Dad and Julie discussing us downstairs. What's next on the agenda? A restraining order for Fran? Boot camp for me? Military school for Schmule? God, they'd eat him alive.

I push open the door. Curled up in bed, my brother faces the wall, bare feet sticking out as usual from under the covers. "Are you awake?" I sit on the edge of his mattress and rub his back. "I'm sorry, Schmoo."

He twitches under my hand. "Me too."

"Why are *you* sorry?"

"For not hiding that picture. I stuck it in with my underwear. I didn't *think* he'd look there," Schmule adds resentfully.

"That's my fault. I should've warned you better." Why didn't I? I should have known Dad would go ballistic if he saw that picture. How could I let Schmule bring it into the house?

Hindsight, blah, blah. Because it never occurred to me Dad would root through Schmule's belongings in search of contraband. Now I wonder, does he not stop with my mail? Does he paw through my room, too?

Schmule draws an imaginary picture on the wall with a fingertip. "Who cares? I'm glad I made him mad. Maybe he'll send me away."

"Back to Fran, you mean?"

"No, to fucking South Africa."

A chill sinks over me, a terrible premonition. "Dad'll never send you back."

"Huh." His finger moves faster. First up and down, up and down, then around in a circle, then up and down two more times. In the dim light from the hall I can see what he's writing: the word "Mom," over and over on the wall.

M-O-M . . . M-O-M . . . M-O-M.

94

In the morning, Schmule executes a perfect turnaround. He apologizes to Dad for sneaking over to Fran's. I huddle on the stairs, listening in astonishment, trying to hear over Klara bashing dishes around in the kitchen.

"So don't be mad at Shawna. Okay, Dad?"

Ah, "Dad." The magic word.

"I made her do it. It was my idea."

An outright lie, to Dad's face, no less.

"I just wanted to see my mom. I miss her, ya know?"

Dad finally speaks, but not unpleasantly, "Sam, please. You know she is not your mom."

No argument. Not a word of protest. ". . . I know."

"And your sister should have known better than to pull such a stunt."

Schmule lies again without hesitation. "I made her."

"No, you didn't 'make' her. Shawna's seventeen. I expect better behavior out of her. And from you, too," Dad adds, softening more.

"Okay," Schmule mumbles. "But don't be mad at Shawna."

Dad refuses to commit himself. "If you're ready for school, I'll drive you today. Better gather up your books."

Strained pause. "Um, why can't Shawna take me?"

"Not today, Sam."

Great. Dad'll never trust me again.

They catch me lurking, but neither of them says good-bye; Dad breezes past and Schmule trails behind him, staring down at his shoes. As soon as they're gone I check my phone, and oh, holy hell, I knew it—no freaking service!

Next he'll probably steal my car keys. Obviously I won't be chauffeuring Schmule around any time soon.

I hear the clatter of broken glass in the kitchen. It's Klara, emptying a dustpan over the wastebasket. "What'd you do with the picture?"

Klara smacks a hand to her throat. "*Mein Gott!* Do not jump out at me like that!"

"The picture, Klara!"

"No picture. Just a broken frame."

"No picture of my mom?"

She shakes her curly white head firmly, and then squawks a warning about broken glass as I fish through the trash myself. All I come up with is a handful of coffee grounds. Dad, evidently, already disposed of the wedding picture.

"Dammit!" I scream.

Ignoring Klara's openmouthed stare, I slam out and drive to school in a fury. I know why Dad's so offended by that picture: Mom and Fran, together, on the happiest day of their lives? An image, I'm sure, Dad can happily live without.

But it wasn't his to destroy. Now Schmule has nothing.

At school, LeeLee bounces frantically by my locker. "Omigod, what happened? I tried calling you, but something's wrong with your phone!"

"We got busted, of course. And Dad canceled my phone."

"Oh, ma-an. How bad was it?"

"Bad, bad, bad. He wouldn't even talk to me this morning."

"Sorry," she says sadly. "I couldn't think fast enough."

"Well, I figured this would happen sooner or—"

"Oops!" Devon knocks me into LeeLee as he saunters by. "Sorry, girls. I mean, guys."

Before LeeLee can interfere, I shout, "Keep your paws to yourself!"

Unfortunately, he halts. I'd sort of hoped he'd move on. "So I see you two lovebirds are back together?" He kisses the air.

LeeLee advances with, "Ya know, Connolly—"

But I step between them. "You'd like me to be a lesbian, wouldn't you, Devon?" I stare ferociously into those amazing green eyes, wondering how I could've fallen for this snake. No, he's lower than a snake. A snake egg maybe, squashed into slime by a dirty boot. "At least that would explain why I find you so, so *putrid*."

Devon's face contorts. "You freaks make me sick. Hey, next time you hook up, why don't you take some pics? Big market on the Web for that kind of stuff."

"Yeah," LeeLee agrees. "And how much of Mommy's allowance do *you* spend on it, pig?"

Devon half raises a fist. I catch his wrist without thinking and lean in close, never mind that I'm practically inhaling my own heart. "Right. You think you're such a hotshot, pushing girls around?" My voice rises and rises till people in the hall slow and stare. For once I'm glad for the audience. I fling down his arm. "You stay the hell out of my face or I'll have you arrested for harassment. And then I'll *hire* somebody to kick your balls in."

Hatred steams from Devon's green irises, but it's hatred coupled with something else. Acknowledgment, maybe? Now he knows I'm for real, that I mean every word.

With a simple "Fuck you two," he shoves off down the hall.

LeeLee dissolves into giggles. "Wow. Speaking of balls, I'm impressed!"

"Thanks," I say modestly, wishing I'd done this months ago.

Wishing I hadn't given him so much power over me.

I only wish I'd moved that fast when Dad took aim at Schmule.

95

"Your brother is upstairs," Klara informs me when I don't see Schmule around. "He says he is working on a report and does not wish to be disturbed."

Armed with cookies and a glass of chocolate milk, I knock on his door with my toe. No answer, so I singsong, "I brought you a snaack!"

Schmule cracks the door and views me guardedly. Then he snatches the treats and plops back down at his desk. Nibbling one-handed, he types with the other, five fingers flying with mind-boggling speed.

"What's your report about?" I note with surprise that, since last night, he's managed to rearrange his entire room; now his furniture and belongings mirror the layout of the room he shared with Arye.

"The Stockholm syndrome." He withers me with disdain when I wait for further explanation. "You never heard of that?"

"Well, are you going to tell me? Or revel in my ignorance?"

"It's when prisoners start to identify with their captors. You've heard of that girl Patty Hearst, right?" I nod vaguely, pretending to be well informed. "Well, she's a perfect example."

Sharing no more, he just types and munches. I leave with a sigh and throw myself down on my bed. At least Dad didn't take my extension phone away.

I call LeeLee and ask, "Who's Patty Hearst?"

"Oh, you know. That chick who was kidnapped, like, fifty years ago. Why?"

"Schmule's doing a report on the Stockholm syndrome. I just wondered what it was about. I'm too embarrassed to ask him."

"Oh, well, she was like this really rich girl—her dad owned a newspaper or something—and she got kidnapped by these radicals who wanted to overthrow the government. They locked her in a closet, and, like, tortured and raped her. Next thing you know she's holding up banks with machine guns, acting just like them."

"If she had a machine gun, why didn't she escape?"

"That's the Stockholm syndrome," she replies with maddening simplicity. "After being tortured and brainwashed for months or whatever, it was like she was grateful or something when they finally let her out. She *identified* with them. She did whatever they told her to do." LeeLee pauses. "Wait. He's doing a report on this? In fourth grade?"

"That's what he said." I add with a strained laugh, "At least he hasn't called anyone a Nazi lately. Gotta run," I add quickly as I hear Dad's SUV pull up. "The warden's home early."

Dad's flipping through the mail as I descend the stairs. One of these days I'll learn to get to the mailbox before him. Lingering over one envelope, he jerks when I say boldly, "If it's for me, I'm right here. You don't have to open it."

Ignoring me, he throws the mail onto the bar, where I watch him slap together his usual after-work martini. "I need my computer back. And my phone."

"You can have them back when you start acting like a responsible adult."

Well, at least he's speaking to me now. But I have to remind myself that this is not Devon. Tread carefully, Shawna. He's not a snake—he's a raptor. "What do you want me to do?"

"You can start by not lying to me. And by respecting my wishes."

"I already apologized for lying." At least I think I did. I don't quite remember. Or, truthfully, care.

Again, he ignores me. He stirs his drink so hard, the olive pops out of the glass. I shuffle through the envelopes, buying time—nothing for me—and add it to Dad's mishmash of assorted junk mail.

That's when I spy the return address on a big brown envelope. The brochure Julie told me about, the one from MassArt. Yes, it's been opened. "I guess you're mad about this?"

"I wouldn't say mad. Disappointed, maybe."

"I didn't ask for this. It was my art teacher's idea."

"Shawna." Dad picks up the stray olive and pitches it aside. Is it my imagination, or are his hands unsteady? "Why didn't you tell me you don't want to go to medical school?"

"I do want to go! I never said I didn't."

He doesn't believe me.

"I just wonder," I add truthfully, "if I'm cut out for it. I mean, what if I'm not?"

"Don't be—" Dad catches himself, and changes this to, "You know you can't earn a decent living as an artist."

"Mom did." After last night I should know better than to bring up her name. But Dad doesn't react. I finish feebly, "I'm just weighing my options."

"All right. Well." Dad clears his throat, and continues cordially,

"Don't get defensive, because I'm really very interested. I'd like to know what you think these options are."

He can't even be nice when he's trying to be nice.

Thoughtfully, he brushes my hair off my shoulder. Then he turns my face with his hand so I'm forced to look at him. "There *are* no other options. We've planned this your whole life. You've been working your tail off to get those grades. And I don't say this very often, but . . . well, I'm proud of you, Shawna. Very proud."

Oh. My. God. Where did this come from?

Flabbergasted, all I can manage is, "Thanks."

"You're welcome," he says formally.

An awkward silence passes, until I take a deep breath. "Dad, I need my computer for school. I need my phone, too. What if I get carjacked? What if I break down on the highway?"

Dad lifts his glass and studies it closely. "Before yesterday, you've never given me a reason not to trust you. I'm disappointed in you. Disappointed in Sam, too. But Sam's a child. It's up to you to protect him."

Protect him from Fran, he means. Or people like her.

"But I talked to Julie today. She convinced me you don't deserve to be grounded. So you can have your computer back. I'll turn your phone on as well. But—"

I brace myself, knowing what's next.

"—you are not to see, or talk to, anyone in that family. Ever. Again. Do I make myself clear?" I nod, but it's not enough. "Not Francine. Not her son. Nobody in that house. If I need to go to court to get a restraining order against them, then let me know now. The courts are on *my* side. I can't make this any clearer."

"You don't have to do that," I say wearily, reluctantly. "I'll stay away."

"From *all* of them, Shawna."

I think of Fran. And then I think about Arye.

"This goes for both of you," he stresses. "You *and* Sam."

"I heard you, okay?"

A brief flash of annoyance—and then, amazingly, he smiles that old "Dad" smile I miss so much. "You're a good girl. I know you'll do the right thing."

# 96

So, days pass, and we all play normal. Julie does everything but move in with us. Either she doesn't believe what I told her that night, or she doesn't understand it. Or maybe she thinks it'll never happen to her.

I hope she's right.

I'm more worried about Schmule. Lately he's been on his best behavior. It's spooky the way he agrees to go to Mass after Dad essentially begs him, promising he won't have to participate. Schmule kicks the kneeler throughout the whole service, ignoring Aunt Colleen's impatient huffs. Afterward, when Father Bernacki extends his hand with a jovial "I remember you, young man!" he stares in horror at the old priest's vestments and then slinks behind Uncle Dieter as if using him for a shield.

Spooky, too, the way he'll sit with Charles, whispering words into those small silky ears. Words he won't share with me, or with anyone else.

The spookiest thing of all is the way he's finally stopped talking about Fran and Arye.

I still need to let Arye know we can't see them anymore, that I promised Dad I'd stay far, far away. And I've been living in dread that Arye will foolishly call me.

My cell phone's out, because yes, it'll be on the bill. I don't dare e-mail him; knowing Dad, he probably installed some insidious high-powered spyware the second my laptop was out of my hands.

So I think about asking LeeLee to make the call, and realize: what I really want is to hear Arye's voice myself.

Late at night, with Charles lumped between my ankles, I dial Arye's number from my extension. Thankfully Arye, not Fran, answers with a sleepy mumble.

"Don't call me," I whisper.

Instantly awake, he admits, "I almost did. Are you guys okay?"

"Yes. But I can't e-mail you anymore. And you can't call me, no matter what." I tell him about Dad's restraining order threat. "Your mom'll get in trouble. This so isn't worth it."

I don't say what I've been thinking lately—that when I graduate and go off to Kenyon, things might be different. I don't say it because I know there's no guarantee that, even then, I'll be able to defy Dad. He could cut off my allowance, my living expenses. If he cuts off my tuition I'll be completely screwed.

I hear his breath in my ear. "It's okay, Shawna."

"No. It's not."

But it's the way it has to be.

97

It's not like I'm sneaking around *looking* for weirdness. But I stop, silent, at the kitchen door when I notice Schmule at the sink—first studying the label of his antidepressants, then staring down at his other hand. He glances from one to the other in a funny, aching way. The way Charles stares at a bird he knows he can never catch.

"What are you doing?" I ask loudly.

With a yelp, Schmule jumps. A shower of pellets rain into the basin as the pill bottle leaps out of his splayed fingers. "Look what you made me *do*!"

"Get them out, quick!"

"I can't. They're *wet*."

I peer into the sink in time to see the foamy glob of pills dissolve into the drain. Great.

"Don't tell Dad," he begs, scooping the bottle out of the sink.

I catch his wrist as he aims for the wastebasket. "I have to tell him. Now he'll have to call for a refill, and explain." Schmule yanks his arm away as I add, "What were you doing with them, anyway?"

He sends me a killer glare. "What do you think I was doing?"

"That's not an answer!" I yell as he charges out of the room.

Dad's not happy about this. "From now on," he says later, "I want someone to *hand* you your pills."

"It was an accident," Schmule insists. He wisely avoids blaming it on me. "Like you never dropped anything in your life?"

I hold my breath, but Dad doesn't fly into him. "It's a new rule, Sam. If I'm not here, either Klara or Shawna will give them to you. Understand?"

Schmule jiggles a foot. "Yeah. Whatever."

Even that snarky "whatever" doesn't set my father off. I stare in amazement as Dad strides away without further comment. Then I glance back at Schmule, who throws me a smug, metal-mouthed grin.

98

When Dad flies to Tampa for a three-day conference—Monday, Tuesday, and Wednesday—Evil Shawna flips into gear.

I know it's crazy. I know it's dangerous. I know it goes against every iota of self-preservation I possess, and I can't believe I'm considering it.

But why not? Nobody has to know. Schmule can see Fran, I can see Arye, and *nobody'll* find out. With Dad a thousand miles away, it's utterly impossible.

I don't mention my dastardly plan in advance. I drive Schmule to Dr. Silverberg's office on Tuesday and flip through a raggedy copy of *People* for fifty minutes. My moist fingers stick to the pages.

"See you next week, Sam," the receptionist chirps.

Schmule stomps out as I inform her, "His name is Schmule!" and then take off after him.

Inside the car, Schmule pulls out his Game Boy. The beeping drives me crazy, and I suspect he's annoying me on purpose. I let it go. "What did the doc say?"

"You ask me that every week and I always tell you the same thing."

"Which is?"

"MYOB."

Gritting my teeth with every *beep-beep-beep*, I head down Cedar

Road. Instead of making my usual left toward Shaker Heights, I continue north. Schmule, zapping aliens, pays no attention.

"Schmoo. Can I ask you something else?"

"Like if I said no, that'd stop you?"

"Did you tell Dr. Silverberg that Dad hit you that night?"

His flying thumbs slow for a microsecond. "You think I want Dad to go to jail?"

I notice he now says "Dad" even when Dad's not around. "I doubt if he'd go to jail. I just wondered if you'd—"

"Shut up, Shawna. I didn't say anything. Yeesh!"

My relief turns into a peculiar disappointment. If Dr. Silverberg knew Dad hit Schmule that night, would it make a difference? Dad can't deny it; both Julie and I saw it. If Fran takes Dad back to court, would it help her case?

I stop for a red light at Lee Road and continue on toward Coventry. Only when I make the unexpected right turn does Schmule lift his head. By then Fran's house is two blocks away.

"What are you *doing?*" he howls, dropping his Game Boy on the floor.

"You know what I'm doing. I'm taking you to see your mom."

"NO! Turn around right now!"

What the—? "Wait. I thought you'd be happy."

"He'll catch us. He'll find out!"

"He's in Florida."

"What if somebody sees us?" Without waiting for any reassurance, he grabs and wrenches the steering wheel—hard! "No. I said *no!*" One tire slams the curb as Schmule's door flies open. "I'll jump! I swear it! I don't care if I die!"

I yank the steering wheel back and scrunch the brakes. *"Stop it!"* The chorus of horn blasts behind me turns my blood to sludge.

"Go back! Go back!" One Nike, untied, dangles from the car. "Please, go back!"

So there's nothing I can do but turn around and go back.

99

Something dreadful has been released within the walls of my home. Something horrifying and unstoppable, something I can't put a name to.

Something nobody recognizes but me.

On the outside, Schmule has morphed into a "perfect" child. Polite to Dad, polite to everyone, including evil Aunt Colleen. Uncle Dieter takes him fishing and to the Indians' home opener. Now that the weather has warmed up, he helps Nonny plant geraniums. He mimics her Scottish brogue perfectly, much to Nonny's amusement.

And yes, he loves Poppy most of all. He even "plays" chess with my grandfather by pinching Poppy's frozen fingers around the pieces and moving them himself. Poppy, I notice, always wins.

"Penny used to talk about him," Schmule says wistfully.

"She did? What'd she say?"

"That he was the one who gave her that nickname. He called her 'Penny, lass' all the time, like it was just one word. Pennylass," he repeats, testing it on his tongue. "She thought it was funny, like he was calling her 'penniless,' ha-ha."

I feel a tweak of envy. Mom never told me that. "Really?"

"Yep. He said she sparkled like a penny."

Sometimes, when it's just the two of us, we'll talk about Mom. It's like I now share a history with someone other than myself. I can say whatever I like, without repercussion. Something I've missed out on for seventeen years.

The Mom Schmule knew, I find out, wasn't much different from my own: flaky, self-absorbed, but, well, still Mom. Who loved us on *her* terms, not ours.

I can see how he loved her.

Nevertheless, there's something in Schmule's eyes—or, more accurately, something missing. Whenever I hear Dad brag about how well "Sam" is adjusting, I know, with growing dread, he can't see what I see.

Maybe "Sam" is adjusting. But Schmule's fading away.

When Dad hauls us to a studio for a cozy family portrait—he and Schmule in suits and matching red ties—Schmule smiles into the camera, all freckles and braces. Later, when I sit down to copy the picture by hand and add it to my collage, his hollow blue eyes plunge an icicle through my heart.

I try to explain it to Julie when she takes me shopping. Next month is graduation, and I need a dress. I'd rather do this with LeeLee, but Julie insisted. Bonding time, or whatever.

"Julie, he's still depressed, and Dad doesn't even see it."

"He's on medication," she reminds me.

I know that. I hand it to him every day. "Pills won't help. He misses Fran. And I think he's scared of Dad," I add in a small voice.

"Scared? Why?"

Her indifference infuriates me. "Hello, weren't you sitting in the same room that night?"

She knows which night I mean. "He lost his temper. He's not a violent man, Shawna." I give her one of those "looks," a genetic gift from my dad. "Now I don't know what you think happened between your mom and dad—"

I do. I saw it.

"—but I know your father. He overreacted, that's all. He promised me it'd never happen again."

"Did you guys set a date?" I ask slyly.

"Uh, no. Not exactly. I don't think your dad's too eager to tie the knot again."

"Funny. He was pretty damn eager when he thought it'd get him Schmule."

"I'm not discussing this with you," she says, uncharacteristically snappish. "Now pick a dress and let's get out of here."

I vacillate between two, one white, one baby blue. Holding them up, I say, "These are cute, don't you think?"

She points to the blue. "Lovely! That's the perfect color for you."

Evil Shawna jams the blue one back on the rack. "Good. Let's go."

If I hurt her feelings, she keeps it to herself. "Don't you want to try it on?"

"I don't care what it looks like." I just want to graduate and get out of there. I'm sick of books and lectures and endless studying. I'm sick of all the end-of-the-year festivities I can't be bothered to go to. I'm sick of Wade Prep, period, and twelve years of plaid. All I can think about is Kenyon . . . and freedom . . . and maybe Arye.

While waiting in line, Julie confides, "Your dad says you discussed that art school of yours."

"It wasn't a discussion and it's not my art school. Can we talk about something else?"

"Like what?"

Hmm, like, what do you see in my dad? Were you fooling around with him when he was married to my mom? Are you going to make him marry you? Or continue to let him string you along like a monkey on a leash?

The words explode from nowhere: "You never said good-bye to me when you left. Remember?"

She pretends to study a display of marked-down sweaters. "I remember. It was thoughtless of me."

"Thoughtless? It sucked."

No answer.

"So why did you leave in such a hurry?"

"Because I was in love with your father. And no," she adds, reading my thoughts, "we were not having an affair. But I was young, and after your mom left, I thought . . ." Julie falters. "Well, he was devastated. He truly was. So I stayed as long as I could, hoping, you know, he'd see me as more than your nanny. But it never happened." She moistens her lips, examining a price tag. "So, after a while I just had to get out of there. I didn't even know I was going to quit, till I woke up that day and thought, 'I can't face going back to that house one more time.'"

"Till you came back," I remind her.

She nods, battling a smile. "He was so thrilled to see me. It still feels like a miracle."

I roll my eyes. "He's, like, almost sixty, Julie."

"I know that. But you can't always choose who you fall in love with, right? You're not that much younger than I was back then. Haven't you been in love?"

"Next in line!" the lady bellows from the register. I could kiss her.

I drop the dress onto the counter and slap down my charge card. "You can do better, you know. It doesn't have to be him." If the cashier wasn't trying so hard to listen in, I might elaborate on that. Then my cell phone goes off. I scribble my name on the receipt with one hand, fumbling through my purse with the other.

"Arye called," LeeLee announces excitedly. "He wants you to meet him at the Coventry Café at eight o'clock!"

I duck away from the counter. "Tonight?"

"Yeah, tonight! Omigod," she squeals. "Are you two, like, a *thing?*"

"No!" Luckily Julie doesn't possess superhuman hearing.

"I said I'd call him right back and let him know if you can make it."

"Tell him yes!" I shout.

Julie, perturbed, marches over with my garment bag. "What was that all about?"

I smile serenely. "Nothing. Just LeeLee."

# 100

A flash of paranoia grips my gut. It's amazing what runs through your brain when you're about to do something your father might kill you for.

I do want to see Arye. I want to see him so badly it's like a rush of fire through my bones. I didn't realize how much I missed him till I heard LeeLee say his name.

At seven forty-five I approach the den. Dad and Schmule, glued to a James Bond movie, barely glance up. From the looks of that Bond girl in her skintight jumpsuit, I can see how Dad might be interested. But I've never know him to sit through an entire movie. Another first.

"I'm going to the library," I sing out.

Entranced by the thundering TV, neither of them replies. Only Charles whines suspiciously as I zip out the door.

I lag in the doorway of the Coventry Café, and spot Arye in a corner with a cup of coffee. Working up the nerve, I watch him push his glasses farther up on his nose, one toe of his deck shoe tapping the table leg.

Spotting me, he flags me over. "Hey! You made it."

"Well, yeah."

"I was kind of afraid you wouldn't come." Me too. "How are you?"

"Oh, peachy," I say brightly. "You?"

"Great. I got accepted to Berkeley." He adds, not shyly, "Full scholarship."

"Wow, Berkeley?" So he'll be moving to California. "How cool." I try hard not to sound deflated.

"Yeah. But Cleveland State gave me one, too. So I guess I'll stay here."

Oh-h, so he *won't* be moving to California . . . "Wait. How can you give up a scholarship to Berkeley?"

Arye shrugs. "I just figured this might not be the best time to leave my mom." He points to the chai latte next to his coffee. "See? I remembered." I duck my head for a sip as he asks, "How's Schmule?"

"Okay," I fib.

"Good. Tell him Mom says hi. And, you know, she loves him."

I nod. "Sooo . . . why'd you want to see me?"

Straight-faced, he replies, "Maybe I miss you?"

"You do?"

"Yeah. A lot. You want to go for a walk?"

Gratefully, I grab my tea and follow him outside. It's not quite dusk. The evening smells like rain, exhaust fumes, and patchouli incense from a nearby import shop. We wander for a block before Arye reaches for my hand. He pulls me closer till our elbows touch. I scan the traffic, happy to know that Dad's home with Schmule, safely planted in front of the TV. True, there's always the chance of a freak encounter . . .

Arye notices my darting glances. "What?"

". . . Nothing."

We pass a Thai restaurant, a New Age bookstore, and a vintage record shop, then cross the street and head back the other way. It doesn't seem to bother him that I tower over him, though not as much as I used to. He feels warm and solid. I love the way my hand disappears inside of his.

We reach my car, and he tugs on the passenger door. "Drive me home?"

I pretend not to understand the glint in his eye. "Arye. You live right over *there*."

"So we'll take the long way around."

With my stomach twisted in a funny, excited knot, I start the engine and head the other way. When he reaches over to rest his hand on my thigh, the spiral of shock this sends through me turns the street into a blur.

We don't speak. We don't need to. Like Schmule and Poppy, we share the same mysterious wavelength.

I park in the lot of an elementary school, and I swear I don't know who makes the first move. Arye's glasses bounce onto to the dash, and his mouth lands on mine. His lips are softer than I expected and the stubble on his jaw burns my skin. My tongue meets his, and I taste coffee and cinnamon. Our teeth graze. Our noses scrunch together. Thank God, or maybe not, for the cup holders, CD box, and gearshift between us. Not that it seems to be holding us back.

Groping hands. Thunderous panting. I feel teeth on my neck. I touch his lap and feel him straining against his jeans, and how his own eager hands seem to be everywhere at once.

A second later I spot the spinning blue light. I smash my head on the steering wheel as I scramble upright.

"Oh, *crap*," is all Arye can manage.

Knock, knock, knock on the driver's-side window. "Everything all right here? Can I see your license?" I hand it over with petrified fingers. "Are you here of your own free will?"

"Yes! Everything's fine."

He eyeballs Arye as he passes my license back. "Do you have any identification?"

"I don't drive," Arye says sheepishly.

What if he makes us get out? My jeans are unzipped! What if he searches the car and finds the empty wine bottles I never bothered to throw out?

"Well, I think you can find a better place to do whatever it is you're doing. Move along." To be perfectly sure we understand the severity of his message, he waits until I pull out of the parking lot and then follows us for a few blocks before turning down a side street.

Arye quips bleakly, "Yay, Cleveland Heights. Nice to know I live in su-uch a safe community."

"Oh, God, oh, God, what if he runs my plates? It's registered to my dad!"

"We weren't, um, breaking the law."

"But what if they do? I am so fricking dead!"

"Take it easy. He didn't even ask for the registration."

I can't take it easy. I can hear Dad now: *Shawna? I just received a call from the Cleveland Heights Police Department. Apparently one of the officers found you in a compromising position and—who do I say I was with?—I think I deserve an explanation. Was it that Goodman boy? Did you have in-ter-course with him? Did you use a condom?*

I wrench the car to a stop in front of Fran's house. We sit there in uneasy silence as I slowly recover from my meltdown. Then I ask, in wonder, "What just happened tonight?"

"Beats me." Smiling, he lifts a strand of my hair and kisses it. A sweet, funny gesture. "But I hope we do it again."

101

I fly awake in the middle of the night.

"I peed the bed," Schmule says in my ear. "Don't tell Dad."

"You want to climb in with me? Wait! Did you, like, *shower* I hope?"

"Yeah, so, what about my sheets?"

"I'll take care of it in the morning." Nudging Charles aside, I hold up the covers.

Schmule scooches in beside me. "Sorry," he mumbles. "Should I tell Dr. Silverberg?"

"Why?"

"I'm ten years old, duh. Now watch me turn into a serial killer or something."

I don't laugh. Knowing Schmule, this seriously concerns him.

Charles pads in a circle of annoyance, wondering why there's an extra body in my bed. Schmule slides him onto his chest and kisses his head.

"This is creepy," he observes. "Ugh, sleeping with your sister? Aren't there, like, laws and stuff?"

"Hey, you can leave anytime. I won't be offended."

He pokes me with an ice-cold toe, then shoves his feet off the bed. A minute later he's snoring.

102

Because I stay awake for hours thinking about Arye, wondering what might have happened if that cop hadn't shown up, I sleep through my alarm. Forty-five minutes late, I stumble downstairs, where Schmule's eating breakfast in front of the Discovery Channel. "Why didn't you wake me? Didn't you hear my alarm?"

"Hey, I'm the child." He nibbles a frosted Pop-Tart. "You should be waking *me* up."

"It's seven thirty!" I yell. "Move! Where's Klara? Take your pill!"

Klara shows up seconds later, stammering some excuse about a long-distance call from a cousin in Germany. "What are you going to do without me for a week?" she demands as she throws together Schmule's usual lunch: peanut butter and jelly and mayo on rye.

"Where are you going?" I ask. Klara never takes vacations. She rarely takes a weekend off.

"Munich," Schmule pipes in. "That's where those terrorists broke into the Olympics once, and took those Israeli guys hostage." He continues to blab as grumpy Klara hustles him through his routine. "They broke in with machine guns and rounded them all up, and—"

Klara throws him his lunch bag. "Did you brush your teeth, Mister Never-Shuts-His-Mouth?"

"Yes. So then the government tried to rescue them and, like, totally screwed it up, and—"

Flinging up her hands, Klara lumbers out to her car. She honks the horn as Schmule lags back, nuzzling Charles and yammering away. I hate when she does that. And I hate the fact that she drives him to school because Dad, obviously, doesn't trust me yet. Good thing he doesn't know I already broke my promise.

Ignoring Klara's warning blasts, Schmule wanders up as I assemble a fruit salad for my lunch. I've pretty much given up on that cafeteria yogurt. "I need my pill."

"You already took it."

"No, I didn't. You're supposed to hand it to me, remember?"

"Didn't Klara?"

Hand outstretched, he waits with a smirk. I shake out a pill, then hesitate. Maybe I should run out and ask Klara?

"Hello? Happy pill, Shawna!" Schmule snaps his fingers. I pass him the pill. "Will you, you know . . ." He points to the ceiling. "Before Klara notices?"

"I said I'll take care of it."

Upstairs, as I gather up the smelly sheets, I trip over Schmule's bookbag at the foot of the bed. Well, if he thinks I'm running this down to him, he's out of luck.

A red folder sticks out, and I see, printed on the front: *The Stockholm Syndrome by "Sam" Gallagher*. Sam, in quotes, I notice with a renewed rush of despair.

I'm already late, but curiosity wins out. I flip it open, and read:

In 1972 a group of customers in Stockholm, Sweden, were held hostage in a bank by a bunch of robbers for six days. After they were rescued they stuck up for their captors. When the case went to trial they refused to testify or say anything bad about them.

This is what is known as the Stockholm syndrome. This is a very well-documented phenomenon. It has been studied by scientists and psychologists for many years. People held captive start to identify with the kidnappers even if they do very bad things like torture and mental abuse.

At first it is a matter of survival. They depend on the kidnappers for food and water. If they are kept isolated they also depend on the kidnapper for company. Every day they survive, they are grateful to the kidnapper for not killing them.

Usually they get brainwashed. For instance a man might kidnap a child and then tell him that his real family doesn't love him. This is how a kidnapper may get you to believe that nobody wants you. If a lot of time passes and you are still with the kidnapper, you start to believe it. You think that the kidnapper is really a nice person who wants you when nobody else does. Besides, he did not kill you yet.

Finally, if you are rescued, you feel sorry for the kidnapper because after he finished doing all the bad stuff to you, he took really good care of you. You start to see him as a human being and not as some monster. There are stories about people who were kidnapped for years and never escaped even when they had a chance. Sometimes they were afraid to risk it. But

sometimes the victim feels that he is being disloyal.
He does not want the kidnapper to get caught and go
to prison even if the kidnapper deserves it . . .

It's not until I reach the end of the report that I realize I'm an idiot.

Not everyone who gets kidnapped becomes victims
of the Stockholm syndrome. But for some people it
is a way of survival. The worst thing is when the
hostages join up with their kidnappers and continue
to do bad things. Or when they can't forget the horrible things that happened to them. Or when they
feel so guilty, they . . .

Goose bumps prickle my arms. A wave of nausea hits me like a mudslide. I scream out loud when Schmule's phone rings at my elbow.

Dad asks, "Aren't you going to school today?"

"I overslept."

"Is Klara there? I have a conference next week. I want to make sure I have a clean suit."

"She took Schmule to school."

"Sam," he corrects me absently. "Well, tell her I need the Pierre Cardin. The gray one, not the black. And I'm running low on shirts, so she needs to drop those off, too, and—"

"Dad! Stop. I have to tell you something." I eye the red folder. "About"—I force the name out—"Sam."

How do I explain how all the clues add up? All that weirdness with his pills. The day he smacked his face into that desk. How he freaked out in the car when I tried to take him to Fran's. His moodiness, the bedwetting, and now this awful report? Granted, I'm not a five-hundred-dollar-an-hour shrink. But I'm positive Schmule's report is really about himself.

Something is wrong!

Dad sighs into my ear. "Look, honey, I know you still think he's depressed." Yeah, Julie probably related every single word of our conversation. "If it'll make you feel any better, I'll take him out to dinner tonight, just the two of us. Maybe he'll open up to me a bit and we can have a private chat. I'll feel him out. What do you think?"

On one hand I hate the idea of Dad interrogating Schmule over a basket of french fries. On the other hand, if Dad approaches it the right way, he might see for himself what I've been saying all along.

My own sigh of relief almost blows the receiver from my hand.

103

Charles and I hike through the park as the afternoon sun dips lower and lower. Dad's Navigator pulls out of the driveway as we mosey back up the walk. Dad waves at me and Schmule sticks out his tongue. I bet he'd much rather hang out and play video games tonight. Or poke bamboo skewers through his eardrums.

I wonder what Arye would think about this Stockholm syndrome thing. How could *he* not understand the chilling significance? But no point in freaking him out, too. Besides, face it—I'm just looking for an excuse to see him again.

A pulsating heat tingles between my thighs. I shudder deliciously, remembering how he touched me. Well, at least now, without a doubt, I know that I'm attracted to guys. That the strange revulsion I felt for Devon was, well, because it was Devon, ha-ha.

Too lazy to heat up the dinner Klara left for me, I wolf down a bowl of Rice Chex and head to my room. Tonight, hopefully, I can finish up my art project once and for all.

I drag the sheet off my worktable—and freeze.

Insidious scratch marks, carved by something very sharp, replace Schmule's face in each picture I'd already pasted onto the board. Sketches I spent weeks on, copying from photographs, adding tiny, colorful details.

I fall into my chair, sick with incomprehension. Months and months of work, all down the toilet.

Schmule. Who else?

Why would he do this?

When I can breathe again, I peek at the extra photos scattered on my table. My stomach hits my knees. Picture after picture, hopelessly mutilated, Schmule's head scissored out of every scene. Our family portrait hits me hardest of all: Dad, smiling proudly, his hand on Schmule's shoulder; then me, uptight and nervous, although my hair does look fabulous; then a ragged black hole, sandwiched between Schmule's newly sprouted brown curls and sassy red necktie.

My disbelief boils over into rage.

Every. Single. Picture!

My whole project, destroyed.

104

"It's a sign," LeeLee says when I phone her in a panic. "He's cutting himself out of the family. It's symbolic."

"Of what?"

"Did you, like, sleep through junior psych? He's *erasing* himself. Is he giving stuff away, too?"

"Not that I know of."

"Well, good. Because that's *really* a major sign of—" She stops.

"He's only ten years old!"

"What planet are you on?" She listens patiently to my long, miserable silence. "Shawna, please tell your dad about those pictures. And tell that shrink while you're at it."

"What if they think he's crazy?"

"Well, I know you don't want to hear this. But maybe he is."

105

I can't function till Dad and Schmule return from the restaurant. They stumble in, laughing and joking, a gold paper crown crammed on Schmule's head.

"Dad told 'em it was my birthday. Man, all these people came over and sang happy birthday. I got a free dessert!"

Dad plucks the crown off and ruffles Schmule's hair. "Okay, sport, party's over. Get ready for bed now. School tomorrow."

"Can I play my new game for a while?"

"Half an hour. Then lights out, champ."

"Yes!" Schmule arcs a fist through the air and zooms upstairs.

Sport? Champ? Not only am I hearing voices, I'm hearing the wrong words coming out of the wrong people.

Dad hands me a Styrofoam box. "You didn't eat yet, did you? I brought you a salad."

Who is this man who looks so much like my dad? My real dad never brought home a doggy bag in his life.

I drop it onto the table. "Dad, listen. And don't blow me off. I was talking to LeeLee tonight, about depression, okay? And she said—"

Dad's demeanor plummets below sea level. "I don't care what she said. And *speaking* of her, I ran into Deb Connolly a while back. She had some very interesting things to say about her." Dad shrugs out of his suit coat. "Frankly, I'm surprised. I always wondered about that girl."

Well, thank you, Devon or Susan, for blabbing about LeeLee's sex life, to your *mommy*, no less. "You wondered what?"

"Let's just say I had a few doubts about her character. Obviously, I was right."

"What does character have to do with being gay?" Maybe I misunderstood him.

"Shawna, please," Dad says tiredly. "In case you didn't notice, I was in a pretty good mood up until three minutes ago,"

"Being gay makes you a bad person?"

"I never said that."

Oh, yes, you did. I've heard it my whole life. You made me believe it, too.

I'm smarter than that now.

"But look at your mother." Dad stops. Silent, I wait, until he realizes I'm not walking away from this. "What kind of mother leaves her seven-year-old daughter behind? Was she worried about you? Concerned? Did she take me to court when I went for full custody? No! Out of sight, out of mind—and that's what I mean by character. Any other mother would fight tooth and nail for her child. All she cared about was making a name for herself." Agitated, he runs his fingers around his collar. "What the hell kind of character would you call that?"

I sting from the brutality of the words "any other mother." "Straight people dump their kids all the time."

"It's their lifestyle I'm talking about. The promiscuity. Why do you think so many people die from AIDS?"

"Mom and Fran stayed together for ten years. They weren't promiscuous."

"As far as you *know*. You didn't live with them, now, did you?"

As usual, I can't win. He always has a comeback, no matter how illogical.

I try to remember what started this. "Forget Mom. This is about Schmule." Before he can squash me, the words explode from my lips: "I-think-he-might-be-planning-to-kill-himself-or-something."

Dad steadies himself, white-knuckled, on the edge of the bar. "What did you say?"

I repeat it. Not only that, I give him the specifics. Schmule's report for Mr. Gorski. The way he goofs around with his pills. And although I suspect Schmule will never forgive me, I tell Dad about that bedwetting thing, too.

Wisely, I leave out that last episode on the way to Fran's. The less Dad knows about that, the better for all of us.

When I begin to explain about my ruined project, Dad stops me. "Enough," he murmurs. "Christ, I had no idea—"

I melt with relief.

"—you'd pull something like this."

Stunned, I shout, "I'm not pulling anything! Every word I said is true!"

"If he's suicidal, Shawna, then guess what? I'll have to put him in the hospital. Is that what you want?"

I say nothing.

"Is it?" he shouts.

I hold my ground as he takes a step closer. I see, or maybe imagine, his flicker of surprise.

Neither of us blinks.

"I don't ever want to discuss this with you again."

My brain kicks in, telling my legs to move. I'm almost to the door when Dad speaks up. His tone has changed; he sounds torn, ragged. "Shawna. Don't you want to know how it went tonight?"

Sure, Dad. Tell me how happy "Sam" was when they stuck that crown on his head. Tell me how stupid I am for being so afraid for him.

"We had a great time. He ate like a horse for a change. He joked around, told me stories. I had no idea how much fun he could be. He's sharp, too. Oh, the things he comes up with." Dad grows distant, not even facing me anymore. "Do you have any idea how this made me feel? To be sitting at a table, in public, having a good time with my own son?"

He was faking, Dad. He wants you to think everything's fine.

"And yes, he opened up to me. I asked him about feeling depressed, and he said yes, he'd been sad for a while, but now he's happy to be here. He's nuts about your grandfather." A smile plays at his mouth. "And he sure loves you, honey."

I know. I love him back.

I gasp when Dad draws me into an unexpected hug. "You're a good girl, Shawna. But you worry too much. Sam'll be fine, I promise. We did the right thing."

106

Escaping at last, I watch Schmule battle a barrage of virtual zombies. Seemingly hypnotized, he destroys every last one and whoops in triumph.

"Cool game?"

"Awesome! It's new. Dad bought it for me on the way home. You should play with me sometime," he insists for the thousandth time. "I'll show you. It's easy."

"Okay." I study the package: *Revenge of the Bloodlusters*. "What happened to *Yoshi's Island*?"

"Baby stuff. Fran would *never* let me have anything this cool!"

Fran. Not "Mom."

"I can show you now," he adds, with a longing glance at his collection of pricey game consoles, hoping to cajole some extra play time out of me. "Maybe if we're reeeally quiet . . ."

I sit gingerly on the bed. "Not now, because there's something we have to talk about." No recognition. "Those pictures?"

Schmule's eyes flash to the door as we hear Dad's footsteps in the hall. "Don't tell him, okay?"

"It's too late. I already did."

He jumps hard onto the bed, nearly bouncing me off. His icy blue stare slices me with resentment.

I try to explain. "I didn't tell him because I'm mad at you, Schmoo. I told him because I'm, well, worried about you."

"Worried about what?"

"Worried that . . . you might do something bad? To yourself?"

"You mean, like, kill myself?" His stare widens. "Why would I do that?"

"Because you're sad?"

"I'm not sad. Why should I be sad? I mean, look at all those people who, like, live in the slums. All those druggies and boozers, all those homeless people. All the people who get, like, beat up and robbed. I bet they get sad, but they don't all kill themselves, duh. That's, like . . ." His shoulders convulse. Oh, my God—he's laughing! "Jeez, Shawna. You're too freakin' funny sometimes."

"Stop laughing! You had me worried sick!" He stops giggling, and I hear myself rage, "So why did you total my project? I worked on that for months! If I can't figure out how to fix it I'll get a big fat zero."

"I'm sorry, okay? I'm sorry, sorry, sorry!" He throws the sheet over his head and rolls to one side. "Leave me alone. I'm tired."

"I'm not leaving you alone till you tell me why you did it."

A long, quaking silence. Then he blurts out, "Sam."

"Sam what?"

"Sam did it."

"Schmule. You *are* Sam."

"I know!" He whips the covers off again. "I'm Sam. I—am—Sam! Sam—I—am!" He starts laughing again, but not his usual laugh. A harsh and monotonous "HA. HA. HA." Each venomous syllable drawn out and distinct.

I scramble closer, tackle him, and hug him hard. He stays stiff in my arms, his chin a slice of steel digging into my shoulder. Then his violent hug knocks the air out of my lungs.

"I'm sorry I ruined your stuff," he says mournfully against my neck.

"I know." Fighting tears, I rock him the way Poppy rocks in his chair. Back and forth, back and forth. "Are you going to be okay with us?" His head bumps my jaw as he nods. "I mean really, really okay? Because if you weren't, you'd tell me. Wouldn't you, Schmoo?"

"You mean if, like you said, I was gonna do something bad to myself?"

"Are you?" I whisper.

A tiny scoff from the back of his throat. "Duh. Don't be stupid, Shawna."

I sit bolt upright and hold him away from me. He stares back, and yes, I've seen those eyes. I've heard that voice. I know that expression all too well.

"I love you," I say numbly.

He replies, "Yeah. I love ya, too," in his Schmule voice now, not the other one. He watches me slink off the bed and stumble to the door. "Hey, Shawna? If you do want to play *Bloodlusters*, you can have the Wii. I mean, yeesh, who needs, like, three fricking game things?"

Somebody flips a kill switch. Every neuron in my brain fizzles out.

"Didja hear me?"

"I heard you," I say lightly. "So, will you teach me how to use it?"

"Oh, it's a cinch. A baby could figure it out."

"I couldn't."

"Yeah, you could," he insists. "You won't need me. I promise."

107

When I wake up at three and can't fall back asleep, I spend the next two hours trying to repair my project. Thank God it's not due for a couple of weeks. This might give me time to come up with another idea.

Or not.

I leave the pictures as they are, take out my pencils, and carefully copy the few photos I have left. After adding dashes of color, I stand back, exhausted, to survey the finished product. Perfectly sketched scenes, some as small as Post-its, pieced together like a mosaic fresco. Faces of me, of my friends, my family, my dog. My "Life as a Collage" with Schmule's bare foot placed prominently in the center.

Scattered among the hundreds of drawings on the board, multiple gouged-out faces follow me sightlessly. The effect is chilling. I deserve an A for that alone.

I touch the drawing of Schmule's foot. I can almost feel the warm pulse, beating softly under my finger.

Now I know what I have to do.

And I have to do it today.

108

When the birds start chirping outside my window, I shower, wash my hair, and throw on a pot of coffee. Dad strolls into the kitchen at quarter past five. "You're up early," I say.

"I have four C-sections today. The first one's at seven. Quads, in fact. No fertility drugs at all. Do you have any idea what the chances are of that?"

No, but I bet Schmule would.

"What are *you* doing up?" he asks.

"I couldn't sleep."

He nods, possibly remembering our conversation last night. Then, "Well, Klara starts her vacation today. Which means," he adds as he snaps the lid to his travel mug, scoops up his bag, and heads for the door, "you'll have to drive Schmule to school. And pick him up later if you don't mind."

I wait for the caveat—*"And I mean straight to school and straight back home!"*—but he says nothing of the sort. Does he trust me again? Or is this a test?

I doze in front of the news but luckily wake up in time to rouse Schmule for school.

"I'm sick." He rubs his stomach. "I'm staying home. I think that steak last night gave me E. coli." He slaps my hand away as I reach for his forehead. "I *said* I'm staying home."

"You can't stay home. Klara's not here."

"I know that, duh."

Cogs of renewed suspicion clank through my brain. "Well, you can't stay here alone."

"Why not?"

"Because I said so. Now move."

I brush tangles out of my hair, put on some makeup, and slip into my uniform. Soon I'll be shopping for a new wardrobe for Kenyon and I will never have to wear this lame uniform again. I hold my bangs off my forehead and stare at my eyes in the mirror. Pale blue orbs, each in a sea of pink, the shadows below them so dark even cover-up can't save me. Not only do I look like I've been up since three, now my insides squirm like a basket of vipers.

Too strung out for breakfast, I wait for Schmule to make his belated appearance. He meanders down, dragging his bookbag—*thump, thump, thump* as it lands on each step.

"Did you brush your teeth?" I ask. "You have all your stuff?"

"Yes, Mommy. And by the way, I'm still *sick!*"

"What about your report?"

This catches him off guard. "Huh?"

"Your report. The Stockholm syndrome?" I point to the stairs when he doesn't budge. "Go get it."

His freckles disappear in a blotch of fury. "Were you snooping in my room?"

"No, you left it out in plain sight."

"Well, it's not due today."

"So? It's finished, right? You can turn it in early. Go get it," I order.

Seething, he disappears, and returns with the red folder. "You read this, didn't you? You're as bad as Dad."

Ignoring this, I snatch up Charles, who's desperately begging for a ride. Schmule sulkily climbs into the car and sits in frozen silence till we get to his school. "You forgot my pill, stupid."

"Too late now."

"You're supposed to be *weaned* off that stuff, not stop it instantly. I could go into convulsions and swallow my tongue and die. I bet you didn't know that. Ha! Some doctor *you'll* be."

I bite my own tongue as I brake near the entrance. When Schmule grabs the handle, I mirror his movement on my side.

He slits his eyes. "What do you think you're doing?"

"I'm coming in with you."

"Into my school? What for?"

"Because I want to see Mr. Gorski's face when you turn in that report. I want to see what he says when you turn in a project he didn't even assign."

"He did so assign it!"

"Then why don't you want to turn it in?"

"You're nuts. Why would I waste time on a stupid project I didn't have to do?"

"Good question," I agree. "But I think I know why."

"Well, you're not coming in!"

"Oh yes I am." I watch how his fingers open and shut, open and shut on the straps of his bookbag. I know he wishes he could wrap those fingers around my neck. "Okay. Give me the folder." He yanks it out of his bookbag and flings it over. "Do you want me to read it to you?"

"No. I hate you! And I hate your stupid ugly dog." Half rising, he hurls his loaded bookbag violently into the backseat. Charles yelps, and cowers in bewilderment.

Determined not to lose my cool, I open the folder. Schmule

snatches it out of my hand and throws that in the backseat, too. A staring contest ensues, and yes, I'm the first to look away.

I hear the shouts of the kids as they straggle toward the school entrance. An occasional horn. Birds chattering in a nearby tree. None of it really breaks the silence in the car.

Schmule kicks my glove compartment, harder than usual. "May I *please* be excused? Or do you want me to get into trouble for being late?"

"Depends."

"On what?"

I drag air into my lungs. "On whether or not you want to go see Fran."

"Fran?" Schmule kicks again. The glove compartment springs open and my sunglasses tumble out. I'm surprised he doesn't stomp on these, too. "Ha. Ha. Very funny."

"I'm serious. Yes or no?"

"Ya-ah, so Dad can *kill* us?"

"Dad's in the delivery room all day. So do you or don't you? This is our only chance. And if you flip out on me again I'll never take you anywhere, ever."

He watches me dubiously from beneath his lashes. "Yeah, you will."

"No, I won't."

"You never take me anywhere good, anyhow."

"I took you bungee jumping, didn't I?"

"Big deal. One time."

Silence, silence, and I chant to myself: make up your mind, make up your mind!

"Do you want me to apologize?" Schmule asks, confused.

"For what?" He shrugs, so I add, "Well, maybe you owe Charles an apology."

Schmule scrambles around and lifts Charles into the front seat, cuddling him, covering his doggy face with kisses. Charles, always forgiving, kisses him back, his long rubbery body wriggling with delight. "I'm sorry, Charles. You know I love you. I love ya, love ya, love ya . . ."

I turn away, unable to speak. I see a teacher's aide wave a couple of latecomers inside, then shut the door.

Schmule notices, too. "Um, what about school?"

I yank my car into gear. "You know something? Screw school."

He snorts into Charles's fur.

109

Leaving Charles in the car, nosing the half-open window, we walk hand in hand up to Fran's door. Schmule doesn't use his key. Maybe he already feels like a stranger.

Fran goggles through the screen, fingers splayed at her throat. "What happened? What happened?"

"Nothing," I promise her. "We just both blew off school."

Trance-like, she unlatches the door. Schmule sends me a questioning look as if to make sure for the very last time that what we're doing is okay. I nod. He bolts inside before I can change my mind.

I don't know what I expected. That Schmule would throw himself at Fran and sob with joy? That Fran would stroke his head and smother him with kisses, the way Schmule kissed Charles only minutes ago?

That she'd swear never to let him go back with me, never, never, never?

Instead, Schmule says, matter-of-fact, "Hi, Mom."

"Hey, sweetie," Fran replies as if he's only been gone an hour. "Well, this is a surprise. Though possibly not," she adds to me, "the smartest idea you ever had."

"You're welcome," I say sarcastically.

What did I expect? Gratitude? It's my ass on the line, not hers. There's no court order yet saying she can't see Schmule; Dad only threatened that, and only to me.

Of course, after today it might be a different story.

Fran touches my elbow. "Shawna, I appreciate this. But are you out of your mind? First of all, you're supposed to be in school. And when your dad finds out you two missed the same day—"

"I told you so!" Schmule aims this at me.

I didn't think of that. Now it's too late.

He edges toward the door. "I want to go back."

"No, you don't," I say firmly.

"I do!"

"Schmoo, listen—"

He cups his hands over his ears. "I want to go to school. Take me back! Now!"

"Shawna, *take* him," Fran pleads as Schmule hyperventilates before our eyes. "This just isn't worth it."

"Not worth it?" I echo in disbelief. "How can you say that? This is your fault, too!"

"My fault?"

"Yes! Why didn't you fight for him?"

"I did!" she cries out, clutching herself tightly.

"You did not. The judge says, okay, Dr. Gallagher, you get to take him home—and what did *you* do? You just sat there and nodded?"

"They won't give him to me! He is not my son!"

"Yes I am!" Schmule torpedoes forward, flinging himself on Fran. She cowers under his pummeling fists but makes no attempt to stop the assault. "I am! *I am!*" He's crying, Fran's crying, and before I know it I'm crying right along with them.

Exhausted, Schmule sags against Fran. She hugs him ferociously before spinning him around. "Go to your room. Please! Just for a while."

Schmule flees. I'm sobbing so hard I can barely understand my own words. "My mom didn't fight for me. Now you're doing the same thing."

"It's not the same thing."

"It's exactly the same thing!"

"Everything you see, you see in black and white! You're seventeen years old. You have no *idea* how the world operates. God!" she screams, slapping the wall. "You and your smart-ass, idealistic attitude. You know there's no way in hell *any* judge would give Schmule back to me. And you have no goddamn right to come in here and say I didn't try!"

"She didn't fight for me," I repeat stubbornly. I swipe my cheeks, sorry I took so much time with my makeup. "Do you know what that feels like? To know your mom just gave up?"

"She had no choice! He would've dragged her through the mud."

"So what?" I shriek. "She could've dragged him right back. I know what he did. I *saw* what he did. If you take him back to court, you can tell them the truth!"

She stares, stricken. "What are you talking about?"

"Oh, please. You know."

I sniffle into my hands, so she leads me to the sink. I splash water on my face. She mops hers, too, and blows her nose.

At last she asks, as if she missed every word I just said, "Why did you bring him here today?"

"B-because," I squeak between hiccups. "He's going to hurt himself if someone doesn't help him. He's cutting his face out of pictures. He wrote this awful report about people who are kidnapped. Plus he tried to give me his Nintendo. I don't even *play* video games. It's a Nintendo Wii. He'd never part with that." I fall down in a chair and hide my face. "Today might've been the day. He tried to stay home. He figured no one would be around."

"Does your father know about this?" Fran asks hollowly.

"I told him most of it. I don't think he believes me. He thinks I'm jealous. Or maybe he doesn't want me to be right, because *he's* in charge. He's supposed to be in control."

Fran takes my hands and squeezes hard. We sit without speaking as the faucet drips, and floorboards creak above us in Rina's half of the house. The silence between us feels strong and viscous. She grips my fingers tighter, enough to jam my class ring into my skin. "Do you want to tell me what happened? The night your mom left?"

"I'm sure she told you." Of course she did.

"Ye-es, some of it. But she didn't know you'd—"

"I don't want to talk about this now." I twist my hands away and push up on the table. "Look, I've, um, got stuff to do if you and Schmule want to hang out for a while."

"Shawna. Are you sure?"

"Yes. Are you?"

Fran nods. Without asking permission, I walk through the back hall and rap on Schmule's door. Cross-legged on the bed, he looks up from the book in his lap and asks darkly, "You guys done yelling at each other?"

I touch one freckled cheek. "Yeah, you can come out now. It's safe." Unconvinced, he stays put till I nudge him. "Go visit with your mom."

"Where are *you* going?"

"I have some stuff to take care of." I glimpse the title of the book as I give him a hug: *The Complete Poems of Emily Jane Brontë*. "Was that Mom's?"

"Yeah. I like poetry. I write it sometimes. But don't tell Dad, or"—he pulls away from me, arcs his wrist, and wiggles his fingers—"he'll think I'm gay or something." He taps the page. "Herr Gorski's making us read one and then say what it's about. This one's mine."

Out loud, I read the lines highlighted in yellow, never mind I already know them by heart. "'These once indeed seemed Beings Divine; / And they perchance heard vows of mine, / And saw my offerings on their shrine. / But careless gifts are seldom prized . . . And *mine* were worthily despised.'" My forced laugh clears the lump from my throat. "Yah, good luck."

"Aw, I can pull it out of my butt."

"I bet." I kiss the top of his head. "'Bye. And be good."

"Ugh, please. Do you have to slobber all over me?"

"Good-bye," I repeat, in case he didn't hear me.

"Yeah, yeah. 'Bye!" Rubbing my kiss out of his hair, Schmule makes an atrocious face. "And don't hurry back."

110

Back home, after Charles and I take a break, I cart my collage out to the car. He knows something's up and watches intently as I aim the car toward Wade Prep. Awkwardly, I lug the heavy poster through the quiet halls to the art room. Miss Pfeiffer's wiping down shelves, no class in session. "Shawna! What's up?"

"Here's my project. I know it's not due yet . . ." But truthfully, I'm sick of it.

She props it on a table and examines it for a minute. Then: "Shawna, this is amazing! I've never seen anything like—" Then she draws back, head cocked at the sight of those creepy, mutilated faces. "Well. Hmm. I don't quite understand . . ."

"Me either," I admit. I run a finger along Schmule's naked foot, sketched in pencil, veins traced in a delicate gold. "By the way, I'm cutting today."

She's so absorbed in my collage, I don't think she notices me leave.

111

What do you do on a day when the only life you know may blow up in your face at any second?

I throw off my vest and my blazer—the day is warming up—and drive around with my dog with the top of my car down. Charles's ears flutter in the breeze as we swing through Little Italy and then head back uptown. After stopping at Starbucks for tea and a scone, I park on a side street and doodle in my sketchpad, trying to take my mind off things . . . but I can't stop thinking about the night my mom left.

How Mom left, came back, and then left one more time. I always wondered: would she have stayed that second time if what happened in their bedroom had never happened?

I remember the sounds—Dad's voice, angry and muffled, and Mom, in tears. A dull explosion, similar to the one I heard the night Dad slapped Schmule.

Even though I'd been warned to *never open the door when Mommy and Daddy are inside*, I opened it anyway. Nobody noticed the click of the latch. I pressed my face into the opening and saw Mom and Dad on the bed: Mom, underneath him, gasping and pushing and smacking his head, saying, "No, no, stop it!" between choking sobs.

Dad, lunging hard and fast. I didn't understand his words then, but I understand now: "Can Fran give you this? Can Fran give you this?"

He said it over and over. And Mom kept crying.

112

Charles, bored, pats me with an impatient paw. Like people, he gets homesick if we stay away too long. The second we get home he scampers to his dish, laps up a gallon of water, and collapses into a sunlit square under the dining room window.

No blinking red light on the answering machine. Dad, thankfully, hasn't caught on yet.

The palpable emptiness of the house unnerves me. I've never felt so alone, but it's not a true "loneliness."

A "nothingness," maybe.

All I hear is my shallow breathing as I root around for that secret box. The "just-in-case" condoms foisted on me by Dad after my last nightmarish date with Danielle's brother.

What the hell do think you're doing, Shawna Gallagher?

I don't answer because, well, I don't have a good answer.

I kick off my uniform, pull on a hot pink tee and flowered capris, and slide a single foil packet into a pocket. I tell myself that if Arye laughs at me, it won't be the end of the world.

It won't. Really.

113

Parked at the curb, I see him, loping down the sidewalk toward his house after school. I toot the horn. He squints to be sure I'm not a hallucination. "Stalking me again?"

"You wish. Schmule's inside with your mom. I'm just hanging around."

Wondrously, he asks, "Do you know you're insane?"

I smile boldly. "Want to go for a ride?"

"Let me say hi to my brother. Be right back."

The sun, startlingly hot for only the beginning of May, roasts my face in the five minutes he's gone. When he climbs in next to me, and his arm brushes mine, I relish this new sensation that leaves me breathless and off balance. Is this what it feels like to bungee jump? Like flinging your heart, brain, and stomach in three different directions, and not caring if they find a way back to your body?

"When do you have to be home?" Arye asks.

"No time soon."

He shakes his head, mystified. "This is great what you're doing. But if your dad—"

"I can handle my dad." For the first time, I believe it.

"So where are we going?"

"Nowhere. Anywhere."

We head out of Cleveland Heights and ride through the next few suburbs. I steer left-handed, my right one resting comfortably under Arye's. The farther we drive, the faster the blue disappears from the sky. Gray clouds roll in from the lake, smothering the hot sun that previously tried to broil me alive.

Arye rubs my thumb. "Thanks for bringing him over."

"You're welcome," I say formally.

"Stupid of you, but nice."

"I didn't do it to be nice."

"Then why?" When I can't answer, he says, "You know, I still don't get you. You're nothing like the person I knew last year."

"Neither are you. I thought you were a jerk."

"Trust me. You were no prize yourself."

We laugh. Relaxed now, I ease up on the accelerator on a crooked country road and roll the car onto the bumpy shoulder. Through an old split-log fence, we spy a couple of horses, munching grass and swishing their long tails.

"You still think I'm a jerk?" he asks curiously.

"Sometimes. Like, when you give me that look."

"What look?"

"That eyeball thing, like you think I'm retarded or something."

"This one?" He does it, and I smack him—so he takes my face in his hands and kisses me. When a truck roars by inches from my car, he quickly lets go, and points to an alcove of trees. "Better pull over there before we get run off the road."

I obey, hoping we won't get stuck in a ditch. The sun reappears, briefly, to cast an orangey glow on the evergreen branches. Then it disappears, leaving our surroundings gray and almost spooky. A squirrel scampers down one knotty trunk, chatters at us for trespassing, then scrambles back into the branches.

"Want to get out?" I ask, oh-so-casually. "I have a blanket in the trunk."

Arye deadpans, "Not only are you stalking me—now you're trying to seduce me."

"Don't be presumptuous. I'm tired of sitting."

"Well, put your top up, 'cause it's going to rain any second."

I do, and he helps me spread the blanket over the ground. We plop down side by side—and then I watch the sky disappear as he brushes my lips with his own. Again and again.

As the full weight of his body leans into mine, I think about Charles waiting at home. About bungee jumping. About that line from Mom's poem—*careless gifts*—and how, until today, I never knew what it meant.

All these thoughts jumble together as he slips his hand under my tee, under the elastic of my bra. I grasp the back pockets of his jeans to pull him closer. Rigid, breathless, he abruptly stops to smooth my hair back with a sweaty palm. Trembling wildly, I shift enough to pull the foil square out of my pocket. He stares, first with incomprehension. Then with disbelief. Part of me knows he may now think the worst of me.

The rest of me doesn't care.

"You sure?" he whispers.

I nod, so he takes it. I watch a looming black cloud drift closer and closer as Arye rips open the package. I wonder if he's ever done this before. It seems unlikely. It takes him a long time.

Then we roll up in the blanket, wind jostling the pine needles and raindrops splattering our hair. The squirrel chirps from the top of the swaying tree. When I fling out an arm, I'm almost sure he thinks I'm waving at him.

# 114

Later, Arye doesn't say anything lame, like, "Are you okay?" Or, God forbid, "I love you."

First of all, I'm fine. Not the same person, but fine. Maybe better than fine.

Second of all, "I love you" would be a lie and therefore the worst thing to say. Even if it were true, I'm not sure I can say it back.

The rain never increased past a halfhearted drizzle. Now it's stopped completely. How strange it is to be sitting here in the dark, with the owls, and the wind, and all the creepy-sounding insects you never hear in the city. He sees me shiver and takes off his shirt to drape it around me, never mind I can feel his goose bumps when our arms rub together.

I can't believe how I once hated this guy.

We fold up the blanket, and I wonder what he's thinking. Is he asking himself why? I ask myself the same thing and I have no answer. It's not like I needed to prove anything. That I'm not what Devon Connolly thinks I am, or that sex isn't what I saw in Mom and Dad's room that night.

No matter. I feel, well, happy. Like a very happy person.

I let him kiss me once more in the front seat before we head back to the road. His broad hands cradle my face like he never wants to let me go.

115

Funny how we don't speak all the way back to the Heights. But Arye holds my hand tighter than ever, his thumb grazing my knuckles as if memorizing the feel. When we stop in front of his house, his first words hit me without warning. I don't know how he figured it out when I haven't figured it out myself. Can he see inside of me?

"You're not taking him back with you, are you?"

I stroke the flannel cuff of his sleeve and pick at the button. The streetlight shines in my face, and I have to duck my head.

"No," I say finally. "I'm not taking him back."

"God. God." He digests this information while I move on from the button to play with my seat belt. He touches my face again. "Shawna, maybe—"

"Don't! You'll make me cry." No, no, no, I—will—not—cry. "Let's not make it a big deal, okay?"

He draws back his hand. "Does my mom know?"

"I guess she will in a minute."

". . . Am I going to see you again?"

"I don't know. Probably not."

He kisses me hard. I kiss him back, harder than hard. I wish I didn't have to let go, but I can't stay here forever. I ease away and point meaningfully toward his house. Then I stare back into the vivid streetlight till spots dance around my vision. And wait, not daring to breathe, till he's out of my car.

I hear his footsteps fade away on the pavement. I hear the front door shut.

116

My family descends on me like bloodthirsty bats on an injured calf: *Where-the-hell-have-you-been-we've-called-everyone-looked-everywhere-oh-my-God-do-you-have-any-idea-how-worried-we-were-we-thought-you-two-were-kidnapped-and-God-dammit-Shawna-where-the-hell-is-your-brother-where's-Sam-where-is-he-where-is-SAM-SAM-SA-A-AM?*

"At Fran's," I yell over the chaos.

"FRAN'S?"

Dad's bellow nearly causes the two police officers to leap for cover. Aunt Colleen clutches her throat like a silent film star. Julie stares, dumbfounded. Even Uncle Dieter inspects me, momentarily, like I've morphed into a demon. Then he sneaks a smile and studiously looks away.

"Fran's?" Aunt Colleen echoes, composing herself. The one place, I guess, it never occurred to them to look.

"Are you out of your goddamned mind?" Dad bellows.

"Sir," one cop interjects.

Dad flaps him aside, but lowers his voice a decibel. "What, exactly, is Sam doing at Fran's?"

I shrug in kind of a smart-ass way so no one can see how petrified I am. Dad regards me incredulously, then points to one cop and rattles off Fran's address. "He belongs to me. I'll show you the court order if you like. But I'd appreciate if you run over there and bring him back now."

"He doesn't belong to anyone," I shout before the cop can make a move. "He's not a dog, Dad."

"You. Shut. Your. Mouth!"

Julie murmurs, "Jack," but Dad ignores her. Fetching his briefcase from the marble-topped table in the foyer, he slams it on the sofa and rustles through papers.

I face the two cops. "Please don't bring him back. He should stay where he is."

Dad whips out his holy court order. "That woman has no right to my child. Here is the proof. I'm pressing charges, do you hear me?"

"John, wait a sec." Uncle Dieter, the peacemaker, steps in, but Dad brushes him off like yet another pesky insect.

Well, okay, Dad doesn't "brush" him; he roars at Uncle Dieter, "Goddamn it, this is none of your business!" This ticks off Aunt Colleen, so she yells at Dad, and then they both start yelling at poor Uncle Dieter. Meanwhile I'm standing there in Arye's five-sizes-too-big-for-me shirt with two fully armed cops eyeing me, askance.

The nicer one of the two scans Dad's paper. He turns to me. "Why did you take him there?"

I point to my screaming relatives and almost ask: how would *you* like to grow up around these raving lunatics?

I drop my hand, and say instead, "She's his mom, that's why. No matter what that paper says."

The second cop, the less nice of the two, looms closer. "Legally, she's not. And she's in serious trouble now, thanks to you. So are you, it looks like."

"Your father's not"—Good Cop glances at the thundering mob—"violent, is he?"

If I said yes, what would they do?

Dad flies over as soon as he notices me talking to the police. "Wait! Did I give you permission to question my daughter?"

Good Cop answers, somewhat significantly, "Sir, we were asking her if you have a history of violence. You seem to be a bit out of control."

"I am never out of control," Dad states through his teeth. "And you may *not* speak to my minor daughter unless I'm present."

My tongue feels like sandpaper. "What're you afraid of? That I'll say something about Mom?"

Dad's temple throbs visibly. "The police are here because you ran off with your brother. You skipped school. You left no note. You couldn't even call your grandmother, who's been worried sick about you. And when you do show up—what, fourteen hours later?—you tell me you left Sam with that, that woman?"

"What about your mom?" Good Cop zeros in.

Dad answers for me, of course. "My ex-wife left us for a lesbian . . . lover." He stumbles badly over "lover," but regains control. "And that's irrelevant, aside from the fact that it's that *friend* of hers who just stole my son! My God. They could be anywhere by now."

"Tell them the rest," I insist.

"What rest?"

"You know what rest."

"Shawna. Please. *Don't* be stupid."

Uncle Dieter explodes, "*Stop calling her stupid, you son of a bitch!*" and Bad Cop's hand moves an inch closer to his holster. "I swear to God, Gallagher, you say that one more time and I'm personally going to beat the living *shit* out of you."

Dad glowers, triumphant. "You hear that? My own brother-in-law just threatened me. Christ, what a family."

Ignoring her shrill protests, Uncle Dieter steers Aunt Colleen toward the door. He says as he passes me, "You know where I am, Shawna. Any problems tonight, you just give me a call. I'll drive right back here and bust his head in."

"Dietrich!" Aunt Colleen screams.

Uncle Dieter hustles her out. Dad then informs the officers, "You witnessed that!" Amazingly, he seems shaken by the attack. "What the hell got into that man?"

Good Cop watches Dad, but speaks directly to me. "You were going to tell us something about your mother?"

I hug myself. Julie watches wordlessly. No way can I say it with her in the room. "Ask my dad what happened."

"Excuse us." Dad catches my elbow and steers me into the kitchen. "What the hell are you trying to do?"

"You have no right to keep Schmule," I plead. "Please, please, Dad. He *hates* it here. He's homesick. He's depressed. He'll die if you bring him back."

"Of course he's homesick! And *you* aren't helping matters by constantly dragging him back to Fran's. He's barely had a chance to settle in!"

"You don't care about him! All you care about is getting your own way, getting back at Mom. You're, like, this total control freak, Dad!"

"Getting back? Your mother's dead. Nothing I do now makes any difference."

"I know she's dead. But that doesn't mean you don't want to hurt her." My throat constricts. If I cry, he wins. "You made her have a Catholic funeral!"

"She was *Catholic*!"

"She didn't want to be. You did that to her on purpose. And you *knew* it'd hurt Fran. You're not happy unless you're making everyone miserable, the same way you did Mom."

"I did not make your mother miserable."

"No. You just raped her."

Infinite silence. Then Dad says, close to my ear, "I did no— such—thing. Is that woman feeding you this bullshit?"

"I saw you. I know what you did that night."

I watch my father's shoulders sag. When he reaches for me and I jerk away, he seems hurt by the gesture. "Shawna, honey, you were seven when she left. Whatever you think you saw, you obviously misinterpreted."

"I didn't misinterpret. I heard what you said to her. Do you want me to repeat it?"

"What I want," he says softly, a guarded glance toward the kitchen door, "is for you to stop talking about this. Nothing. Happened." In the split second that follows, I almost, *almost* begin to doubt my own memory—but then he clinches it with, "And if it did, how can you prove it? You were a child, Shawna."

Yes. I thought of that. Mom isn't here to tell her story. Fran knows, but she heard it secondhand. Who'll listen to me? Dad's right. I was seven. I can barely remember the name of my teacher that year.

I cocoon myself in Arye's soft shirt. "Even if no one believes me, you know how bad it'll look? What your patients will think? They'll never let you near them again."

Dad's astounded eyes rivet mine. "You'd do that? My own daughter?"

"I'm not doing it! You did it to yourself when . . . when . . ." Ragged sobs escape—maybe I'll lose this one after all—and I rub my face, remembering his terrible words. "When you hurt Mom that night."

"Shawna," he begins, helpless, disbelieving.

"I'll tell people. I will! And I'll tell them you hit Schmule. I'll tell anyone who'll listen." I step closer and note his surprise. "Schmule belongs with Fran. He was never your son! And it's so wrong to try to make him that now."

"Shawna," he says again, but I'm powerless to shut up.

"I know how bad you wanted a boy. And I'm sorry it wasn't me, and I'm so sorry I'm not perfect. But you're right, I *don't* want Schmule here anymore. And I swear to God if you make him come back, I'll tell everyone the truth—about everything, Dad. And then I, I'll just leave."

"Leave? And go where? You're going to Kenyon this fall!"

"Maybe I won't! Maybe I'll go to MassArt and be an artist, like Mom."

"The hell you will. I'm not paying your tuition to any damn art school. You're going to med school."

"Fuck med school! I'm not you. I'm not *you!*"

Dad ignores my choice of words. He stares hard at something in my face I know he's never before seen. Then, quietly, he says, "Why are you doing this to me?"

To him, him, him. Everything's always about him.

"Have I been such a terrible father? Have I ever laid a hand on you, even one time?"

Fresh tears spurt from my eyes. "No, but I wish you had. Because some of the things you say to me are a thousand times worse."

Good Cop coughs apologetically in the doorway. "Uh, sir?" Dad forces his attention to the officer while I bawl noisily into my hands. "About the boy? What would you like us to do?"

"Go," Dad says, almost inaudibly. "I'll handle it. Everything's fine."

Nothing could be further from the truth.

117

Julie leaves right after the cops, with questions in her eyes neither of us try to answer. I microwave, in slow motion, two mugs of water for tea. Dad's not crazy about tea, but he'll drink it if I make it. Personally, I'm not in the mood for anything at all. But it gives me something to do while I collect my thoughts.

He watches me add two packs of Splenda to his tea. "Shawna." I'm right beside him, yet I have to strain to hear his words. "I'm not the person I was back then."

Yes, you are. Only you use words now. Not your hands. .

He sips his tea, cupping the mug close to his chin. "I begged her to come back. I went for counseling. I did that whole anger management thing. I did everything I could, because you wouldn't stop crying for her. But by then it was too late. Fran poisoned her mind. Thanks to her, your mom would never give me another chance."

Awed, I think: he honestly believes that. He'll never see Fran as anything other than the person who stole his wife, his property, the one person, besides me, who belonged solely to him.

Funny how this realization doesn't surprise me. Dad, I know, will always be Dad. Yet I find this reassuring, in a twisted way.

"Sam was born eight months later," he says tiredly.

My ragged intake of air sears my chest. "I know. But you can't take him away like he's a piece of furniture." Dad raises his head. I rush on before he can blow up, or I lose the last of my nerve. "You can't make him love you. Just like you couldn't make Mom."

He plunks his mug down hard. And when he replies, it's the last thing I expect.

"I know," he says hoarsely. "Goddamn it. I *know*."

118

The next day, Julie hands me a paper bag. "It's not a gift. But it's something you might want."

I pull out the wrinkled photo of Mom and Fran. There's a gouge on Mom's chest, and it reeks of coffee grounds. Otherwise, it's intact.

"Don't tell your father," she adds unnecessarily.

More secrets, I think. But I promise anyway.

Then I stuff the picture into an envelope, address it to Fran, and drop it in a mailbox.

119

Arabic Guy's real name is Nabil. I roll it across my tongue: Nah-beel, Nah-beel.

I study his "Life as a Collage" at Miss Pfeiffer's art show. Real photos, not drawings, of a life a thousand ways different from mine. A dark-skinned family swathed in layers. Camels and goats. A bustling marketplace. Burned-out buildings and abandoned artillery.

Beside me, he asks in a soft, semi-British accent, "If you do not already have an escort for the prom, I would be most pleased if you would accompany me."

Hello! Prom is, like, two days away? We've barely exchanged five words all semester.

Evil Shawna thinks: Why are you asking me *now*? Did everyone else turn you down?

Pathetic Shawna thinks: Oh, no! Dad'll strip-search the poor guy, alert Homeland Security, and cordon off every suburb east of the Cuyahoga River.

Perfect Shawna says: "Thanks. I'd love to go."

My collage comes in second. I'm fine with that.

120

The morning after my graduation party, LeeLee twists sideways to view her butt in my mirror. "Be honest. Do you think these shorts make my *culo* look, like, excessively big?"

"Yes." Well, she did ask me to be honest.

Her reflection flips its tongue out at me. Then she wedges her *culo* down on my bed between my two overloaded suitcases. "I still can't believe you blew off MassArt. Even after your grandmother offered to pay?"

"Oh, please. You know it's always been Kenyon. I'm not changing my mind now. Besides, it's not like I can't take art classes there, too."

"Yah, whatever." She picks up my *Welcome to Scotland* folder and thumbs the pages. "So how long are you and your grandma gonna be gone?"

"Till the week before school starts."

I feel a ping of excitement. My graduation gift—touring the British Isles with Nonny for three weeks—is perfectly doable now that Dad hired around-the-clock nurses to care for Poppy. Nonny was mad as hell at first, because no nurse in the world can be good enough for Poppy. She got over that as soon as she discovered she can now sleep, undisturbed, all night long, and come and go as she pleases.

"What time does your plane leave tonight?" I ask LeeLee.

"Seven thirty." She squeezes herself and squeals, "Ooh, I can't believe I'll be living in frickin' New York City! And rooming with Tovah? Omigod, she's so-o excited. It's all she talks about."

All LeeLee talks about, too. But this I keep to myself.

LeeLee adds, "You know what else I can't believe? That you made up with Susan. And she was *civil* to me last night."

Of course Susan had to be civil; it was a small party, only LeeLee, Mel and Danielle, Jonas, and Nabil. We grilled outside, danced on the deck, and splashed around in the pool till well after midnight. I got some great gifts, too, including an art book from LeeLee, a diary from Susan, Godiva chocolates from Jonas, and a jangling ankle bracelet, imported from Lebanon, from Nabil.

Ah, Nabil. Pool water glistening on his deeply tanned skin. The gold cross dangling on his rippling chest. His sexy white smile, his laugh, his accent, his everything. And no, he didn't try to jump my bones after the prom.

Dad sneered when Nabil, resplendent in his tux, showed up on prom night and slipped a lily corsage over my waiting wrist. Well, Dad, you can sneer all you like.

"Have you talked to, you know . . ." LeeLee doesn't say their names.

"I promised Dad I wouldn't," I admit.

"Like that ever stopped you before?"

"It's different this time."

"That's a big bummer, Shawna. 'Cause you and Arye'd make a cute couple if he'd, ya know, grow a few inches, maybe join a gym . . ."

"LeeLee. Stop."

"Okay. Gotta run anyway." Her fierce hug explodes the breath from my lungs. "Send me lots of postcards, 'kay?"

"I will," I promise. I add, hugging her back just as hard, "I'm happy for you."

"Me too," she mumbles, and takes off.

I didn't tell her the whole truth about MassArt. Knowing LeeLee, she'd rant and rave and accuse me of "sacrificing" my own happiness. But not going to art school isn't a sacrifice. Isn't a true sacrifice something that helps you become a better person? Or, possibly, makes somebody else happy? So maybe this is only a half a sacrifice, because I know Dad's happy I'm going to Kenyon after all.

I'm not proud that I blackmailed my dad. But Dad nailed me, too. Because this is our mutual agreement:

1. I will go to Kenyon, as planned.
2. I'll keep my mouth shut about what he did to Mom. And to Schmule, too. I will never breathe a word.
3. I will not under any circumstances see the Goodmans again. If Dad has no son, then it's only fair that I have no brother. A "clean break," Dad called it.

He meant "All or nothing."

As for Dad's part of the agreement:

1. Fran keeps Schmule.
2. Dad, like me, will not call, or visit, or do anything at all to disrupt their lives.
3. Surprise. There is no number three.

So I got my way and, yes, Schmule's with Fran. But I pay for this every day in small, cruel ways. Like when Poppy bobs excitedly as soon as he hears my voice—and the bobbing slows to a disappointed quiver when he sees Schmule's not with me.

When I pass my brother's room and see all the stuff that Dad, so far, has refused to get rid of. Or when Dad sits in his study, silent, dejected, and I know he's thinking about the son who really isn't his son.

Or when I used to find Charles on Schmule's old bed, perplexed and lonely.

I haven't seen Arye since that day on the blanket. I changed my screen name and blocked his number from my cell.

And I'm trying every second of every day to forget the feeling of his hands on my face.

All or nothing, Dad.

At least I have his shirt.

121

Realizing how thirsty I am, I venture downstairs to brew some iced tea after LeeLee leaves. I stop dead in the kitchen and stare at empty space where Charles's dishes used to be. He's only been gone two days. I may never get used to it. But I promised myself, after crying for hours, that I'd be strong, strong, strong, and keep in mind that it's for the best.

Obviously I couldn't take Charles with me to Kenyon, right? Who'd take care of him here while I'm away? Feed him? Walk him? Love him the way I've loved him for ten years and exchange those sloppy, lovable doggy kisses? Nonny's too old. Aunt Colleen's too bitchy. Julie lives in an apartment with a snarky Persian cat. Dad works long hours and travels all the time; in fact, he and Julie are together in Greece right now. Still not married. No longer discussing it, either.

Because I couldn't exactly do the deed myself, Uncle Dieter volunteered. The last time I saw Charles he was prancing on a leash on the way to my uncle's car, tail wagging like a metronome at warp speed.

My baby, my Charles.

Frighteningly close to tears again, I carry the iced tea back to my room—against the rules, ha-ha—and drag my laptop closer. I need to write some good-bye letters, especially to Susan and Nabil, though something tells me, yes, I'll be hearing from Nabil again.

I spot an e-mail from LeeLee, forwarded to her from Tovah, forwarded from somebody else. LeeLee sent this yesterday? She never said a word.

I stare, confused, at the original sender's name: BUNGEE1202.

I only know of one bungee fan who was born on December second.

The e-mail reads: *Careless gifts may be despised, but your gift to me will forever be prized. I love you! I love you! Many good-byes.*

And when I read the P.S.—*Charles sends kisses!*—I feel the mosaic edges of my heart shift closer together.

ACKNOWLEDGMENTS

Many thanks to my family and friends, as always, for their love and support; to my awesome agent, Tina Wexler of ICM; to editors Caroline Abbey and Michelle Nagler, and the rest of the Bloomsbury crew who worked so hard to bring Shawna to life; plus a very special thanks to Jill Davis.

I'd also like to thank the dedicated members of my weekly group, my first readers, all my wonderful friends on LiveJournal and AWR, and my old TCU buddies (I miss you guys!).

JEANNINE GARSEE grew up in Cleveland, Ohio, which is the setting for *Say the Word* and *Before, After, and Somebody in Between*. As the author of three "practice" novels before she was out of high school, she never wanted to be anything except a writer—but she fell under a strange, insidious spell and found herself in the nursing profession instead. Jeannine now works as a psychiatric nurse in an inner-city hospital and lives with her family in a southwest suburb of Cleveland. She is currently working on a new YA novel about a bipolar teen who sees ghosts—both real and imagined.

www.jeanninegarsee.com